ALSO BY A.M. SHINE

The Watchers
The Creeper
Stay in the Light

A.M. SHINE

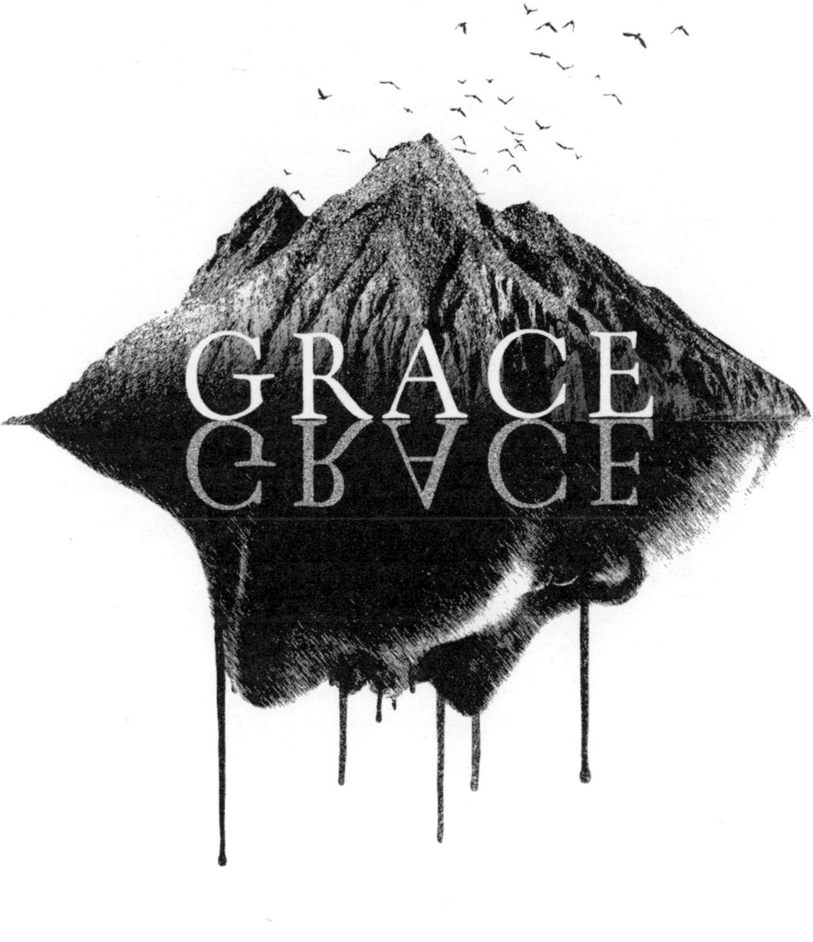

GRACE

An Aries Book

First published in the UK in 2026 by Head of Zeus,
part of Bloomsbury Publishing Plc

Copyright © A.M. Shine, 2026

The moral right of A.M. Shine to be identified
as the author of this work has been asserted in accordance with
the Copyright, Designs and Patents Act of 1988.

All rights reserved. No part of this publication may be: i) reproduced or
transmitted in any form, electronic or mechanical, including photocopying,
recording or by means of any information storage or retrieval system without prior permission
in writing from the publishers; or ii) used or reproduced in any way for the training,
development or operation of artificial intelligence (AI) technologies, including
generative AI technologies. The rights holders expressly reserve this
publication from the text and data mining exception as per Article
4(3) of the Digital Single Market Directive (EU) 2019/790.

This is a work of fiction. All characters, organizations, and events portrayed
in this novel are either products of the author's imagination or are used fictitiously.

9 7 5 3 1 2 4 6 8

A catalogue record for this book is available from the British Library.

ISBN (HB): 9781804547984; ISBN (XTPB): 9781804547991;
ISBN (eBook): 9781804547960

Cover design: Jessie Price | Head of Zeus

Typeset by Siliconchips Services Ltd UK

Printed and bound in Great Britain by Clays Ltd, Elcograf S.p.A.

Bloomsbury Publishing Plc
50 Bedford Square, London, WC1B 3DP, UK
Bloomsbury Publishing Ireland Limited,
29 Earlsfort Terrace, Dublin 2, D02 AY28, Ireland

HEAD OF ZEUS LTD
5–8 Hardwick Street
London, EC1R 4RG

To find out more about our authors and books
visit www.headofzeus.com
For product safety related questions contact productsafety@bloomsbury.com

Prologue

DECLAN

'Take Gracie to her room and don't come out, no matter what you hear.'

Chrissy's parting glance was a snapshot of contempt, the worst of him having finally awoken the worst in her, and it was no less than he deserved. Their daughter had been warming by the fire, ten toes aglow, at peace amidst the panic. Her pyjamas were too short in the ankle and mottled overall with tired stains and bobbles. A new pair might have scrunched Gracie's little face up into a smile, but Declan never considered that until Chrissy's jewellery box had been stripped as clean as their savings. It would have been nice though to see it one last time: something so rare as a smile in a home where sorrow had long outstayed its welcome.

'What are you going to do?' Chrissy asked him from the doorway, holding on to Gracie's skinny shoulders, her hands hidden neath those curls shimmering bronze in the half-light.

The woman's eyes were dead as her voice, and it harrowed Declan to meet them.

'I don't know,' he replied, giving her an honest answer for once.

His family receded into the darkness of the hallway before he'd chance to say sorry. Not that a word could have fixed the damage he'd done. Declan heard the door to Gracie's bedroom click softly into its frame. Cold floorboards creaked under Chrissy's feet before the chest of drawers was dragged across them. Bedsprings squeaked, lively enough to hint at who was responsible. A whisper was shushed. And then, in a house whose sounds travelled lightly as powder on a breeze, there was silence.

He'd spun so many lies around their innocence, entwining their fates with his own. Chrissy couldn't have known how dire their situation had become. If she had, then she was a far braver woman than Declan had ever given her credit for.

Sending them over to the mainland wasn't an option, not after what happened to the Corcorans. Nothing in nature could have risen the waves to rage the way they had that morning. Declan had never seen anything like it. The rocks skirting the shores of Croaghnakeela could raze the strongest hull to scrap. And after the capsize and the screams, the islanders had huddled together – united in shame and horror – watching as the blood of five bodies exploded in the seafoam. Declan still saw it whenever he closed his eyes, a scar on the mind, a memory scored too deeply to ever be forgotten.

He reached for the bottle glowing amber on the coffee table. A half-glass was poured before the trembling became too much to bear. Fingers flexed and clenched, reaching for a hope that wasn't there. Declan never let slip any clues as to what he was thinking unless he was selling them for a reason. But all those tells he'd taught himself to conceal at the poker table were now exposed, and the truth was bleeding from him like an open wound.

With the whiskey gulped back, he slammed down his glass. Chrissy would have heard it: his last drink, as if she'd have thought it possible until now. Declan slouched back in his armchair – a threadbare throne for a goddamn fool – abandoned by every doomed soul that'd ever crossed his own. The fire drew his gaze. The golden light of its flames sparkled atop the salt that Chrissy had sprinkled in long battlements along the hearth. Declan fidgeted around that band of pale skin where his father's watch used to be. Lost now, like everything else. A lifetime of regrets spiralled maddeningly around his thoughts – torturous glimpses of all those godsends he'd taken for granted, coupled with the solemn surety that they would never be his to hold again. A gambler's remorse. The pains of lost possibility. It's true what Fergal had said about him: if good luck were a blessing, then Declan O'Dwyer was more cursed than the Devil himself.

'Where are you, you bastard?' he grumbled, searching the shadows that draped between the lamplight of the room. 'Why don't you just get it over with?'

Declan still disbelieved that it had come to this. But the island was dying long before anyone realised it. If there'd been some early symptoms of its sickness, then nobody had the good mind back then to see them. And now it was too late. Croaghnakeela had become a black heart festering in the bay, its inhabitants no better than maggots writhing in its salty air, waiting for dark wings to descend and devour them.

He had visited Finnerty's that afternoon, desperate enough to cast off his pride. The very air on the island felt tainted on that walk, soured by some sepsis rising up from the soil, as though a bloated corpse were bleeding rivers of black beneath it. Trees were few on Croaghnakeela, but amidst that westerly gale their leaves shivered like a thousand cymbals in the silence. And all the while that hill in the island's centre seemed to billow like some monstrous lung, as if the damned rock they lived on was alive, not just with life, but with hate and malice and an evil that no man could reason with.

The pub was a short walk from door to door, and yet Declan's shirt was soaked through when his knuckles found its wood. Firelight streamed down its two teary windows. But in lieu of the music and the laughter that'd once met his ears, there was only the reluctant rhythm of John Finnerty's shoes, approaching more out of obligation than the man's own free will. His pub had been a safe place for so many for so long. But nowhere was safe anymore. And some had learned that lesson in the worst ways imaginable.

The door cracked open just enough for John to peer an eye out. 'What do you want, Declan?' he asked, stern but unsteady. 'Shouldn't you be at home looking after Grace?'

Every other family on the island had locked themselves away to guard their young, lining their doors and windows with salt, as Chrissy had done. Not one amongst them could explain how they'd been taken. There was no sign of entry. No weaknesses that an intruder could target. Little consolation to those parents who'd awoken to find their child's bed empty. Three nights. Three more missing kids.

'I need a loan, John. It needn't be cash, so long as it has some value. I need something to give him.'

The publican's eyes narrowed. 'I've nothing to share, Declan. You know that. Whatever I've left I need to keep my own safe.'

'Please,' he said, closing his hands in prayer. 'I've lost everything. Chrissy has no idea.'

'Go home, Declan. For once in your life would you ever look after that family of yours. You shouldn't have left them to come here. Charity died on this island a long time ago.'

With that said, the door closed, and the click of Finnerty's footsteps faded behind its wood, leaving Declan to traipse home, alone and none the richer.

The lamps in the sitting room now flickered like a flurry of winks forced on the eye. He looked to the hallway, that which led towards Gracie's bedroom, and imagined his wife and child bundled up under the duvet, Chrissy hugging their daughter close, caressing her hair, listening out for those same haunting footsteps that had visited them these past nights.

The light bulbs faltered again, their filaments fizzling like scorched insects that'd flown too close to a flame.

'You're here, aren't you?' Declan asked as a sudden chill slithered over the knots of his spine. 'You don't have to do this, you know. We could come to some—'

In a blink, all of the lamps died in the same second, leaving only the firelight to gleam across the table's dusty lacquer. Declan needed to know that he wasn't to blame – that the game he'd played had been rigged from the start – and the proof he needed was right in front of him.

'I never had a chance, did I?' he whispered, snatching the deck up in his hand.

The cards, so familiar to Declan's touch, were shuffled effortlessly, almost confidently, as if their dealer stood a chance of winning. The room grew colder. The flames burned a little weaker, like orange petals wilting in a frost. The cadent swish of the cards had drawn the evil closer, irresistible as blood to a beast. Declan leaned over the table and slid his glass aside. Chrissy would have heard that too. She'd probably guessed what he was doing. Her husband never did know when to quit. He squeezed the deck in his hand, faces flat on his palm, breathing hard like a fighter stepping up to a bigger man.

'What do you say?' he grumbled, eyeing up the darkness flanking him on all sides. 'A quick game of higher or lower? Who knows, maybe you'll let me win this time.'

He slid off the top card and placed it down on the table.

Eight of hearts.

Of course, it had to be. The only number in the deck that offered him no advantage.

'Higher,' he spoke aloud, knowing that the other could hear him.

Declan drew the next.

Seven of hearts.

He'd left his hope at the door that night. Jesus, he'd abandoned that old dog long before it ever came to this.

'Higher,' he repeated as his nervous fingers pinched another card and set it down.

Six of hearts.

This was the way of it. Nothing he could do would ever change his luck.

'I know you're there,' he said, casting his eyes about the black, seeing nothing and hearing less.

The next card was held aloft before he put it down.

'Higher,' Declan shouted, pursing his eyes shut.

Chrissy would have been listening. She'd have heard the desperation in his voice.

He opened his eyes and there it was, lucent in the firelight: proof of the trickster.

Five of hearts.

Declan threw the remaining cards towards the fire. A few

found its flames. Others scattered on the floor or were swallowed up by the darkness on either side.

'All hearts,' he muttered, running a hand down his face, 'you son of a bitch.'

The air was tightening like a noose around his neck. Declan picked up the dice – six in all – and rolled them in his cupped hands, counting each precious moment, indulging one last time in that gambler's optimism that maybe – just maybe – he could win this round.

'Even numbers,' he declared, casting them across the table as the first tears glazed his eyes.

The dice scattered, tumbling and cracking, until they came to rest in a perfect line.

Declan held his head in his hands, mesmerised by those numbers face up by the firelight – six little dots spread across six dice. *Odd*, every single one of them. Luck like that wasn't possible. But never was a card drawn or a die cast without that thing watching from the darkness, torturing a man's hopes into something unrecognisable.

Misty shadows infested the light in slow and sinister increments. His nostrils flared at the stench, like a bonfire of dead bodies burning, only without the smoke; Declan's regrets were suffocating enough.

'Is there nothing else I can give you?' he pleaded, looking to his empty glass.

The room darkened as the firelight rolled into the hearth like a golden rug.

Declan hastily poured out one last measure. A quarter of the whiskey bottle remained. Maybe Gracie would have a taste for it someday, though he sure as hell hoped not. His little girl was better than that. He brought the glass to his nose, inhaling deeply as a tear trickled down his cheek, but there was only that noxious taint in the air, denying him even that last pleasure.

'There must be something else you want?' he whispered, his heart thrumming with a pain that coursed across his whole chest, like a closed fist beating on the dark underside of a coffin lid.

From the darkness, footsteps stormed behind Declan's shoulder, each one a roll of thunder that quaked through the floor. And there they stopped, behind his chair. Declan raised the whiskey to his wife and child. He hoped with all his heart that Gracie was too young to remember him and the horror that he'd invited into their home.

'I'm sorry,' he mouthed to them.

Chrissy would have heard his glass fall to the floor.

And then, only silence.

I

Grace

The tides had gnawed deep into the coastline, leaving the land jagged and torn from an eternity of tooth marks, and with only the salt water to cleanse its wounds there was everywhere a feeling of neglect and pain, of a sorrow that time hadn't consoled. A sludgy algae had long breached the shore, laying its putrid beaches on the still water and growing bright as fox fur across banks of stone. And where a narrow quay beetled out above the slime and seaweed, Grace saw what she'd come for: her ticket to the truth.

'Okay,' she muttered, bracing herself with hope and a sense of helplessness, 'let's get this over with.'

The tour boat was a tired little vessel that would have looked quite quaint on a postcard, sunken on some wave-washed sand and rotting in the rouge of a bloody sunset. Its red and white paint had paled to a sickly coral and cream, and the deep gouges across its hull would have given the gutsiest sailor cause for concern. Two rows of plastic seats were drilled into its deck, each holding its own puddle of seawater, and the wood overall had warped from damp, swelling here and there in painful welts, some boards more beaten than others, all of them abused.

Grace approached it with slow, hesitant steps, secretly praying that this wasn't her lift. But the pier was otherwise abandoned save for a lone seabird circling overhead, probably just as baffled as she was as to how that boat was staying afloat. Its cabin was no larger than a wardrobe, with the last of its paint peeling like sunburnt skin. And as she neared the ledge, she noticed someone shifting behind its murky glass, presumably Maloney, the captain in charge of ferrying her across that afternoon.

'Hello,' she called out, but the wind swept her voice inland, leaving the man none the wiser that she'd spoken.

Grace, content to wait, stuffed both cold hands into her coat pockets and peered nosily onto the deck. A few wooden crates were sealed and stacked between the seats – proof enough that this was indeed *her* boat, sorry a fact as that was. The priest had mentioned that she'd be travelling as part of their next delivery – some fleshly cargo that none on the island had ordered.

'This should be fun,' she whispered wryly to herself, glancing back at her car and its comforts, unappreciated until now.

Maloney stepped out into the open, garbed head to toe in a black rain coat and barely scratching five foot. 'Grace is it?' he called out, squinting like a nocturnal creature called abruptly from its cave.

'That's me,' she replied, choking on a lungful of wind. 'Father O'Malley said you'd be able to take me over today.'

Maloney leapt onto the pier, gifted pace by the gale lashing at his back. He was lean as a whippet, with weather-beaten skin brindled and misshapen like old peanut shell. Whatever vices had taken their toll on the man, vanity certainly wasn't one of them. His tweed cap was squeezed down atop two pointy, protrusive ears, and this batlike resemblance was furthered by that long coat swishing around his feet like wings at rest.

'You're late,' he said, manoeuvring around so as to steal some shelter from her body.

'I know – sorry about that,' she said, suffering a handshake limp as it was meaningless. 'I took a few wrong turns along the way and had to backtrack. My GPS didn't realise that the roads around here are... well, roads.'

His eyes tarried on Grace's long red hair whipping around her head like wildfire. ''Tis no bother. I'm happy to wait, especially seeing as you're paying for the pleasure and all.'

The priest never mentioned the possibility of any hidden fees when they'd spoken. But her memories of that conversation were a patchwork of half-heard words whose seams Grace was still stitching the threads through.

'How much do I owe you exactly?' she asked, frowning down at him, suspecting that she was being casually taken advantage of.

'Well, considering the cost of fuel and whatnot,' Maloney replied sheepishly, 'I'd have to charge you maybe fifty to take you over today.'

'Fifty euro?' she repeated, incredulous. 'But aren't you going out there anyway?'

'Aye, euro,' was all he said, ignoring the question as he extended his hand like a hungry child. 'And cash is king, as they say.'

Grace slipped the backpack from her shoulder with a snap sigh of frustration and made a slow show of unzipping its pocket and retrieving her wallet before picking out Maloney's prize. Only then did she behold the ferryman's lurid smile in all its glory – nightmare fuel at its most potent.

'Climb aboard there and make yourself comfy,' he said once the deal was done, balling the note up in his tiny hand. 'We'll be on our way soon enough. And pay no mind to that wind. So long as the water behaves itself, I should be able to get you over in one piece.'

'That's reassuring,' she whispered to herself.

If Maloney had heard her, then Maloney didn't care.

Grace's eyes narrowed as she gazed out across the bay. There she saw the island for the first time, weak as a watercolour in the mist. She had never heard of Croaghnakeela before *that* phone call. Strangely enough, neither had anyone she'd asked about it. But there it was, haunting the horizon like a ghost ship, seen only by those who knew to search for it.

'What's it like out there?' she asked, awed by the bleakness of it all.

'On Croaghnakeela?' Maloney replied as he went about untying his boat from the shore. 'I couldn't tell you. I've never set foot on it myself, so I'm not really the man to be asking.'

She stared down at the crates on the deck and then back to her captain, puzzled. 'But you make deliveries to it, don't you?'

'Aye, but like I said, I don't set foot on it.'

The fact of the man standing on solid ground in that moment meant he wasn't entirely beholden to the open seas.

'Why not?' Grace asked. 'Is there someone out there you're trying to avoid?' This last question was smoothed out with a smirk.

Nothing like a little cheekiness to lower someone's defences, and Maloney's were raised twice his height. Greedy little gremlins like him probably couldn't count all their enemies on two hands. She watched him chew over his answer for a moment, and judging by his frown he wasn't particularly enjoying the taste of it.

'If I told you, Grace,' the captain replied with a solemn eye, eerie as it was unexpected, 'I don't think you'd want to believe me.'

The call had come in two days earlier.

It was gone six o'clock. The bay window of *Silke's Rare and Old Books* held a slow but steady cascade of raindrops – an opaque collage of water and streetlight, reimagined with every stroke of wind. Grace was still sat at her desk, sorting through the latest batch of Penguin Classics under the light of a green banker's lamp. A local collector – an old, cobwebbed creature with too much money and a hoarder's appetite for rarities – had written up a list of those he was missing. And so, before those skinny paperbacks ever touched a shelf, she had to set some aside. Not that Grace minded. They were the easiest sales of the week.

Her last remaining customer had been perusing the classics catalogue for the past half an hour. This was shelved in the back room, where a velvet couch had slumped like a beanbag in its far corner. The ceiling was perplexingly low in that part of the shop. And anyone who spent too long sniffing around its brittle pages always came out with a stoop and a dusty tickle to their nostrils. The SORRY WE'RE CLOSED sign on the door should have been flipped by now. But given the state of the evening outside and Grace's reluctance to be a part of it, she didn't mind sharing her shelter a little longer than usual. And besides, she still had work to do.

Another delivery had come in that afternoon. Grace was only getting around to the last few boxes now, carefully drawing incisions across their tape with a letter opener. Most she knew the contents of. One of them she didn't, and it was this box that she'd set aside from the rest. Carrie wouldn't forgive Grace if she opened it without her.

In spite of the weather, it hadn't been a bad Thursday's trade by any means. Grace had sold a French Dickens before lunchtime – *Les Papiers Posthumes du Pickwick Club*. Three volumes. Not the most valuable edition. But a sale was a sale, and they were rarer than the books these days. The usual parade of browsers had trickled in and out as the day grew older, each one darkening the damp trails across her carpet. A few of them had even bought something. A student, still shy of twenty, had audibly gasped when her eyes aligned with *Poe's Popular Tales*. Green hardback with an engraved spine, its typeface so small as to cram his life's work into a modest five hundred and forty-eight pages.

Grace had watched her count out her purse, even the loosest change: the dirty, coppered kind that people store in grubby savings jars but never spend. She'd minded how the girl's excitement dissipated as she came up short. Fifty euro was a fair price for an 1893 third edition. But this was the kind of reader who'd cherish that book for the rest of her life, keeping it dry and clean and loved. And so it sold for twenty. Her smile alone was worth the loss.

The bell chimed above the door.

Grace looked up to see Carrie standing half in, half out, shaking the rain from her umbrella. The woman's red trench coat was soaked from the waist down and her high boots shone glossy from the flood.

'Please don't drag all that rain inside,' Grace said to her, smiling sadly at her carpet. 'Nobody's ever going to buy a wet book.'

Carrie turned to her, wild-eyed, hair smeared to her forehead like freshly washed chives. 'Everything in this country is fucking wet, Gracie. There's not a whole lot I can do about it.'

Grace stood up from the desk and walked stiff-legged over to her. 'Leave the brolly by the door and give me that,' she said, reaching for her coat. 'I'll hang it by the radiator.'

Carrie slipped it from her shoulders and handed it over like a soggy rag. She looked back at the sign on the door, and then cast a glance about the shop, where unsteady towers of books had been built on the centre table from the day's delivery.

'Are you still open?' she asked disbelievingly.

'Kind of,' Grace replied. 'There's someone in the back.'

Carrie set her handbag on the floor between her feet with enough care to hint that it held something special. She peeled it open, revealing a bottle of wine cradled like a newborn in a chunky scarf.

'Well, can you kindly tell them that you're closed?' She smirked, kicking off her boots so that they landed in a heap by the door.

A bookshop was one of the few places where someone could hide out for a day without actually spending a cent. And whoever had made their home in the back room had buried himself in there like a thirsty tick, leeching on Grace's goodwill. But luckily she kept a brass tea bell on the desk for such impromptu evacuations.

'You can do the honours, if you like?' she said.

Carrie giggled as she skipped over to the desk and plonked the bottle atop it. The flat of her palm poised over the bell. She closed her eyes and took a long, steadying breath before slamming her hand down repeatedly on its ringer.

'We're closing up now,' she called out, firing her voice like a volley of cannon fire across the room. 'If you want to buy anything, now's your last chance.'

The bell's tinkle still lingered in the air as the floorboards creaked at the far end of the shop. Grace's last customer was blatantly brooding over a bruised copy of *Ulysses* as he approached them. His tweed blazer and neatly cropped beard hinted at the notions to come. The man's neck was moulded into a hunch, as was to be expected, only adding to his carefully curated intrigue.

'Picking up some Joycie, are we?' Grace said as he handed her the book. 'It's a lovely edition, isn't it?'

'It's a masterpiece,' he replied in a posh Dublin brogue. 'Everyone should read it.'

'That's the kind of high praise I like to hear.'

The bastard scoffed at the remark. 'Uh, it's James Joyce.'

'I know, I can see that.' Grace smiled through the regret at opening her mouth.

'It's a classic,' he said, puffing out his chest.

'I suppose that's why it's in the classics section,' Carrie put in, slouching back in Grace's chair and crossing her socked feet atop a box.

The customer eyed her up and down disapprovingly, but he was shrewd enough not to talk back. Grace held out the card machine, whose single beep concluded their transaction. Her vintage cash register, heavy as a small house, had been bypassed yet again. She still thrilled at the sound of its metallic ping and how it made every sale feel like a celebration. As soon as the door closed behind him, Carrie was on her feet. The sign was snapped around, the blind was wrenched down, and its latch was twisted like a knife.

'I bet he hasn't even read that,' she said, dragging an extra chair over to the desk. 'Lads are always carrying around fucking *Ulysses*, thinking it makes them look intellectual.'

'Have *you* read it?'

'Absolute shite.' She grinned. 'I managed a few lines in college before I realised the folly of it all.'

'Uh, it's James Joyce,' Grace said, mimicking the customer's accent. 'It's a masterpiece.'

'Open that, please and thank you,' Carrie said, sliding the bottle across the desk towards her.

Grace's closest friend was a wisp of a woman with a bob of blonde hair. Red lipstick popped on the palest skin, and whenever Carrie smiled she looked exquisitely wicked. Even though she was now in her late thirties, her dainty face looked fresh out of secondary school. And that rebellious pout of hers put her firmly in the bad bunch – those misfits who smoked behind the bike shed and chewed gum with an open mouth during class. They'd met through a mutual acquaintance who'd since evanesced into the social ether. It was an unspoken practice amongst the Irish to trade friends between groups – odd shapes trying to find the right fit – and she'd clicked with Carrie immediately.

'What's in the box?' she asked, poking the last of the delivery with her toe.

'No idea,' Grace replied, twisting the corkscrew deeper with a satisfying squeak, 'but you're welcome to have a look.'

'Really?' Carrie said, sitting forward excitedly. 'It's another mystery box?'

In the wheeling, dealing world of rare books, buying a dead man's possessions was natural as the seasons. Collectors liked to imagine they owned their libraries. But they were no more than custodians. These books were around long before they were, and they'd be filling up somebody else's shelf space long after their bones had turned to dust.

'Who died this time?' Carrie asked, drawing the box between her legs.

'Jesus, you make me sound like a grave robber!'

Carrie smiled up at her. 'This is the nearest thing in the world to legal grave robbery, and you know it!'

Grace grinned as she poured her out a glass of wine. 'He was a solicitor. Cancer got him, I think. He left his home to the three offspring, and they've since torn the place apart, selling whatever they can. Most of the library went to auction a few weeks ago. But they discovered a few more books stashed away in the attic. I bought them as soon as they were listed.'

'Do you know what they are?' Carrie asked.

'Not a clue. The dead man's kids just wanted them sold, and I was happy enough to oblige.'

Carrie rubbed her hands together. 'So these could be worth a bomb, yeah?'

'Or absolutely nothing,' Grace replied. 'Trust me, I've bought enough of these *mystery boxes* to not raise my hopes too high.'

She was sitting, glass in hand, watching Carrie scratch around the tape with a long fingernail, when she heard a faint knock on the front door. Grace turned in her chair. With the blind drawn, she couldn't see who it was. But given the hour of the evening and the fact that she'd seen Carrie flip the sign to *closed*, whoever it was could wait till morning.

'They must think it's a twenty-four-hour bookshop,' Grace said, shaking her head.

'What?' Carrie asked, eyeing her up as if she'd just uttered something stupid.

'The knock,' she explained, waving a hand towards the door.

'What knock?'

'You didn't hear it?' Grace asked her.

Carrie shook her head disinterestedly before dipping both hands into the box. Grace, meanwhile, was scanning the rainswept window, expecting to see the smudgy shape of a face peeping inside. Carrie's cackling snapped back her attention.

'Check these out,' she said, holding a magazine in each hand, grinning those ruby lips from ear to ear. 'You're now the proud owner of a dead solicitor's porn collection.'

'Show me,' Grace said, reaching over to take one from her.

The January 1990 front cover of *Playboy* had a sultry brunette peeling her dress past her thigh. *Tom Cruise gets intense*, was its leading article. That Grace could believe. It wouldn't be like the Cruiser to dial it down a notch.

'Do they go back far?' Grace asked, flicking through its pages.

'Back to the seventies, by the looks of it. Mostly *Playboy*. But there are also copies of something called *Mayfair*. Jesus, Gracie,' she whispered, 'what would your mum say about this? Her little pride and joy becoming a merchant of pornography.'

'She'd be laughing as much as you are, I'd say. Are they all in this condition?'

The magazine in Grace's hand was mint. Not a dog-ear. Not a crease. Not a stain, thank God. It was as though the horny solicitor hadn't even opened it.

'Pretty much,' Carrie replied. 'Why, you're not actually going to sell these, are you?'

'Sure, why wouldn't I? There aren't many bookshops with a vintage porn section. The way I see it,' she said, returning the magazine to the box, 'people are too embarrassed to buy porn if it's, you know, modern or whatever. But these will be sold in a week. Trust me. These can be passed off as collector's—'

A heavy hand hammered on the door, a single thud whose wooden echo tremored throughout the entire shop, jolting Grace forward in her chair.

'What's gotten into you?' Carrie asked, giggling to herself.

'We're closed,' she shouted, turning around to glower at the door.

'Who are you talking to?'

Grace frowned at her, confused by the joke. 'I'm talking to whoever nearly just broke my door down. Jesus, word must have already spread about the porn.'

Now it was Carrie's turn to play the confused card. 'I didn't hear anything, Gracie.'

There was no way that could be true. Usually Carrie's humour was cleverer than this. That knock had come so violently, she was surprised it hadn't shaken a few books from their shelves.

'Piss off,' Grace said to her, forcing a weak smile as she drew the wine to her lips.

'Honestly, there hasn't been a tap on that door since I got here. I don't know what you're hearing. What are you now, thirty-four? This could be early onset dementia. You know yourself, it's all downhill once you're past your twenties. And you've been hearing and seeing weird shit since the day I met you.'

Grace partook of another sip and watched her, waiting for the slightest smile to crack between her lips. Carrie was joking, obviously. But she was too damn gifted at hiding it.

'Okay, screw this,' Grace said, putting her glass down on the desk and jumping to her feet, the last of her patience having been stolen without its thief even needing to step indoors.

The shop was on a narrow, cobbled street with a dozen or so terraced houses and a closed-down café. Any noise, especially of the loud variety, had no rightful business being there. And what she'd just heard was disturbance enough to kick-start a local petition against her. Most of the neighbours were retired hermits who lived vicariously through their cats and peered out from behind their curtains like wanted fugitives whenever the peace was compromised.

Grace didn't dither for a second, not even to lift the blind. She clicked the latch and jerked the door open, eager to catch the culprit in the act. The wind raced inside around Carrie's umbrella – felling it like a tree – and she stepped out to where fat blobs of rain leaked from the gutter overhead.

'Hello,' she shouted, searching the lightless alcoves that ran along the walls on either side, listening out for some childish snickering or the splash of tiny footsteps.

But there was nothing. Only a silence that left her wholly dissatisfied.

'What are you doing?' Carrie asked, swirling her wine before the lamplight.

'They must have run off,' she said, standing in the doorway.

'*Who* are you talking about?'

Grace squinted through the rain one last time before closing the door, her fingers fumbling as the latch was returned to its locked position.

'Did you see anyone run past the window?' she asked, suspecting now that maybe Carrie wasn't in on the joke; she couldn't seem to care less about it.

'I wasn't looking. I was too busy admiring the porn.'

Grace's hands instinctively began arranging books on the centre table, like a dealer shuffling a deck, her hands working blind as she kept a wary vigil over the door.

'Okay, well, there's someone out there,' she muttered, more to herself than to Carrie.

Just then, the phone rang – a red rotary with no volume below deafening. It seldom made a peep during the day, never mind after hours when every other shop in the city had dimmed their lights and drawn down their shutters. Following the disturbances of that night, any noise other than the chinking of wine glasses made Grace uncomfortable.

'You going to answer that?' Carrie said, nodding at the phone.

Grace was too distracted to talk shop, but also too curious as to who was calling at that hour to let it ring out.

'Can you get it?' she asked. 'Just find out who it is and tell them we're closed.'

Carrie reached casually for the phone. '*Silke's Rare and Old Books*,' she chirped, posh as humanly possible, 'how may I be of service to you on this grand soft evening?'

Grace watched her friend's debonair charade darken before her eyes. Whoever was speaking on the other end of the line, they hadn't called the shop to talk about books – that was sure.

'She's beside me,' Carrie said before holding out the receiver. 'Who is it?'

A sudden flare of sea spittle drenched the side of the boat.

Croaghnakeela was creeping into view, like a mound of dead leaves afloat on the ocean. They were close. But that creamy mist still veiled the air between them, muddying the island's details into mulch.

'Did you used to run tours out here?' Grace asked, leaning into the windless shelter of Maloney's cabin.

'Aye,' he replied, turning his head a notch but keeping one hand steady on the wheel. 'Seasonal fare. Any port between Clare Island and Inisheer, depending on demand.'

'Did you ever bring tours out to Croaghnakeela?'

The captain shifted his weight uncomfortably in the strange silence that followed, as though he were waiting for the question to politely excuse itself. But Grace stayed by the door, keeping him locked in there with it.

'Never to *that* island, no,' he eventually replied, albeit grudgingly.

The odd inflection to his answer hadn't passed unnoticed.

'Why not?' Grace asked, to which the man finally turned to face her.

If his knitted brow were any indication, Maloney was more fond of delivering cargo that didn't travel with a thousand unsolicited questions.

'That's Lavelle's island,' he replied, his beady eyes smouldering in the half-light of the cabin. 'And dead as he may be, I know better than to set foot on it. And that's all I'll say about that.'

'Lavelle?' she repeated, grinning at the captain's cryptic manner of speaking. 'Who was he: a landlord or something?'

'Just a name,' Maloney said, snipping that particular line of questioning with a dramatic suck of his gums, 'and not one that you should be speaking so long as you're staying there. They don't like to talk about him.'

The captain didn't exactly like to sing about the man himself.

Dull vibrations rumbled throughout the cabin. Even the grimy windows surrounding them like smoke were seen to rattle.

'Do a lot of people live on the island?' Grace asked, curious as to how many more shaded answers she could extract from her captain before his patience was pitched overboard.

Maloney shook his head. 'Less and less every year, I should imagine. There hasn't been a child on Croaghnakeela for decades now. So I suppose it's only a matter of time before the old guard die out. It's sad when you think about it. An island without children can't make much of a future for itself now, can it? But sure, for better or worse, you'll see for yourself soon enough.'

Grace wasn't letting the ferryman off the hook that easily. 'You're telling me there are *zero* children on the island?' she said, her eyebrows arching in disbelief. 'What happened, did they all grow up?'

She only realised the indelicacy of the question once it'd been asked, and by then it was too late to take it back.

'A few did, I suppose,' Maloney replied, glooming over his answer. 'Most of them weren't so lucky.'

Grace held the man's gaze, unsure if she owed him an apology. But before she could open her mouth – to dig herself even deeper into that hole – an impish little grin cracked across his cheeks.

'You've really no idea what you're landing into, do you?'

Grace took the phone, and Carrie guided her to sit down by the lamplight of the desk. She held it hesitantly for a moment, looking worriedly to her friend as though she'd just passed her a live hand grenade.

'Grace Silke?' the priest asked, warmly and ominously sympathetic – a tone they must have taught at the seminary given their fondness for entertaining bad news.

'Yes, speaking.'

'My name is Father Richard O'Malley, Grace, and I'm terribly sorry to be calling you in work like this, and at such an hour. I've already taken the liberty of contacting your parents. I hope you don't mind. But you see, I needed to make sure you were aware of your adoption before reaching out to you.'

Only her closest friends knew the truth of her heritage, and they'd collectively deemed it as something taboo for reasons she never really understood. Grace had been in her early teens when she'd learned that she was a second-hand daughter. The revelation came as no surprise really, or so she felt at the time, though hindsight can be an unwieldy gift to wave around, especially for one so young. The dissimilarities between Grace and her parents, both the emotional and the physical, far outweighed any strained congruities, and so the blank years in her past suddenly made a sort of sense. She was almost embarrassed that she hadn't copped it sooner. Surely the absence of any baby photographs would have perked the suspicions of a sharper adolescent. Add to that, there was no historical record of her until she'd started school. It was as though a stork had delivered her to its front step just as the bell rang.

'It saddens me to be the one to tell you this,' Father O'Malley said, speaking softly, his every word an embrace, 'but your biological mother – the woman who gave you up for adoption, that is – has passed away.'

The priest's words didn't register immediately. Grace's first thought – the only thought – that sprang to mind was that the man had obviously called the wrong person.

'Grace?' he said, reminding her that she still held the phone to her ear. 'Are you there?'

'Yes,' she replied, though it felt like a lie.

'You never knew your parents, did you?' he asked.

'No, I don't think so. I mean, no. I didn't.'

Grace wasn't sure what she knew anymore. Somewhere in that empty space that her adoptive parents so carefully guided her around like a bottomless pit, there was still *something*. Maybe it wasn't anything as appreciable as a memory. But it had always been there, in the periphery of her life, some residual feeling that time couldn't clean away.

'What was her name?' Grace asked, the words slipping her lips as a whisper.

A question she'd pondered more than any other.

'Christine O'Dwyer,' the priest replied, 'but we called her Chrissy.'

Grace held her eyes shut as the name was chiselled across her mind.

'How did she…' The words got caught up behind her teeth.

'I'm afraid that Chrissy was sick for some time, Grace,'

Father O'Malley replied. 'But you'll be glad to know that she passed away peacefully.'

Carrie was waiting in the wings to rescue her. She'd noticed the obvious signs – the shock, the confusion, and that most startling sense of sadness that made Grace's green eyes sparkle. But she also marked the red spit of wine in the dregs of her glass. Amends were made. The glass was filled and set on the desk beside her, because sometimes that's all a friend can do.

'Do I still have a *biological* father?' Grace asked, hating the word for sounding so forensic.

The priest sighed. 'No, unfortunately, Declan has been gone for many years now.'

Christine and Declan, and their daughter...

Grace didn't know what else to say. The once orderly queue of questions occupying her mind had fallen into chaos, and so she held the phone in silence, quietly grieving a life she couldn't remember.

'It was Chrissy's wish that she be cremated immediately upon her passing,' Father O'Malley said, guessing perhaps – had Grace not lost the power of speech – that her next question would have concerned her mother's funeral. 'Her ashes have already been interred in her family's plot. I can't imagine how you must feel. This is a lot for anyone to take in. But it's my responsibility to let you know that in her last will and testament, Chrissy left everything she had to you, including her home.'

'Okay,' Grace said. Even her own voice seemed distant now, and she wasn't one hundred per cent certain if she'd spoken that word or simply imagined it.

'This is probably not the time to discuss such matters,' the priest continued, 'but I would be more than happy to sell the house for you, if you wish? That was what Chrissy wanted me to do. I could send her possessions over to the mainland for collection. This would save you the inconvenience of travelling to—'

'No,' Grace interjected, accidentally raising her voice. 'I want to go. I want to see where I came from.'

Silence on the line. A long breath – ever so thoughtful, ever so concerned.

The Isle of Croaghnakeela darkened as they seesawed towards it. Details were awakening in the mist. The craggy coastline descended at a hundred odd angles like a collapsed causeway, all cockled edges and wave-washed cliffs. It was as though the island were another vessel, approaching them at a speed far greater than the captain's faded little tour boat.

Maloney came pacing past after the engine cut. 'There you are now,' he said, staring proudly at the shore as though he himself had built it. 'I told you I'd get you here in one piece.'

Water sloshed the hull in loud gulps, and Grace had to dig her feet into the deck just to keep upright. There was only one place to safely dock – a skinny shoulder of stone that jutted out from the coast. The rest of the island was guarded by an impenetrable ring of rock, their shadows perforating the tide like a trap for any so foolish to attempt a landing elsewhere.

'It was *your* decision to come here, wasn't it?' the captain asked, looming by her side.

Strange question, but then nothing about Maloney was borderline normal.

'I guess so, yeah,' she replied, stepping away from him, 'why?'

'Just saying is all. You're here because *you* chose to be. All I did was give you a lift.'

His beady eyes suddenly snapped inland, like a cat who'd spotted a mouse scurrying across the pier. The captain's head cocked to one side. Had he heard something that Grace hadn't? It was as though the ghosts of Maloney's past were all whispering in his ear.

'Come on,' he said, hastening her off the boat, 'quickly now.'

A child could have cleared the gap. But a child probably wouldn't have imagined the grim reality of being crushed and drowned to death at the same time should she have fumbled it. Grace waited for the boat's weathered side to bob closer to the pier, conscious all the while of Maloney standing behind her, goading her on like an impatient shepherd.

'Is the church far from here?' she asked him, still gathering her courage.

These were the questions she should have been asking.

'Not far,' he replied, dragging one of his crates towards her. 'Sure it's only a small island, Grace. Nothing is ever far away here.'

Since learning the truth of her adoption, she'd pictured a long shelf of books organised chronologically. And on the very left, where the first spine should have been, there'd always been one missing. But that lost book did exist. All she had to do now was reach out and take it. And so, before another thought could hold her back, Grace touched onto dry land, her legs so weakened by that single leap of faith that she'd almost collapsed on arrival.

'There you go,' she heard Maloney call over the wind, 'you're a far braver soul than I am.'

The crash of his first crate startled her forward as he pitched it onto the pier.

'There'll be someone coming to collect these soon,' the captain said, wiping his brow. 'Probably Brendan or some other busybody. Either way, I'm sure whoever it is, they'd give you a lift to the church, if that's where you're headed.'

She couldn't think of anything worse – forced to make small talk with a stranger who probably knew more about Grace than she did about them.

'I think I'll walk, thanks.'

'Suit yourself,' Maloney shouted, already backpedalling towards his next crate. 'Have your priest call me when you want a lift back. Or just be here, same time, same day, next week, and don't be late. I won't be hanging around for you. Like I said, this is Lavelle's island.'

A week wasn't exactly ideal. She'd have to ask Carrie to keep an eye on the shop while she was away. But it was Grace's fault that there was no one else to cover at such short notice. She'd grown too fond of her own space between the books to even consider hiring someone.

'I'll be *here*,' she said, pointing down to where one of the captain's crates had toppled over on its side, scattering a bag of loose apples across the pier.

Maloney squinted down at the spilled fruit. 'Just make sure you are.'

Grace offered him a half-hearted salute and left the sea urchin to brutalise his delivery in peace. Never in her life had she witnessed a job carried out so poorly and with such blatant mean-spiritedness, and the islanders were probably paying a small fortune for the service.

A gaunt little path led off from the shore. Even the seabirds must have shared Maloney's aversion to the island, as the grey sky was clear of all but its clouds. And that sense of emptiness, like a hollow stomach in need of nourishment, was enough to make Grace feel more than a little lonely. Carrie had offered to come. Now she wished she'd taken her up on that offer. It was then that she heard the softest sound on the breeze, so utterly unexpected given the abandonment surrounding her, and yet it came so clearly that she spun around, searching for its source.

'Hello?' Grace called out. 'Is someone there?'

Where the windswept rise led further inland, there wasn't another soul to be seen anywhere. She looked back to the pier. Maloney had since skulked back into his cabin and it was empty save for the wooden boxes he'd pitched ashore. But Grace *had* heard it. Of that she was certain.

It was the laughter of a child.

2

MALONEY

The captain never relaxed until his boat had drifted a safe gap from the pier. He knew better than to step onto Croaghnakeela for any reason, even the lucrative sort, but no one else was willing to make that crossing, and Brendan – the islanders' fucking pit bull – paid him well enough. Better than he ever had, for that matter, and Maloney had only himself to thank for that. Three years back, he'd upped his fee. Caught the tight bastard off guard, so he did, right in the cold heart of a cruel and fallow winter when their needs were at their most desperate.

'Pay or starve, 'tis nay bother to me,' the ferryman had said to him, bold as brass and braced for impact.

He didn't doubt that Brendan could throw some weight behind a fist. But the old lad wasn't stupid. He knew when the high ground wasn't his. And so a new price – one more agreeable to Maloney's interests – had been agreed upon. There were days when the captain regretted not asking for more, if only to know for any future dealings just how far he could push it. But he'd probably have traded a few teeth for knowledge such as that. And despite what people may have said about him, Maloney was never a greedy man. He just wasn't the kind to leave any juice in ripe fruit when he held it in his hand.

Something on that island wasn't right. That's why he slammed his boat through the waves the way he did. There was no telling who was watching or what could be lying in wait for him when he was casting those crates ashore. And the fog on Croaghnakeela ran thick, especially this time of year, when the days were at their shortest. He'd asked Brendan about it more than once. All he'd ever got was a stern eye for an answer, and that was before he'd squeezed the last drop of patience out of the grumpy bastard.

But Maloney didn't need to beg for scraps under Brendan's table. He'd heard his own share of stories from other seafaring souls like himself – whispers more chilling than the sharpest easterly, and not the kind a man should ever speak aloud before checking his company. There'd been a spate of deaths on the island some thirty-odd years ago, or so a lad called Duggan told him once. The population – and the poor old fuckers who still lived there – had never really recovered. Happy families weren't exactly crying out to move to sad places, and the clouds over Croaghnakeela rarely lifted. So it was that the island was left to rot, like a spoilt carcass that not even the crows wanted a bite of.

Things washed up there, apparently. Old things, he'd heard people say. Evil things that no man on this earth should ever come into contact with. To be fair, Maloney scratched little sense from those warnings. But there was another rumour too. Supposedly there'd been a monastery on the island once upon a time, though the ferryman had caught no sight of one ruined or otherwise as he'd navigated its coast over the years. All he knew for certain was that no amount of prayer or holy water could save that place. But then, if there was any truth behind the tattle, it wasn't with the coin of Christianity that the damned thing was built. Pagans, or so they said, had made a home for themselves on Croaghnakeela long before there was ever a priest to wave his fucking book around. And sure the Devil himself wouldn't have a handle on what kind of horrors that crowd were worshipping.

Maybe that Grace woman would come back in a week's time with something spicy to share with him. Maloney would be the one asking the questions on that trip. That is if she were ever seen again, God bless her innocence. The fog on that island had a bad habit of making people disappear.

The boat's engine was humming away, primed and waiting patiently for its homeward journey. But not yet. Maloney snatched up the mooring stake from beside his wheel – galvanised steel and nearly as tall as him. He never travelled to Croaghnakeela without it. Risky as it was lingering by that rock for any length of time, he'd never chance bringing anything back off it. The captain could forgive himself many an indiscretion, but not that one.

The wind nearly took him off his feet when he padded out of the cabin. It was no day to be out at sea, and the weather was making a point of reminding him of that. Maloney crossed over to the port side and, with his cold fingers tensed around the stake, peered over to inspect the hull. The usual scratches – flesh wounds that looked worse than they were. The same flaky paint. Nothing else. Maloney expelled his relief in a foul breath and stepped back, more balanced on that deck than he was on any land.

But something was awry. Call it a sailor's intuition. There

was a tremble to his legs now that he only felt when he was being watched. He looked back to the shore, so distant now that he couldn't pick out much of it.

'I can't see *you*,' Maloney grumbled, searching the mist for movement. 'But I know you see *me*.'

He'd only ever caught glimpses of it, years ago, back when his eyes still held some focus. But that'd been enough to make a cautious man out of him. Whatever it was, he wasn't sure he even wanted to know anymore. But so long as it stayed on the land and Maloney kept to the water, there'd never be a reason to cross paths.

He shuffled to starboard, wise to those unseen eyes feasting on him from afar. Same stance, weapon at the ready, always anticipating the worst, like any good captain should. Once this side was checked he'd be on his way, back to a hot stove and a pint of porter and an extra fifty for the tin. Maloney couldn't keep from chuckling at the thought of what that Grace woman had paid him. Maybe he could have milked her for more. But then, that would have been greedy of him, and he didn't need a reputation like that lingering after he was dead and gone.

The captain leaned over the gunwale, still grinning away to himself, when suddenly the whole deck tilted hard to that side. The water had risen so wickedly beneath him, seizing its chance to deliver the man into its depths. Caught off guard, with his mind still counting out his day's earnings, he'd no hope of saving himself, and the ocean didn't suffer the slightest ripple when he slipped beneath its surface. It swallowed him whole without a bite. Maloney's body was wrenched deeper, so swiftly, so violently that in his last moments he'd pawed around his ankle, convinced that some anchor were dragging him to his doom. But there was nothing to feel or see amidst that growing darkness, and the man's lungs had gorged their fill of icy water before he'd even realised he was dying.

The engine purred on, and Malony's faded tour boat became just another ghost adrift off the coast of Croaghnakeela.

3

Grace

Autumn's cold was never so sorely felt nor were its colours ever so absent as on that walk. Luckily, Grace had had the sense to wear her green woollen coat, as it was by far the warmest layer she owned. It'd come with a belt, but somewhere between her apartment and the bookshop it'd slipped its hoops and taken to the wind. She liked to imagine it was still out there somewhere, travelling the world, marvelling at sights a whole lot more uplifting than what the Isle of Croaghnakeela had to offer.

The roar of the waves had softened to a whisper as she'd made her way deeper inland, following a skinny clay path that was somehow more exposed and unwelcoming than the island's pier. Any trees were bare and haggard old things, wistfully awaiting some axe to put them out of their misery. And the walls divvying up the land were low enough to step over – their tumbledown stones sunken in the soft earth and streaked with sallow stains, long outliving the careful hands that'd built them. Grace almost felt sorry for the place. Wisps of white mist still haunted its fields in a shallow fog, making cobwebs glitter like silver dreamcatchers. But that low cloud that'd shrouded the island in secrecy from afar was now thinning out like cotton wool pulled apart in the breeze. The sky felt a little less suffocating, even if it hadn't lightened a shade since she'd landed. It was as though Croaghnakeela were trapped under the belly of an upturned bowl, forced to endure the same dreary dome until the ocean rose up to devour it.

A hill loomed in the island's centre, its body a broken rampart of rock and bare earth. Houses were scattered around its southern side – near enough to visit each other, but not so close to disturb. Grace counted maybe twenty that she could see, but most looked uninhabited. A few had extensions of crude blocks attached to their sides, as if the owners had given up on the renovations shortly after they'd begun, leaving hollow rooms and empty frames for storm winds to scream through. A lone resident had taken the time to paint their home a pale magnolia. The other dwellings had all blistered in the cold, their concrete darkened in dreary patches as though a cancer had grown through their walls unchecked. And amidst them, squared off like a tombstone, Grace saw Croaghnakeela's church, where Father O'Malley was expecting her.

She pinched the phone from her pocket and rang Carrie, as promised, to let her know she'd arrived safely. A lonely bar of network coverage was kind enough to keep her on the grid, but Grace was still surprised when the call connected.

'Where are you?' were the first words Carrie uttered.

'Where do you think I am? I'm on the island.'

A long sigh of relief. 'What's it like?'

'Honestly,' Grace replied, checking over her shoulder, 'it's pretty bleak. I've been walking for like twenty minutes now and I still haven't seen anyone.'

'Where are they? Aren't these islands meant to be mad for their trad sessions and all that? The tourists love them.'

Grace scoffed. 'Not this one they don't. But don't worry, I can see the church, so that's where I'm headed now.'

'Do you have any... how... stay...'

That last bar on her phone was struggling to keep up with the conversation.

'Sorry, Carrie, you cut out there. I didn't catch a word of that. The coverage is awful out here. I won't be back for a week. Can you check in on the shop for me while I'm away? Carrie... can you hear me?'

She waited for some response, any indication that her words had been delivered, but there wasn't even a disjointed syllable snapped out of context on Carrie's end. And Grace still had so much to tell her. She hadn't even mentioned the weird little bat who'd ferried her over in his toy boat.

'Shit,' Grace muttered, squeezing her phone out of frustration before dropping it back into her pocket. 'Talk to you later, I guess.'

Father O'Malley must have a landline she could borrow. How else would he have contacted her in the first place? There was no need to start fretting about her precious books just yet. She'd felt the first pangs of separation anxiety when she locked the shop door behind her, leaving an empty bottle and a box of porn within view of the window for all the neighbours to gawk at. Even if the books were safe, her social standing on that street would always be in some state of peril.

The first lightless bungalow that Grace encountered was aligned with the laneway, and there was nothing to stand between her and sneaking a closer look inside. Its door was rotten. The ravages of damp glistened around its base like sickly black eggs about to hatch, and she didn't need a local's knowledge to surmise that nobody had lived there for a very long time. Curtains had been drawn across its front-facing windows, but one was parted just enough to peep through. Grace cupped both hands on either side of her eyes as she leaned in closer. The sparse daylight stirred some shadowy shapes within its darkness, but nothing was whole. After so many years of maddening abandonment, the contents of the house must have forgotten what they were. Shrouds of fleecy dust draped their surfaces, and any colours the room might have once held had lost their identities too. They now merged into a collective membrane of muddy greys and browns. But *something* caught her eye – a movement in the stillness.

Grace jolted back from the window, certain that someone had been standing in the far corner of the room, ogling her as she'd stared obliviously into their home.

'Shit,' she whispered, retreating further away, 'sorry.'

Creeping around the island and spying in people's windows probably wasn't the best tack if she was to be stuck there for a week. Grace would be blacklisted before she'd even had the chance to introduce herself. But it didn't make sense given the building's dereliction. The front door would have collapsed from its hinges if anyone had put a shoulder into it. There was no way someone could still have been living there, in dampness and in squalor, denied all but a spit of natural light.

Grace scratched her feet back towards the window, convinced that the darkness had deluded her. There she stole a timid glance to where she'd seen that figure in the shy light of the room. And to her relief, the corner was empty.

'You're seeing things again, Gracie.'

She continued her journey up the pathway, at one with the silence, for there wasn't a sound yet in the air to disturb it.

The church was a build so devoid of imagination that it brought to mind a stable of stone. Though its white paint popped against the sky, this was hardly a feat in itself, seeing as the clouds bulged overhead like black cotton sacks about to burst. Skinny windows of stained glass offered no hint of their craft or colour. That was reserved for the devout – those indoors, creaking pews under bums and whispering into their rosaries. For anyone standing outside, especially on a day as dull as this, they just looked like run-of-the-mill windows, ungodly at best.

Father O'Malley had been politely adamant that she visit him immediately upon her arrival. He did, after all, hold the keys and directions to Grace's inheritance. But there was someone she wanted to say hello to first, whether she felt ready for their reunion or not. Casting a searchful eye over the cemetery, there was only one grave whose soil was freshly mounded and free from the unkempt grasses that grew so liberally elsewhere.

Damp as the grounds may have been, she couldn't feel her feet on that walk.

'Hey, Mum,' Grace whispered, offering her tombstone a short wave, 'remember me?'

All those questions she'd carried like a cross over the years, it was sad that this was where she'd finally lay them to rest, with her mum's ashes, buried beneath the earth amongst a family she'd never known – her family, once upon a lifetime.

'I would have visited you sooner. But no one knew where you were.'

It was perhaps the saddest aspect of Grace's adoption: that the parents who'd raised her for four years had wished to have all trace of their existence erased. No records preserved the history of where she'd come from. All she'd brought to the mainland was a name, and her adoptive parents were kind enough to let her keep that when all else had been lost.

'I don't know why you gave me up, Mum. I'm sure you had your reasons. I just wish I'd met you before today. Maybe you could have told me. Maybe we could have spent some time together. I don't know, maybe you'd have liked that.'

Grace's eyes lifted to the church. A priest was stood by its open door, clad head to toe in his best black, watching her. What else had the man to do but guard his house of God like a watchdog in a white collar?

'There's Father O'Malley now, Mum, spying on us.'

Or was it? The voice she'd heard on the phone had held such a distinctive, cask-aged warmth, making Grace imagine someone much older. A daughter standing by her mother's grave didn't exactly cry out for company and light conversation, and yet the priest was now trudging between the tombstones towards her, hands in his pockets, carrying the weight of the island's sins on his shoulders, fittingly solemn given the scene surrounding him.

He offered a coy wave as he stepped within earshot. 'I'm not interrupting, am I?'

The voice was the same.

'No, not at all, Father,' Grace replied.

His polished black shoes sank without a sound into the

wet grass as he padded over to Grace's side, ever respectful, as though he'd played this role a thousand times.

'Keeping Chrissy company, I see,' Father O'Malley said, turning his head to share a smile.

'Just introducing myself, Father.'

'Please,' he said, 'call me Richard. Everyone's always calling me Father. I guess it wouldn't be so strange if I wasn't the youngest person on the island.'

The Father O'Malley in Grace's mind had been an elderly chap in his eighties, probably handsome enough during his wild days in the seminary, but an old-timer nonetheless, with a worn picture of the Virgin Mary in his breast pocket and an insatiable fondness for boiled sweets. She'd imagined grey hair and similarly ashen skin – any colour between black and white, if only to match up with his outfit. But *Richard* couldn't have been much older than Grace. He was possibly even younger. The autumnal palette that the island was so lacking seemed to exist entirely within the man's beard. His hair on top was darker than the rest, long and drawn back behind his ears, and his eyes were some of the brownest she'd ever seen, squinched up beneath heavy eyelids and gleaming golden in the dim daylight.

'How was your crossing?' he asked.

'It was... interesting,' she replied, smirking over at him. 'Maloney is quite the character, isn't he?'

'*That* man,' he said with a sigh. 'He didn't try to swindle you, did he? I told him not to. I even threatened the bastard with God's wrath if he did.'

Grace chuckled. 'He stuck me for fifty euro.'

'Of course he did,' Richard said, smiling embarrassedly as he cast his eyes to the sky. 'I'm sorry about that. I wish there'd been some other way to get you over here. But Maloney's the only man with a boat who'll come out this way, though his time isn't cheap. And just you wait for next week when he's bringing Finnerty's kegs over and collecting the empties. He'll charge extra for the *labour*, as he calls it, even though Brendan has to do all the heavy lifting with Maloney watching him from his deck.'

'What exactly is it about this island that has him so nervous?'

'I wish I knew,' the priest replied. 'Something happened here, long before I ever arrived, Grace, that I think everyone is trying to forget. But I wouldn't trust any rumours you've heard from the likes of Maloney. You know yourself, the Irish love nothing more than a good story. And we're so isolated here, heaven only knows what they're saying about us.'

'Maloney told me there are no children on the island?'

'Now, sadly that is true,' Richard said, clearly more comfortable than the captain had been in discussing the topic. 'Would you believe I haven't seen a child in six years? Never thought I'd miss the little buggers. And it's a strange thing; the absence of children just makes a man feel… older, I suppose. There's only a handful of families left on the island and I know they don't like to talk about it.'

'That's weird,' Grace said, frowning over at the man, doubting her own hearing more than his honesty. 'I was sure I heard a kid laughing at me when I got off the boat.'

The priest shook his head. 'That's impossible I'm afraid, unless our man Maloney is smuggling them over. Oh, and before I forget,' he added, rooting around in his pocket, 'I do believe this is yours.'

Grace picked the lonely key from his palm.

'It's a fine house,' the priest added. 'Chrissy kept it pristine over the years. You can't miss it actually. She never could understand why the others left theirs so plain, and so hers is the only one that's been painted.'

'The magnolia house?'

'Yes, that's the one.'

Grace's heart – its strings so knotted and sore – swelled with pride.

'You don't have to stay there, you know,' Richard said. 'I can talk to Finnerty, if you like? There's an empty room or two above his pub. I can have him prepare a bed for you.'

'I'll be okay,' Grace replied, grateful for the thought.

As the key was pocketed, a woman caught her attention. She was treading slowly up the path towards the church, shoulders stooped, her head bound in a black scarf. The only discernible trait at that distance was her age. Grace smiled at the sight of her, braving the journey to visit her God in person, making sure the day's prayers were hand-delivered. Richard delighted at the sight of her too, though he seemed to source more joy from Grace's natural reaction to the woman.

'Bridie is one of my regulars,' he said as together they watched the woman enter the church. 'She comes every day. It does her good to see people, to be a part of this world, to know that she hasn't been forgotten. But there are others here on the island, Grace, who aren't so fortunate.'

She'd seen it with her own eyes. Those living alone, too wary to step outside onto streets they no longer recognised. No more familiar faces. No friends to visit them. The longest days are those spent missing all that you have lost, knowing that your happiness and the hope of its return count amongst the absent.

'It's sad when people are forgotten,' Grace said, wondering where the priest was leading the conversation and how long it would take him to get there.

'May I ask you something, Grace?'

'Of course, Fa...' she replied, catching herself in time. '*Richard*. Sorry, I can't promise I'll get used to that.'

'There's a woman in the village who, I believe, could use some company,' he said, respectfully discarding his smile. 'It's just an idea, of course. Please, by all means feel free to say no. I understand that, given the circumstances, you may wish to be left alone, to grieve and, I suppose, make sense of all this.'

Even when stood amidst that chill, Grace gleaned some warmth from his eyes. 'Who is she?'

'Harriet,' he replied, a name fondly spoken. 'She's lived here all of her life, if you could call it that. Life, I mean. Poor woman.'

'Is she very old?' Grace asked.

'She's... let me think.' Richard tilted his head back in thought. 'She would still be in her seventies, so not especially.'

'And she lives alone?'

'She does.'

'Has anyone visited her like this before?'

'Unfortunately, no. Just me. Time tends to leave some people behind, and Harriet is one such soul. She had a terrible life and I think that good company could be a means to move on from her experiences. You have that special something. I don't mean empathy or kindness, though I can tell you have those in droves. You are Chrissy's daughter, after all. How can I describe it? Some people don't just feel the sadness and the loneliness, Grace, they see it. They truly see the person in a way that others cannot. And I think that's what Harriet needs, a friend, if only to remind her that friends – wonderful gifts that they are – still exist.'

Grace felt almost obliged to offer some kindness back to the man.

'When do you want me to visit her?' she asked, committing there and then to his proposal.

'When are you free?' he replied, inviting that smile of his back on stage for an encore.

'Anytime really. I'm stuck here until Maloney's next delivery.'

That was if the little captain didn't skedaddle back to the mainland without her, though the lure of another crisp fifty was probably bait enough to hook his interest.

'How about I visit Harriet and run the idea by her. I'm sure she's grown quite tired of entertaining me in her home. It could be nice, perhaps, all going well, if you were to meet her on Sunday? And then we can take it from there.'

'Okay,' she agreed. 'So, tomorrow?'

'Yes, of course,' he replied absently. 'Tomorrow's Sunday, isn't it?'

The priest was looking elsewhere. Anywhere, it seemed, other than at Grace. His hands were shoved back into their respective pockets, stuffing some unspoken truth in deeper.

'What's wrong?' she asked, calling him out. 'There's something you aren't telling me.'

'There's something that I'm reluctant to tell you,' he replied shyly, with a very particular smile that made him look even younger.

The man *had* been holding back on her. Whatever would Jesus have to say about this? Grace kept her grin in check, though she still took some delight in grilling a priest in his own churchyard.

'Go on so,' Grace said, awaiting his confession. 'What are you *reluctant* to tell me?'

'Harriet's husband passed away some years ago,' he explained, 'and she's lived on her own ever since. In the same house, might I add, that they shared when he was alive.'

'Okay,' Grace said, surprised by the truth's simplicity, 'there's nothing especially unusual about that, is there?'

'No, I suppose not.'

'What condition is the house in?' she asked.

'Condition?' Richard echoed blankly.

Grace held his gaze. Wasn't this an obvious question?

'Ah,' he said eventually, 'you have no need to worry. The house is actually in very good condition overall. Better than most. Mind you, it does have a strangely austere feel to it. Harriet's late husband – Valentine was his name – had an aversion to clutter, I think. So it's all quite empty really. More a house than a home, I believe is what they say.'

'Valentine?' Grace repeated. 'That's a name you don't hear these days.'

'Indeed, you don't,' the priest agreed. 'Fashions change, even with names.'

'Does she miss him?'

'Quite the opposite, actually,' he replied. 'Harriet is convinced that her dead husband is still with her.'

'Oh,' Grace whispered, drawing a hand to her lips, 'that complicates things.'

Had the priest genuinely considered not sharing this information? His intentions may have been in Harriet's best interest, but he was well out of his depth if the woman was suffering a mental illness of sorts. Dementia and Alzheimer's weren't cured with a little company.

'Harriet's mind couldn't be sharper,' he added, marking her concern. 'She's not sick. I can tell you that now without an iota of doubt.'

'Then what is she?'

'She's terrified, Grace,' he replied, letting that comment hang in the cemetery's soundless air.

Grace's eyes strayed to her mum's name, wondering if she were listening in, curious as to what kind of woman her daughter had grown up to be. Harriet's case was getting more and more complicated by the moment, but that should have encouraged, not dispirited, her willingness to help.

'She won't open up to me,' Richard continued. 'But if you could talk to her, I think that would really help. She's lonely, Grace, and she's old. Fears come naturally. And the poor woman has no idea that—'

Grace raised a hand, cutting the priest short mid-sentence. 'Okay,' she said, beaming brightly to apologise for the interruption. 'I'll see what I can do. But, Richard, the woman might need professional help. Do you understand what I'm saying? Like a nursing home on the mainland or something. And without regular carers, anything could happen and you wouldn't even know. She could have a fall. She might forget to buy enough food. I don't…' She stopped herself. 'I don't know. But I'll do what I can.'

'Of course,' he said. 'It would mean so much to me, if you could.'

Given Grace's swelling curiosity surrounding her old family home, her feet were now itching to leave and find some shelter before that brood of black rainclouds spilled their guts.

'Tomorrow,' she said, turning her shoulder slightly to advertise her departure, 'we're going to visit Harriet?'

'Yes, of course. Sunday, tomorrow.'

Grace felt mildly chuffed that the priest had deemed her the best candidate for the job. It was, she liked to believe, a tribute to her mum's character that he would trust her after so short an acquaintance.

'Does she really believe he's still alive?' Grace asked as the distance widened between them.

'No,' Richard replied, 'she's quite aware that her husband is dead.'

'So Harriet thinks that she's being haunted?'

'Oh, I'm afraid it's worse than that. I don't want to say too much in case it colours your opinion of the woman. It's best, I think, if you find out for yourself. I'm sorry to have kept you. But thank you, Grace, for your time and understanding.'

With that the priest retraced his path between the tombstones, plodding clumsily over clots of weed.

'Hey,' Grace called after him, to which he turned, 'why doesn't Harriet have any friends? You said she'd lived here all of her life.'

'Her husband,' he replied ruefully.

'What do you mean?'

'Valentine Lavelle wasn't a nice man, Grace. It's important that you remember that.'

4

ROBIN

The wind and the water, those two restless sharks that forever stalked the west coast. They kept its shores safe from absolute silence, whistling and roaring, and warping those last lonely hawthorns so that none stood straight. The young priest felt it too. They all did. Croaghnakeela wasn't just inhospitable, it downright hated everyone that stood on it. Six years gone and still Robin hadn't acclimatised. It was safe to assume by now that he never would.

The day had soured around four o'clock, making fortresses of homes and deeming Finnerty's pub the safest place to hide out, as if the islanders needed an excuse. Still, it was hard to condemn them. The publican took good care of those who filled his till, and the ashes in his hearth rarely settled. It was a haven from the cold, if nothing else – a reason to sit together and share in the silence that clung to their tongues like a bad taste.

The sacristy was the warmest part of the church. Boxy as it was, it felt like home to a priest who for a while didn't think he'd ever have one again. God's plan for him certainly wasn't without a few questionable surprises. Its walls were a smoky grey and so similar to stone that a retouch of white paint would only spoil the effect. The radiator stored a low heat courtesy of the collection basket. Mahogany panels across the wardrobe and cabinets gave it the feel of an office, somewhere for Robin to sit, to rest, to read, and to write as he was now. He'd jotted down a short note for Grace – Chrissy O'Dwyer's daughter. Careful words sprinkled with care about the page. Nobody knew Harriet like Robin did. But she was that oyster he couldn't shuck – the one soul that wouldn't open up for him. But maybe, or so he hoped, Grace would succeed where he had failed.

Sincerely yours, he wrote.

No matter how he practised his signature, it never flowed naturally from his wrist.

Father Richard O'Malley.

It was an old island surname. The bishop thought it would help him fit in – a shiny accessory to spruce up his disguise. There were times when the sound of it passed right over him, like a dog who'd only memorised half a dozen words. Robin would tap his ear with an apologetic smile whenever he missed it. There were some who only spoke to him in raised voices now, but he'd no choice but to play along. Regardless of his youth, their priest was their Father, and Richard O'Malley was his name. In the eyes of the church and the world it conquered, Robin Thompson no longer existed.

He was surprised when the bishop let him remain in Ireland, though being transferred to Croaghnakeela did feel an awful lot like exile. He understood the church's reasons. The scene he'd caused was loud. It'd drawn interest, and not the kind he had hoped for. It was easier for everyone – himself included – to simply move on, to disappear and let time do the forgetting for him. Priests had no familial ties. No identity other than their calling. It was sad for him to leave and probably sad for a few to see him go, those who understood. But they weren't many. Gossip doesn't heal like the truth. It goes gangrenous, and by God does it spread.

A few had asked after his old parish when he'd arrived, more so out of politeness than genuine curiosity. Even that lie was forgotten before it could be cross-examined. Robin's past had been cleansed by the salt water when he'd made that crossing, ever mindful of the fact that it was a one-way journey and that his life would be forever changed from that day forth. Fresh air. Fresh start. But even that optimism aged like everything else.

Croaghnakeela had its secrets too. Robin knew that when his feet first touched its soil. The waves there broke the shore in a light mist that tasted too much like death. And it wasn't the sleepy kind of silence that kept the island so still. Whispers don't work when they're all a people speak. Something happened there that it wanted to forget. Sealing their lips was a way to pat down the soil. Talking only disturbed it. But Robin knew better. The truth never stayed buried, and the silence never got any easier, no matter how they may pretend.

Saturdays were the quietest in church. It was the day when the islanders raised all those wholesome sins for their next confession. Finnerty would lock them in after hours, covering up the windows so that God couldn't catch sight of them – the Almighty's omniscience trumped by a thin pair of curtains. It was never the stout. For whatever reason, that drink was blessed as the sacrament. No, whenever there was a row or a raised fist, Robin knew what was to blame. He'd peel the word from their lips like the skin from an unripe orange. It was as though they were betraying an old friend, a repeat offender at that, leading sober men astray and sending more than a few careening into some moonlit ditch on their walk home.

'It was the whiskey, Father,' they'd whisper from the thatched shadows of the confessional.

One would swear the smell of it robbed a man of his own free will. The priest would offer his tired sympathies and prescribe three Hail Marys to clear the conscience – no more, no less, though he doubted many took it seriously. Sometimes he'd throw in that same sage advice he'd considered printing in every church pamphlet: *would you not just stay on the stout?*

'I'll try, Father,' they'd reply, adding that lie to their next confession.

Robin had read through the week's newsletter, counting the typos. None too grievous this time round. He'd laid out his vestments for the following day's mass and tidied around the room as though any aspect of it were ever out of place. It was the nerves, so needy for distraction. He hadn't sat still since speaking to Grace. The key to Harriet's door was slipped into the envelope, sealed and pocketed. Chrissy's girl could help. He was sure of that.

More fool was he to think that a daughter should borrow her mother's likeness. Grace had inherited so much from her father, in looks at least. Same green eyes, like Connemara marble, perfectly cut and polished, and a curio she might have resented had she known where they'd come from. They didn't catch the light, those eyes, they devoured it. Robin had only seen Declan in photographs. He'd been handsome, no doubt, and the priest thought it peculiar how that translates to beauty. Smaller face, same sharp bones, but with a softness that her father never had to his own. It was, in essence, Chrissy's kindness sealed and stored in a roughly cut locket. She also had her father's red hair, curled and coppered as though to touch it would slice you open and call for a tetanus shot. It rolled down to her shoulders, thick, effortless, and probably the envy of many. But all that mattered was her compassion – that gift so rare.

He stepped out of the sacristy on the off chance that anyone had come looking for him. There was only Bridie as per usual, rosary in hand, oblivious to his head poking out. The colours that stained the glass were darkening, each passing hour adding another glob of black to their palettes. Autumn's night was a curtain. It'd drop without Robin realising its cue had rolled around again, and he was getting worse at keeping track of it. Time had never been his friend. Whereas there were those who saw it as something steady, like a pool of water they could gauge from one end to the next, he saw the ripples that they couldn't. The past, the present, the future – when you splash a stone in there, they're all the same.

Bridie's presence between the pews was a given. She hadn't missed a day since the accident; content to sit and pray, to talk to God directly in her own way. Robin had considered introducing her to Chrissy's daughter. But Harriet's dilemma was far more pressing, and it wouldn't do to take liberties with Grace's good nature.

The church was his sanctuary. Those who only crossed its door on Sunday never realised just how safe a place it was – a far sturdier bastion than Finnerty's had ever been. Robin had told them in no uncertain words, too many times now to merit repeating himself again. Suffer nightmares for long enough and they'll eventually feel like dreams. But that doesn't mean they slept any better.

It was common enough to lock up the church earlier on Saturday. Only Bridie was ever any the wiser, and if Jesus himself rose on the island he'd probably be tempted into Finnerty's with the rest of them. He could sit in the back row and nurse his sore head during mass the next day. Robin knew that Bridie would sit there until he went about turning off the lights, and he'd rather she leave whilst there was still some pale in the sky.

'I'll be closing up soon, Bridie,' he said, his voice's echo lingering somewhere in the ceiling. 'Will you be okay finding your way home?'

Robin knew the answer. But he still asked every day. The woman tilted her head – the subtlest of gestures, only noticeable because the priest knew to look for it. Her family were aware she was there. He had told them, and he'd promised to keep an eye on her. In a way, which surprised him, they had understood.

He considered calling into Finnerty's himself. Far from a weakness, it was one of his weekend treats, and Robin liked to imagine that the islanders better enjoyed their pints knowing that their priest was a party to them. That was his excuse anyway. If you can't beat them, join them.

He stepped back into the sacristy, relishing in its warmth before meeting the chill evening air. The wind was singing over the naked land, awakening all those natural, living things that knew as well as Robin did that something horribly unnatural lived amongst them. The kind that caused shadows to shift in the cold, like bones reaching up, searching desperately for some kind of innocence, if ever there was any left on that island.

He patted down his jacket and felt the envelope in its pocket and the spare key he had for Harriet's. When Robin returned to the altar, Bridie was gone. The door was ajar, as he had left it. He stood a moment, breathing in that cool silence, reminding himself that it was just a name.

Father Richard O'Malley.

Nothing had changed. He still had his responsibilities. And he'd only God to thank for that.

5

GRACE

This was where Grace had spoken her first words, taken those first uncertain steps, and where – despite these momentous achievements – the decision was made to give her away. Unlike that hovel she'd peered into earlier, her mum's door held a long pane of frosted glass above its letter plate, and it had received a glossy coat of blue paint in the not-too-distant past. She had cared for her house. She'd kept it alive by feeding it some colour when all those around it were left to starve. Grasses had grown untamed within its tiny garden, with a few clumps of weed taking shelter neath the sills of two latticed windows. Nature must have seized on her mum's illness as an opportunity to expand. But it was positively manicured compared to what she'd passed on her walk to its front step.

'It's just a door, Gracie,' she whispered, toying with the key that Father Richard had given her. 'All you have to do is open it.'

She wanted to enter. And yet something was holding her back. Bungalows, especially the small ones, don't tend to draw any profound feelings of fondness or revulsion. But

Grace knew without being told that she wasn't welcome there. Whatever unaired hopes her mum may have held for her daughter's future, she was certain that avoiding this house was of the highest priority. It was the eeriest epiphany, and it came not as a warm ray of light but rather a sudden chill that coursed right down to her toes.

'I'm not staying above the pub,' Grace muttered to herself, pinching the key harder as she imagined the islanders' many eyes all turning to gawk at her.

Determined, she clicked open the door with a brave turn of its key. It swung inward with the faintest press, its handle knocking on the wall within. Reluctant as the light was to enter, it ventured so far as a line of white powder on the wooden floor. It'd been poured across the threshold, not a foot from the step, and done in such a way that could only have been intentional.

'Maybe I'm not so alone here after all,' Grace said, assuming it to be rat poison as she listened out for the pitter-patter of tiny feet scuttling across the floorboards.

One wall of the hallway was lined with a queue of black binbags, all strangled into knots as if awaiting collection. Not the most welcoming of parties. But then, she wasn't exactly expecting colourful bunting or balloons given the circumstances. Had her mum prepped her belongings like this? The priest did say that she'd been ill for a long time. Grace couldn't imagine a sadder chore: to pack up your worldly possessions in anticipation of the end – to finally realise their worthlessness in the grander scheme of things.

Grace sidled inside, back to the wall, taking care not to drag her feet through the powder. If it wasn't healthy for the rat, then it probably wasn't great for her boots either. An oval mirror was hanging by the door, unseen until she came face to face with it.

'Good Lord,' she mumbled, trying to mash some shape back into her hair.

Grace wondered how many times her mum had stood in that same spot. Had they shared the same face, the same hair, the same imaginative eyes? The impossible riddles of her past were on the cusp of unravelling and nothing would ever be *the same* again.

The first door on her right led to the sitting room: a squared-off space with a sunken couch by the wall and an armchair facing the fireplace, its grate swept clean, with a scuttle of coal and a neat pyramid of briquettes built beside it. More white powder lined the brown tiles of its hearth.

'Seriously?' Grace sighed, horrified at the thought of a bloated rat creeping down the chimney. 'How is that even a thing?'

There was a coffee table in front of it, and in the corner stood a bookcase, stripped clean. Tattered as the furniture may have been, it was the fact of it being so empty that saddened Grace most of all. She'd probably been too optimistic in her hopes of finding a home. Instead it resembled an outdated showroom, desirous of some swift refurbishment or the strong swing of a well-aimed wrecking ball. But something *had* been left behind. Her eyes were drawn to the mantel – to the only embellishment that remained after all else had been bagged and relegated as rubbish to the hallway. The photograph's glossy colours had aged over the years, but it was her mum, seen for the first time, holding a baby Grace in her arms, complete with curly red hair and that look of primitive bewilderment that comes to babies so naturally – proof that her life hadn't begun on her first day of school.

'Hey, Mum,' she whispered, lost for words in that most singular of moments.

Grace had hoped that they'd shared so much in common, with age being their sole distinction, but there were few, if any, similarities between them. Jet-black hair draped down to her mum's shoulders, freshly combed and silken in the camera flash. And she had the kindest face, round-cheeked, with squinty brown eyes that did more than twinkle, they glowed with a warmth that rivalled even the island's priest. She tried to imagine how the woman might have aged between that moment and her passing. Had time ravaged or enriched her beauty? Was her life one of happiness or one of regret? There was so much that Grace still didn't know.

As she returned to the hallway, she felt instinctively drawn to one door in particular. It was as though a memory from another life had just trespassed into this one, upsetting the scales as the past suddenly outweighed the present. It was her old bedroom, novel to the eye and yet so intimate to the soul that it set her whole body atremble. She looked to the bed with its perfectly laid pink linen, imagining the ghost of the other Grace lying across it – the Grace who'd lived within these walls before the island cast her ashore, confiscating all but her name. The tasselled lampshade on the nightstand, the chest brimming fat with board games and jigsaws – its every artefact felt so intimate. Stepping back in a daze, she drew the door closed and stood, eyes held shut, forehead pressed against its wood.

Carrie had been right. She shouldn't have done this alone.

At the end of the house, a stream of leaden light trickled across the tiles of the kitchen floor. Akin to the other rooms, Grace found it clean and orderly, reinforcing the suspicion that her mum had been preparing the house for sale. Countertops had been scrubbed and bleached. No perishables remained. But thankfully she did find four cans of soup in a top cabinet, so she wasn't going to starve. Though Grace hadn't considered that dilemma until she'd laid eyes on them.

'Right,' she said, placing two cans down and swivelling their labels around to face her, 'what's it going to be?'

It was then – standing alone in the calm of her mum's kitchen, deciding between tomato or cream of chicken – that she heard it: the same laughter, those stifled little giggles that could only have come from a child.

Grace looked to the kitchen door, uneasy now. 'Is someone there?' she called out.

A quick succession of footfalls suddenly hammered down the hallway.

Grace couldn't believe it. They were actually inside the house. Her nervousness was usurped by a far more proactive sense of annoyance and so, eager to catch the little scut who was responsible, Grace stormed across the kitchen. She hadn't heard the front door open nor had she heard it close. And yet outside, standing on the front step, behind that pane of frosted glass, she saw the dark shape of a young boy, no more than ten years old.

'Hello,' she shouted down to him, startled by the echo of her own voice. 'You know you're not allowed in here? You can't just come into someone's house, or did your parents forget to teach you that?'

The glass blurred the child's features into their basest form and colour, but he wasn't seen to react at all. It was as though he were staring at her, just as Grace was staring at him, his skinny bones rigid and unmoving.

'Stay there,' Grace said, squeezing clumsily past the train of bags, her frustration on a low simmer. 'Just don't fucking move, please.'

Locking one eye on the child and the other on her feet proved trickier than she'd expected. The rubbish had splayed in parts after she'd disturbed it, leaving scant floor place to aim for, and it came as no surprise really when her foot snagged on something hard, sending her crumbling forward.

'Oh, come on,' she grumbled with one hand sunken out of sight and the other pressed to the wall, her distemper divvied out between the bags and the boy.

But even as Grace sank deeper into that pile of God knows what, she was aware of the silhouette still standing by the glass, offering some reassurance that her quarry hadn't already scarpered off. She was surprised not to hear the little shit laughing at her.

'Hang on,' she called out as she struggled to clamber back onto her feet, more focused on the floor than the door. 'Don't go running off any—'

Grace's heart sank when she looked up.

Where the boy had stood only a blink of an eye earlier, there was now only the grey light of a long and haunting day darkening in the frosted glass.

6

BRENDAN

Every family on the island had gathered under Finnerty's roof that evening. Brendan was roosted on his usual high stool, heel of the counter, the farthest a man could sit from the door. The pub was a long gallery of a room, and from there Brendan could keep an eye on its comings and goings without ever turning his head. Walls were cluttered with bric-a-brac – nets and useless tools, mostly – and framed prints darkened under dirty glass. Sawdust scattered the hardwood floor. Amber was the light, warm as whiskey. Every day, without fail, the stone hearth kept the flames on and the layers off. Most arms slipped their sleeves before opening the door, knowing full well to expect a heat that'd make a teetotaller thirsty.

The usual musicians were by the window, pints on the house for so long as they kept the silence out. Donal Holleran – late fifties now – on fiddle. He'd been playing since they dropped the bow in his cot. Best there ever was on the island, no question. He could knock out a tune and be watching the news at the same time and you'd never know. The last of the Tierneys – Ray was his name, sixty-one years under his belt and still tone deaf – was thrashing the guitar. Fucking eyes closed and grimacing as though playing a few chords sent him into a trance. Too many notions and not enough practice was Brendan's take on that lad. If he'd open an eye, his fingers might actually find the right fret for once. Holleran would throw him a look of daggers here and there, resisting the urge to wrap all six steel strings around his neck.

Brendan didn't play. The only music he understood was in the ocean and its waves. The shell of his boat had come from his father. He'd taught him how and where to sweep the nets, out there without a lifejacket, still a child. He'd learned more than that since, but he still ascribed it all to the old man. Brendan's hands were once the hardest on the island, and they were still there for anyone who needed them, same as his father's used to be. That much was taken as gospel by those who knew him. But his bones had ached worse than ever these past winters, the fingers especially. Mutinous pirates no longer did as they were told. It was as though the sand had settled in between their hinges, forever crunching and crackling. Getting old never meant life got any easier. His father had warned him as much.

Brendan scanned the faces lining the bar taps. Such a solemn bunch of bastards. There was hardly a word whispered between them. They'd known each other all their lives and could pass now as strangers. The way most of them stared glassy-eyed into their drinks, you'd swear it was poison Finnerty was pulling. That's partly why the music was welcome – any excuse not to strike up a conversation with the dour sod sitting next to you. But then, Brendan knew they had their reasons, no more than himself.

Gerard and Laoise Cunnane were there. His pint near

empty. Her wine untouched. Quiet couple in their sixties. Kept to themselves mostly. Held hands as if the wind might take the other away. The widow Mary Malley had her hunched back to Brendan, watching the fiddle-playing, lost in the notes, and happily alone in company as usual. Connor O'Toole was there with his daughter. Whereas he was thin as a stick, Sarah carried a shape to her. Still single though, to Brendan's knowledge, not that the island was exactly rippling with suitors; on the cusp of turning forty now but still the youngest local left alive. Both were pale as the other, with hair black as pitch. Words passed back and forth between them like an unwanted gift, and neither shared a smile. Eoin Murray was there, the survivor of a dead brother, never the same since. Tadgh Scuffel, too, with his wife, Maggie. Only he ever called her Margaret. Close enough to marry the woman but not to call her fucking Maggie. Ridiculous. She'd aged beautifully. And yet there she was, tied to the arm of that smug mutt with more hair above his lip than on his spotty head. And at the opposing end of the counter, facing Brendan but rarely meeting his eye, was Fergal Wilberforce. Fat bastard with a mouthful of wet brown teeth and a beard that still held the cream from last week's stout. Closest seat to the door because he crawled out most nights.

There were two generations in that room – saddest dying breed of bastards Brendan ever met. His crowd were all in their late fifties or sixties. And the younger ones – for loss of a better word – were either edging forty or past it already. Every year they each got older, and every now and again their number would lessen, leaving another empty stool by the bar. Chrissy was their latest loss, God love her. She'd known better than anyone that Croaghnakeela was no place for a child.

'You all right for a pint?' John Finnerty asked, nodding down at Brendan's glass.

He hadn't realised he'd emptied it. Ladders of cream still held strong. He mashed his palm across the bristles of his beard – a habit of his when considering another.

'Go on,' he replied, 'and would you tell the lads to quit the music for a moment? I want to have a word.' This he added with a glum wink that was understood.

Finnerty hesitated nervously before retreating to the other end of the bar. He caught Donal's eye as the other gobshite still had his closed. Drawing a flat hand across his neck cut an instant silence. Not a single head turned to the musicians. Instead they all looked to Brendan, as though they'd been dreading this conversation all evening.

'We're all here,' he said, now stood from his stool, leaning two heavy arms on the bar, 'and it's time we talked about what's been going on. I know some of you don't want to. But I don't think we've a choice in the matter anymore.'

A few heads bobbed gently up and down as though disturbed by a draught.

'Would I be right in saying that you've all heard it?' Brendan asked.

Firewood cracked and split in the silence. It warmed their arses but not their willingness to speak up. He knew they'd all been suffering these past days, hoping the evil would just keep on walking if they ignored it. Brendan wasn't sure which he pitied more – their cowardice or their optimism. But there was certainly no home for the latter on Croaghnakeela.

'Footsteps,' the widow said. 'Downstairs, two nights ago. So loud that I swear they shook the house.'

Their bodies shifted in closer to each other, like animals

tend to do when they're cornered, as though some strength in numbers could miraculously boost them up the food chain. Eoin Murray steadied a hand around his pint. They knew his brother's death wasn't an accident. And he did too. The hottest room on the island suddenly didn't feel so warm.

'Is that the same for everyone?' Brendan asked, calmly as he could.

He looked to each person individually. Only Connor O'Toole had the courage to speak up.

'We heard a knocking on the door,' he said, looking to Sarah by his side. 'Quiet the first night. But it's gotten louder.'

Finnerty topped off Brendan's pint and handed it over. It was a rare day that you'd see a tremble to the publican's hand and yet there it was, aired to all those who didn't know where else to look.

'Cheers, lad,' Brendan whispered through his silvered whiskers, embarrassed for the man.

It was O'Toole's daughter who voiced what they all were thinking.

'Why now?'

She was probably too young to remember him. But she'd come to his funeral like the rest of them, and she'd heard the stories too. They were never intended to scare anyone. They were only ever meant to be a warning.

'It's been thirty-odd years,' her father put in, voice as light as his body. 'We all watched the bastard being buried, didn't we?'

'We were all there, Connor,' Brendan agreed, taking a long draw of his pint.

'It doesn't matter a shite what was in that casket,' came the low thunder of Fergal Wilberforce. 'What we buried that day was flesh and bone. And we all know that the Bodach doesn't need either of those fucking things to make our lives a misery.'

Brendan placed his stout down gently and sucked in its cream from his beard. Wilberforce may have been a drunk. But Wilberforce wasn't wrong.

'But we've had peace here for years,' Maggie Scuffel said, to which her husband reached an arm around her shoulder, pouting that little moustache of his like a terrier guarding its bone.

'Peace?' Wilberforce scoffed. 'Just because you removed his mark from your land doesn't make it yours again. We're still in his fucking debt unless you've forgotten. And he won't rest until he gets what's his.'

'Do we know how Chrissy died?' the widow asked.

'Chrissy was sick for a long time,' Brendan replied sadly.

'Her daughter landed in today,' Sarah said sullenly. 'I saw her walking back from the cemetery. Does she know anything about this?'

'Impossible,' Brendan replied. 'Chrissy kept her safe from all that. It broke her heart, but she had her gone from this island soon as she could. If only we'd been so brave.'

That closing sentiment echoed in the silence that followed. One dream stretched thin between a whole community – to be gone from that place, to stop looking over their shoulders, to be free from the horror that stalked their days and dreams with pounding steps.

'What can we do?' Finnerty asked, his eyes panning those lining the bar before finally falling back on Brendan.

'I don't know,' he replied, mooning over the question. 'Like Connor said, we put him in the ground. What more could we have done?'

'Burned him,' Eoin Murray snapped, bitter as the day his brother drowned.

Laoise Cunnane, squeezing her husband's hand as always, leaned forward to meet Murray in the eye. 'And how do you intend on explaining that to Father O'Malley, Eoin? We can't exactly dig him up without him asking why, can we?'

'How much does the priest know?' Finnerty asked, throwing the question in the air for anyone to catch.

'Sure he's only been here a few years, and we haven't been especially honest with him now, have we?' was the widow's answer. 'Even the priest before him, Father Maguire, only came to the island the day after the bastard died. He held a funeral before he did a mass. Never a good omen. He should have known this place was doomed from the start.'

'Richard knows enough to leave us be,' Brendan said. 'More, I reckon, than we give him credit for.'

'He's a good man,' Sarah added.

To that everyone nodded in mute agreement.

The pub's windows had dimmed like lanterns leaking oil. Too short were the days. Too long the nights.

'So, he's back?' Wilberforce grunted.

'It would seem so, Fergal,' Brendan replied, frowning at the man. 'Unless some other dead bastard is visiting your home without need for a key.'

'But why now?' Finnerty asked, standing between them like a jittery referee.

'Maybe he was never gone,' Wilberforce replied, speaking more soberly than Brendan had ever heard him. 'Did you ever think about that? Maybe he's been stepping into your homes all this time, keeping an eye on ye. Maybe something has given him back his fucking power and he's here to collect what we denied him.'

Brendan watched the others pale around the room. Whatever was happening, scaring the shite out of everyone wasn't going to help matters.

'For fuck's sake, Wilberforce,' he said, staring him down across the pub. 'You can't say—'

The filament in every bulb flickered.

And then they died.

A hymn of gasps filled the darkness. Someone suppressed a shriek. There was only the flames behind their backs, and yet their presence was no longer felt. A room so warm – so stifling that no skin within was ever dry – was now icy as a tomb. Lips shivered. Cold fingers balled up into painful fists. Together they watched the firelight flicker across the low ceiling, making glow their barest features. And they watched in disbelief as the flames weakened, darkening and darkening, until the dark was all there was.

Heels clicked on the path outside, getting closer by the second, where the faint moonlight settled on the sills like fallen ash. The footsteps reached the door. Everyone sucked in that cool air, holding their breath in anticipation of what was to come. And then, in a blinding second, every bulb was reborn and the hearth's flame licked back to life. Brendan jolted back from the lip of the counter, his large hand choking his pint glass near to shatter. No eye blinked. None shifted their gaze an inch from that door as it drifted inward.

Father O'Malley had never been more welcome.

'I must be losing it.' He laughed through his own bafflement. 'I could have sworn the lights were out. And there was me thinking I wasn't going to have a cheeky scoop before I head off home.'

If the priest had glimpsed the fear across all their faces, then he was a wise enough man not to mention it. His eyes sought out Brendan at the back of the room, and a subtle wink was all it took for him to ask that same old question without speaking a word.

What are you all so afraid of?

7

GRACE

It was midday when she set out for Harriet's. The same clouds from the day before still held the sun hostage, billowing black as bonfire smoke behind the distant hilltop and steeping down its sides in candyfloss tufts of white. Skies like that did more harm than they did good. They undermined the hour, making Croaghnakeela forever feel on the cusp of twilight. Grace just hoped for the islanders' sake that one of Maloney's crates had been chock full of vitamin D tablets, otherwise their bones and spirits would split long before the winter had had its heartless way with them.

With the front door locked and standing alone amidst that dank, misty air once again, she'd waited a moment, listening, half-expecting more laughter, but hearing only the low warble of the wind. That silence – so dispiriting twenty-four hours earlier – now came to Grace as a comfort. The island obviously wasn't so lacking in children as the captain and priest would have her believe. But at that hour, the islanders – and any fucking kids – should have been locked up in church under Richard and God's joint supervision, gifting her a narrow but hopefully sufficient window to reach the old woman's home unhindered. Seeing as she was marooned on Croaghnakeela for a week at the very least, eventually she'd have to introduce herself. But today was not that day.

She tested the door handle one last time before leaving. God bless any burglars with a mind to break into *this* house, with only a few soup cans left for stealing. She'd find their mangled bodies stuck halfway up the hallway, weeping into binbags.

'Okay, let's get this over with, shall we?' Grace said, patting around her coat pockets. 'We have our keys, our directions, and… we're good to go.'

She'd stayed in her old room that night. The bed was too narrow to toss and turn her way to sleep. And so, with no other choice, Grace had lain on her back, staring at the starry stickers glowing on her ceiling, watching them as she must have done as a child, with the same wonder, gleaning the same comfort, because despite all that had happened since, she was still that same girl. Why shouldn't she still love the stars?

The envelope was on the floor by the door when she'd padded into the hallway, hunched over and hollow, suffering the feel of the cold floor seeping through her socks. The radiators had warmed up eventually, but the walls and windows were so paper-thin that the draught stole the heat faster than they could make it. Taking up the envelope, she saw there was no stamp, no address, just *Grace* written in the most elegant of hands and the weight of something small sealed inside it.

'Seriously, Richard,' she'd whispered, tearing it open. 'This is not what we discussed.'

Grace might have to tell Jesus about this, that Father Richard O'Malley – his sworn and celibate spokesperson on the island of Croaghnakeela – had a nasty habit of dodging the truth. She let the key drop into her hand and unfolded the letter.

Dear Grace,

Please do forgive me for not staying for a chat. Time has gotten away from me today and there's much to do before the pews are packed and everyone's crying out for another top-notch mass on my part.

I did really enjoy our chat yesterday, and I hope you feel as welcome as you are on Croaghnakeela. I'll be the first to admit that my parish is unlike any other, and its isolation has certainly whittled away at its charms over the years. But you know where to find me should you have any questions in need of answering.

You'll find enclosed a key to Harriet's house, and I've jotted down a few directions below. She would be only too delighted to meet you. Please feel free to visit her at any time that suits you this afternoon. It would be best, however, if you made your way home before dark. I know that it's a habit of hers to retire early, and such is her politeness that she'd never tell you this herself.

I look forward to talking to you soon.
Sincerely yours,
Father Richard O'Malley
P.S. That offer to stay above Finnerty's pub still stands, should you change your mind.

Harriet's home was north of the hill, where the stones rolled deepest inland and the wind did more than whistle, it screamed like a dying beast. Whether by disfellowship or its own discretion, it had been built apart from the islanders' community. If Croaghnakeela was the loneliest rock on the west coast of Ireland, then this was by far its loneliest house, and Grace could already feel her sympathies for the woman bulging in her heart as she made headway towards it.

Richard's directions were hardly necessary. Only one path led to where Grace was going, surrounded by an uneven expanse of misty marshland and stone. The far-off crash of the waves filled the air like radio static, crackling and hissing over the horizon. And as she rounded the hill, Harriet's home could be seen in the distance, tall and grey, standing like an ancient tomb amidst the fog. It was the largest she'd seen on the island thus far and fell in line with Grace's presumption that her husband had been some sort of landowner. That might explain the man's disrepute. Public opinion rarely had a kind word to say about *the big house.*

The Lavelle estate was a lifeless tract of land, dark above as below on a day that still petered on the brink of darkness. A spine of gravel led in a long line from the gate to its door. Brown grasses coated its acreage like a massive scab, so wizened that a passing shoe could split them in half. Even in the daylight, windows were as shadows – black squares on an ashen wall. It was a soulless building, devoid of any architectural subtleties, as cold and unwelcoming as they come, and the last place on earth that Grace fancied visiting. She was no stranger to these abstruse intuitions, but this one was especially repellent.

Dark clouds rolled in relentlessly from the west. But none had brought rain. Not yet.

Grace unlocked her phone with a cold swipe of her finger.

'Can't say I'm surprised,' she whispered, as if she'd have

miraculously discovered a network on the other side of the hill.

Her mum's house was sadly lacking in a landline, and she'd forgotten to ask Richard for use of his phone when they'd spoken. Hopefully, Carrie would check in on the shop once in a while, like she did whenever Grace was away. But if the delivery drivers left her latest box of books out in the rain, there'd be hell to pay. Maybe she could claim the loss back with her insurance, though no one would ever believe the value of some of the editions she was waiting on. For now, however, Grace had other worries to tend to.

Harriet's home felt even more oppressive up close, but at least the air had calmed in its shelter. Neither the wind nor the light were welcome where Grace now stood, wondering how anyone could live in such a place. She tried to peer through the lace curtains, but the shadows outnumbered the shapes. It was as though a dark fog were trapped inside, obscuring the slightest detail and suffocating the room in darkness.

A circular pewter plaque was set into the door, engraved with the letter V. Whereas everything around it had dulled over time, this seemed to almost gleam in that dimmest of daylight.

'Valentine Lavelle,' Grace spoke aloud, recalling the name before rapping on its wood, nervous now, doubting herself.

What would she and Harriet even talk about? Old people liked to share stories from their youth, didn't they, reminiscing over lost value and longer summers? Or was that ageism at its worst? Hopefully, the woman held an interest in books, rare or otherwise, though any library – much like Harriet herself – would have surely mouldered from dampness in that house. Some people were no stronger than the paper they read from.

Maybe her late husband had kept a porn collection hidden in their attic. Stranger coincidences had happened. That could be a fun, if bizarre, conversation to keep their friendship afloat in its infancy.

Still Grace waited. But still no reply came.

A horrible niggling suspicion rippled under her skin. *What if Harriet had suffered an accident?* The very act of mentioning such a possibility in the cemetery might have goaded fate into kicking her down the stairs. If Richard had spoken to her, like he said he would, then she should have been expecting her. Grace couldn't walk away now, not when an image of an old woman passed out pale on the floor was all she could see.

'Harriet,' she said, speaking directly to the door. 'I hope I'm not disturbing you. Rich... I mean, Father O'Malley asked me to pop by and say hello.'

If the woman was in there, then she must have heard her. Big stone houses like that amplified every sound that disturbed their dust. And yet, leaning her ear into the door to listen, there wasn't a whisper from within. Luckily, or perhaps the opposite were more true, Grace had the means to take matters into her own hands.

'Father O'Malley gave me a key,' she said, louder, as she picked it from her pocket. 'He told me to let myself in, Harriet, so I'm going to come in now, okay?'

The lock was stiff, its inner workings caked in a brittle rust, and Grace had to wiggle the key back and forth before it clicked. She eased the door in the shortest inch, just enough to be heard more clearly.

'Harriet?' she said softly, eager to explain herself. 'Like I said, Father O'Malley told me to come over and introduce myself. I think he mentioned it to you yesterday. I'm Christine O'Dwyer's daughter.' It felt surprisingly liberating to say it.

Shadows recoiled as Grace pushed the door open. Everywhere, dust glimmered in the gloomy air. She edged in for a better look. To her left she saw a fireplace framed in cut stone. Two wooden chairs were on either side of it. This was probably the warmest room in the house – somewhere to sit and stay alive. Grace imagined Harriet spending her lonely hours there, beside the hearth, hands outstretched to catch the last of its embers, dreading the dampness of her bed upstairs. Or perhaps she slept by the fire on the worst nights, with a blanket pulled up to her chin, counting the hours until the dawn light tinged the window's lace with silver. The stained linoleum floor was dog-eared and riddled with mildew, and cracks had split like broken cobwebs across the ceiling.

Aside from the two chairs, the room was bereft of furnishings. But there *were* signs of life. The shuffle of tired feet had cleared a path through the dust, most notably by the fireplace and the short walk to the door on the far wall, nearest the stairs, possibly the kitchen. A mug was set atop the hearth, and beside it, Grace saw a battered Bible. And there were the makings of a fire – coal, firelighters, and a box of matches – of which she assumed Richard had been the sponsor.

'Hello?' Grace said in her loudest indoor voice. 'Is anyone home?'

The key had fit. This had to be the right house.

Veiled light leached through the lace curtains as Grace crossed the room, her footsteps echoing in the emptiness of a home as dead on the inside as it had seemed from afar.

Could Harriet have gone to church? That would have made a favourable explanation for her absence.

A floorboard suddenly creaked overhead. There was someone up there.

'Harriet?' she repeated, peering over to the stairs, wondering how the woman might react to a stranger landing in on top of her, expected or not.

She was going to find out soon enough.

The stairs had softened over the years, and Grace couldn't help but cringe at the squeak of each step, expecting the whole case to collapse beneath her at any second. Old stone she could trust. Wood just got meaner with age. There was a small window awaiting her at the top, admitting just enough light to show the way. She climbed with both eyes fixed on her feet, taking due care to avoid any particularly mouldy patches, but she stopped when a door was heard to whine open behind her. It'd come from downstairs.

'Harriet?' Grace said again, descending as she'd climbed, with her hands pressed into the walls as though they were trying to crush her.

Harriet must have been busying herself quietly in the kitchen, as a corridor of light now shone through its open door. Grace peered down into the half-lit pall of the room, and there she saw her, sitting in the chair to the right of the hearth, hands neatly laid on her lap, staring with the widest and whitest eyes at the intruder in her home.

'You shouldn't be here,' she whispered. 'If he sees you, he'll follow you.'

Words spoken so swiftly that Grace had to take a moment to isolate their sounds.

'Who'll follow me?' she asked.

But the woman shook her head like a child, refusing to speak their name.

She was as fine-spun and fragile as Grace had feared. Harriet had withstood the years, but they'd each taken a piece of her as recompense, whittling away at her softness, like a sculptor trying to fix a mistake in stone, leaving lines too sharp and the flesh too little. The woman's hair had greyed to near white on the longest wisps that fell like the island's mist past her shoulders. Yet her face was petite and pretty, and though its skin had aged, her eyes retained their sparkle of innocence.

'Is *he* here now?' Grace asked, unsure if she was fuelling the woman's delusions, playing accomplice in entertaining this phantom guest that Richard had warned her about.

Harriet tensed in her chair, back straight, and stared at the collage of stains on the ceiling, searching for some sound above their heads.

'No,' she replied, breathing softer now, 'not at the moment.'

The building was too decrepit for anyone to keep their presence a secret within its walls, especially upstairs, where the simple act of standing still would have drawn pained creaks from its wooden floor.

'My name's Grace, Harriet. You might have known my—'

'How do you know my name?' she interjected nervously.

'I spoke to Father O'Malley yesterday and—'

Harriet's eyes darted to the front door. 'How did you get in?'

It was as though the woman had snapped out of a daze. Grace had left the door open in the hope of making the room less dreary, but the stubborn daylight seemed determined to stay outside. There must have been a playbook of ways to approach and befriend a woman in Harriet's situation. But creeping into their home without permission and snooping around the stairs probably wasn't one of them.

'Father O'Malley gave me this,' Grace said, producing the key from her pocket to support her case. 'Didn't he tell you that I was going to call over today?'

'Father O'Malley,' she repeated absently, turning to look at the charred hollow of the fireplace, 'he's very sick.'

'Well,' Grace continued, 'sick or not, he asked me to visit you. He didn't come by here yesterday to tell you?'

'No,' she replied, shaking her head, 'I don't think so.'

Harriet looked anxiously around the room. The jury was still out on whether the priest had been telling porkies again. He might have visited, like he said he would, or maybe the glow behind Finnerty's windows had waylaid his best intentions.

'Would you mind if I sat down beside you, Harriet?'

The woman glanced at the other chair, her eyes lagging for a second on the mug and Bible on the hearth. 'You have to keep your voice down,' she whispered.

Grace walked gently over to the front door and drew it closed, and then she approached the chair and put her hands on its backrest. 'May I?'

'Yes, please, but you mustn't talk so loudly.'

'Okay,' she agreed, taking a seat, mirroring the woman's whisper. 'I won't, I promise.'

Grace examined the inside of the mug beside her: drained dry, leaving a sad-looking teabag at its bottom like a child trapped down a well.

'I'm sorry if I startled you, Harriet. I honestly thought you were expecting me. Father O'Malley told me as much.'

The woman nodded uneasily.

'I'm originally from around here actually,' Grace said, even though that truth still felt a little uncomfortable to wear. 'The island, I mean. You might have known my mum. Chrissy O'Dwyer?'

Harriet shook her head. 'I don't have any friends.'

Grace's heart tensed like a fist. 'You have Father O'Malley?' she said, leaning forward, keeping her voice low. 'He told me how much he enjoys coming over to visit you.'

'Father O'Malley said that?' Harriet asked shyly.

'He did. And is he the one who brought you all this?' she asked, glimpsing down at the bag of coal.

'Yes,' she replied, smiling now as though the thought of having a friend made the darkness of that room a thousand shades lighter.

'He's a very nice man, isn't he?' Grace said, trying to keep the words flowing between them.

'Yes,' Harriet agreed, 'but he looks so sickly these days. I'm awfully worried about him.'

Were they talking about the same priest? There were a few early grey hairs sprinkled about that beard of his, but other than that, Richard looked remarkably healthy.

'He mentioned to me that you lost your husband?' Grace said.

Harriet toyed with her wedding band, like a puzzle that held some answer she'd spent a lifetime trying to unlock. Grace felt so unprepared for this conversation. It was like being back in school again, sitting an exam she hadn't studied for.

'When did you lose him?' she pressed, eager to fill in those pages that the priest had left blank.

'A long time ago,' Harriet replied, her eyes falling over Grace's shoulder, 'before anyone even realised he was gone.'

The woman's thin lips creased into a smile at whatever she'd seen. Grace turned in her chair, and there – on the window ledge outside – she saw the slender silhouette of a cat.

'Is that yours?' she asked.

'No,' Harriet replied sadly, 'but she comes to visit me most days.'

'What do you call her?'

Harriet shifted happily in her chair. The topic of cats was obviously one she enjoyed.

'Tiddles,' she said excitedly.

'Does she ever come inside? There's nothing a cat loves more than a warm fire.'

'No,' Harriet replied, glancing down at her shoes, 'she's not allowed.'

This fact seemed to deflate the woman's spirit.

'Here's an idea,' Grace proposed, 'how about I get a fire going for us? And don't worry about the coal – I can bring another bag with me the next time I come over.'

'You'll visit me again?' Harriet asked, perking up but still speaking in that same whisper.

'Of course,' Grace replied, smiling as broadly as possible. 'I'd love to.'

'I'll make us some tea,' Harriet said eagerly.

Before Grace could offer to do it for her, the woman's shoes were shuffling towards the kitchen, tracing the same worn path through the dust. Richard had at least been honest about the woman's mind. Aside from her initial bemusement, which was reasonable given the circumstances, she seemed relatively lucid. That being said, her allusions to another presence in the house would have to be confronted eventually. But the time for that would come.

Grace knelt by the fireplace and went about shovelling a low hill of coal atop a firelighter. She vowed to clean the grate on her next visit, but her first priority was to stoke some heat into that house. A kettle was heard to click in the room next door. Grace was glad that Richard had asked her to do this. At least she could now say that she had a friend on the island. And, by the looks of it, Harriet needed one just as much as she did. A match was strook alight. Its flame took greedily to the firelighter, gilding her face with a warmth that she'd all but forgotten the sensation of. And then, as she kneeled on that filthy floor, dusting the black from her fingers, a hard step sounded in a room above. Could it be that there *had* been someone upstairs? Grace looked over to see Harriet standing at the kitchen door.

'He's back,' she said, her eyes flushed with terror. 'You have to leave. Please, don't let him see you. If he sees you, he'll follow you. I don't want him to follow you.'

Grace staggered back onto her feet. 'Who is he, Harriet?'

'Please,' she replied desperately, 'you must go.'

The woman was upsetting herself. And Grace knew too little of her wounds to heal them with a few words.

'Is it Valentine?' she asked her. 'Is that who—'

'Don't ever speak his name,' Harriet snapped. 'Please, go now while you still can.'

So heartfelt and affecting was her fear that Grace did as she was told. Fortunately, the flames had taken to the coals, and some warmth would remain after she'd left.

'Okay,' Grace said, not wishing to further her distress, 'but I'll come back, all right?'

'You don't understand,' Harriet said. 'He'll never let you leave.'

Another resounding thud came from the ceiling. There *was* someone up there.

Grace opened the door. 'Don't worry about me, Harriet,' she said. 'I'll visit you again tomorrow. We might even bring Tiddles inside too. Wouldn't that be—'

'Run,' the woman said, staring her in the eye, unblinking, 'while you still can.'

Spooked by the woman's warnings – with the door closed behind her – she broke into a hasty walk down the pathway. Harriet's fears were contagious and Grace wanted nothing more than to be far from that place. Gravel crunched and sank beneath her feet as she stormed towards the gate, her heart set on getting home as soon as possible. Between her laboured breaths and that restless wind sweeping through her hair, she discerned another sound in the air. This time it wasn't laughter. It was something much worse.

She dug in her heels – more stubborn than she was brave – committed to proving, if only to herself, that she'd imagined it. But there it was, as clear as those footsteps that'd chased her from Harriet's door. So melancholic, so unmistakable: the weeping of children. Their voices were too many, all bawling their little hearts out – inconsolable and truly terrifying in light of the loneliness that surrounded her. And no sooner had their eerie lament touched her ears than the silence was restored.

Grace looked back to Harriet's. Her eyes were drawn to the three front-facing windows on the first floor, where those heavy steps had pounded. The rooms were lightless as before. And yet, there was someone there – a shape darker than the air surrounding it – standing behind the besmeared glass of the centre pane, watching her. Harriet's warnings returned to Grace as she felt the other's gaze wash over her like a wave of ice water.

If he sees you, he'll follow you.

8

ROBIN

Routines and rituals brought their own comforts, and Croaghnakeela's priest oft enjoyed this quarter hour upon a Sunday afternoon, when his parishioners shuffled their feet in an orderly queue to bid him good health. They were a tight-lipped bunch, even after their respective skinfuls, and so this was an opportunity to exchange a shake of the hand and a quiet word – to offer some assurance that their priest was there should they have need of him. Not that any ever followed through on the invitation. These people were faithful only so long as the weekly mass kept them detained between the pews. After that, no one trusted their God to keep them safe.

The islanders' beliefs were founded on more than Christianity's teachings, and Robin had learned over the years to respect their secrecy and the odd traditions it kept alive. What they practised was unlike anything he'd encountered in scriptures sold or secreted. It seemed much older in origin and, as such, like a seed buried deep in their collective psyche, it wasn't so easily removed – not without understanding what shared experiences had planted it there.

'God bless you, Father,' the widow Mary Malley said to

him, squeezing his right hand with both of hers, their fingers calloused and cold to the touch.

'And you, Mary,' he replied, placing the flat of his palm over their union. 'It's a chilly one today. Are you still making that trek to the hilltop?'

'Aye, that I will, Father. Sure it wouldn't be Sunday now, would it, if I didn't pay my way like the rest of them.'

Every Sunday, without fail, the islanders performed the same solemn pilgrimage. No matter how the elements racked their ageing bones, still they ascended that hill like a line of ants, loyal to some loftier power than common sense. Brendan McMorrow was the only one who'd linger on the lowlands, offering a helping hand around the church grounds, as he would on this day, with the promise of pruning back the briars that'd made a nest for themselves by the western wall.

Atop the hill there survived the ruins of a church, built from the same grey stone it stood upon, with no records tying its allegiance to Christianity. Perhaps an archaeologist could make better sense of it than Robin had. In his six years of mostly idle research, he'd failed to identify any clues as to its origin, though in his defence there was very little left to examine. Those few symbols that had withstood the ravages of time were far beyond the priest's field of expertise.

Its most fascinating aspect, however, was found within the remnants of its walls, where a circular well had been constructed in its centre. The priest posited that it'd once been a stairwell of sorts, but the interior of its throat – or as much of it as he could see from above – looked relatively smooth and lacking in any means of passage. Regardless, it was certainly a curious addition to the aisle of any church, assuming the building had indeed been a place of worship. All he knew for sure was that the well went deep, possibly down to the very ocean itself. The ancient stone that lined its circumference bore three hundred and sixty-five perfectly notched lines, hinting perhaps at some astrological significance, though Robin had neither the books nor the knowledge to pursue the theory any further.

This was the oddity that beckoned his parishioners to perform the strangest ritual of their day. They would gather in a sombre circle and drop a few coins into its unfathomable depths. It was a joyless affair, and no prayers were ever spoken. Not even a wish. Robin had overheard a few of them referring to it as payment, but the identity of who or what they were paying remained a mystery to him, as did the size of the debt they each felt obliged to lower in painful increments, breaking their bodies upon the Sabbath, all for the sake of a cleaner conscience.

With her focus now tied up somewhere around Robin's feet, the widow moved aside to let the next body through. John Finnerty, one of the chattier ones when the mood took him, but a respected keeper of the islanders' secrets all the same. He wasn't a bad man by any means. But he kept his friends close if only to hide behind them, too timid in spirit to stand up for anything bar the ever-increasing price of a pint.

'Are you well, John?' Robin said to him.

The publican looked especially shaken, as though he'd stared at his clock all night, worrying about the morning. He could barely bring himself to look his priest in the eye, not unlike the widow before him. Whatever had so chilled their hearts the evening before had yet to thaw completely, frosting over what little remained of their already sketchy social skills.

'All's well, Father,' he lied, reaching out his hand blindly to be held.

Robin squeezed it tight enough to draw the man's gaze. 'If there *was* something, John,' he said, low enough to keep their conversation sacred, 'that was troubling you and, God forbid, might be a trouble to someone else, you'd be sure to tell me, wouldn't you?'

Finnerty would have run back to the safety of his pub in that instant had Robin not held him to the spot, trying to ferret out some truth between the lies.

'Of course, Father,' he replied, slipping his hand free.

It was a coward's grip, held only so long as it'd keep him safe. Robin watched him leave, head bowed, pacing along as though his priest were chasing him.

Each of them in their own curious way evaded the truth of what was haunting them. Robin knew what to expect by now, and yet the mood on this Sunday was particularly uneasy. The priest caught sight of Tadgh Scuffel muttering in his wife's ear, dawdling in the doorway, sharing whispers that looked on the brink of raising to a row. When everyone had passed outside but them, he shooed Maggie ahead, and she turned a brave and beautiful face to Robin, as she always did. He could only imagine how striking she must have been in her youth — the kind of face that men were slow to look away from and women were quick to envy.

'Good to see you, Father,' she said, letting her warm hand slip into his.

'And you, Maggie,' he replied, all too aware of Tadgh watching him from the doorway; her husband never did like anyone's skin meeting hers, even if it was only their priest.

The woman was gone before he could spark up anything more stimulating than the bare pleasantries, and no sooner had she turned to walk away than Tadgh was standing in front of him, close enough to smell last night's whiskey on his breath. There was a ruddy sheen to his fat cheeks that looked out of place on a day so cold.

'Everything okay, Tadgh?' Robin asked, taking the man's hand and squeezing the sweat from his palm. 'You seem a little out of sorts today.'

'I was wondering if I might have a word with you, Father,' he whispered, 'in confidence.'

This was a first for any of them.

'Of course,' the priest replied, containing his surprise as best he could.

Scuffel looked to those who'd already departed, as though he were in some way betraying their trust in speaking with Robin like this. His movements hadn't passed unnoticed. A few glanced back at first, and then – chained as one by their many whispers – all heads turned to ogle them.

'Can we speak inside, Father?' he said, drawing back into the shadows of the church.

'What's troubling you, Tadgh?' the priest asked him directly, drawing a panel of the door closed behind them to keep their conversation safe from any prying eyes.

The man couldn't stand still. 'I know this isn't your problem, Father. It has nothing to do with you, and that's the way it should be. But I don't know what else to do. I mean, we talk and we talk in that fucking pub but there's never anything said that'll save us. We thought it was over. And it was. There was peace, Father. You've seen it yourself. We thought we'd heard the last of him but—'

'Slow down, Tadgh,' Robin said, placing a firm hand on the man's shoulder, 'and just tell me what the matter is.'

Scuffel looked on the verge of a nervous breakdown. 'I've

been hearing things in my home,' he replied, glancing to the door. 'Margaret has too.'

Robin adopted a frown to air his concern. 'What kind of *things* exactly?'

'Footsteps, Father, just like before.'

The priest crossed his arms and stroked thoughtfully around his chin. 'And tell me, when did you first start hearing these *footsteps?*'

Tadgh wasn't the most popular man on the island. But it wouldn't have been like any of Robin's parishioners to break into another's home, even if it was only to give the old sod a good scare.

'They started this week, Father, on the night that Christine O'Dwyer passed away.'

'Okay,' the priest said, baffled as to the connection, if that's even what the man was hinting at. 'And who do you think is responsible for these footsteps?'

Tadgh was kneading his hands together, trying and failing to keep them steady.

'It's *him*, Father.'

Ever since he'd arrived on Croaghnakeela there'd been whispers of *him*.

'And *who* are you talking about?'

'You really don't know, do you?' Tadgh replied disbelievingly. 'You've no idea what he made us do!'

'If you'd only tell me, then maybe I could—'

The aisle darkened as the fat form of Fergal Wilberforce materialised in the doorway like a cloud blotting out the sun, startling Scuffel away from the priest's side.

'Fergal,' he yelped, his voice breaking, 'what are you doing here?'

Wilberforce stared the man down. It was how a wolf looks upon his next meal, salivating at its weaknesses, the fear, and the flesh.

'Are you not coming with us, Tadgh?' he said sternly. 'I'm sure you wouldn't want Maggie making the journey up that hill alone now, with just us for company, would you?'

'No, of course not,' Scuffel said as he slinked like a chastised schoolboy towards the door. 'I'm sorry to have troubled you, Father.'

'It's no trouble,' Robin replied, honouring the man's desire for secrecy. 'Like I said, I'm always here to listen.'

Wilberforce lingered in the doorway after Tadgh had gone, watching the priest, gauging with a steely eye and a firm hold on the silence just how much he'd been told. Neither man spoke, and without so much as a goodbye the brute turned his back and trudged out into the open. Fergal was outspoken as they came, but never with his priest. And Robin knew that the white collar around his neck was all that had kept him safe from a rough round of words.

He walked to the altar, with only the echo of his heels for company, pondering what Chrissy could have to do with all this. The general mood on the island had no doubt curdled since her passing, and Robin had experienced enough in his lifetime to no longer believe in coincidences.

Her death *had* affected them. If only he knew why.

Tadgh Scuffel made the link, and so it was safe to assume that the rest of them had too. Chrissy had so little left to her name when she passed. The only wealth the woman had was in that house, and she'd been steadfast in her wish that that wealth find its way into her daughter's hands. Chrissy trusted her priest to stay true to her will. And she died in the belief that he would.

'Grace must never know where she came from, Father,' she'd said the last time they'd spoken.

Secretly, Robin had disagreed. Unanswered questions, he'd learned, are a cruel burden for any soul to carry. Would it not have been kinder to tell her estranged daughter the truth, if only to shed some light on those lost years? He would, of course, still follow through on Chrissy's request, selling her house and any valuables that may profit Grace's future. But maybe this was one instance when her priest knew best.

'Don't let her come to this place,' she'd asked of him. 'She must never step onto Croaghnakeela. It's best, Father, if she doesn't know the cursed thing exists. Can you promise me that?'

And in his prayers, Robin still sought forgiveness for breaking the dying woman's wish.

9

Grace

The glass in the door was still chattering as she slid the chain across its lock.

A sharp stitch of pain had made that last mile a torture, like a rusty blade drawn back and forth between Grace's ribs, agony enough to make her eyes water, and yet it hadn't slowed her down. With Harriet's warnings too raw in her mind to be reasoned with, that presence in the window had spurred her on as she'd fled the woman's estate. But in spite of the myriad throes that'd risen against her, it was how that unsettling feeling of being watched persisted – even with the house no longer in sight – that'd pushed Grace to reach beyond her limits. She must have looked over her shoulder a hundred times, if not more. And yet, alone as she was, she couldn't shake the suspicion that she were being followed – that no matter where she ran to or how well she hid, her capture was inevitable as the coming of the night.

The land itself seemed to awaken as she'd scrambled home. Everywhere its shadows were rippling, restless and alive. Grasses, once so limp, had quivered with a sick excitement, licking at her ankles as she'd passed them by. Every brown stream leaking through the fields pulsated like a vein, as if each one were fed from some dark heart buried neath the island's surface. And through those silken wisps of fog clinging to the hill's eastern side, she'd seen the islanders climbing to its summit. Galling as the wind was amidst the low stones and swampland, it must have been a whole lot worse up there. But Grace was glad that their dour little procession ran a safe distance from her own course. She hadn't the headspace to make polite conversation with any of them. There was only one person on the island of Croaghnakeela she needed to talk to, and that was Father Richard.

There'd been someone in Harriet's top window. Of that, Grace was certain. But if her husband was long dead and mourned by none, then *who* was the woman so scared of, and was the priest even aware that another inhabited her home? To think that had Harriet not stepped out of the kitchen when she did, Grace might have reached the top of the stairs. She could have come face to face with whoever it was that held such an abusive sway over the poor woman's happiness.

If he sees you, he'll follow you.

And what happens if he catches you?

Still breathless, chest heaving, Grace waited for her heart's beat to soften. The island's air was more stagnant than the very soil it crept through. It'd stripped her throat, making every dry swallow a chore. And she could feel the first sprouts of a headache pressing against the backs of her eyes. Grace was a reader. She was *not* a runner. And her wilting body was a tragic testament to that. She looked down to her feet, where she'd unknowingly kicked through the white powder when she'd fallen in the door, disturbing its perfectly laid line. But the rats were the least of her worries now. She couldn't shake the look on Harriet's face from her mind, and the fear in her eyes especially. At least the priest had been honest about one thing when they'd spoken – the woman *was* terrified.

Grace panned a hand across the wall as she side-stepped the first bag standing in her way, cursing the lot of them under her breath but nonetheless respecting them for what they were. Her toe collided with something hard, possibly the same guilty party that'd tripped her up the day before. She gave it another gentle kick as punishment and felt the glassy thud of a bottle, heavy enough to suggest it hadn't been emptied before being binned. The possibility of something tastier than tap water was too tempting to pass by.

The bag's knot was stretched loose. A fleecy blanket was dragged out like loose intestines. Reaching her hand down deeper, squeezing through clots of clothes, dreading the furry feel of a rat, her fingers clasped their prize. To Grace's surprise, a bottle of whiskey was duly rescued from death row. Somebody had already enjoyed a decent enough go at it. But a quarter remained, still perfectly drinkable, unaffected by the years that'd dulled its label. Grace had never been much of a whiskey drinker unless it were softened out with a splash of ginger and chocked full of ice. But maybe a stiff glass was just what the doctor ordered after the day she'd had. A bowl of soup was hardly the best medicine to steady her nerves.

'Thanks, Mum,' she groaned as she stood back up.

What else was there to do? Grace's inheritance hardly resembled a home anymore. Aside from the sad shrine that was her old bedroom, its rooms were cold, empty spaces, with nothing to offer but the hapless feeling that she'd arrived too late for a party – one that she was beginning to suspect she hadn't been invited to in the first place. There would have been a letter. There would have been something. Her mum obviously couldn't bring herself to disturb the memories left behind by her daughter's absence, but she'd removed all else, closing that door on her life like a tomb.

'You didn't want me to come here, did you?' Grace whispered sadly.

She dragged her legs into the kitchen and set the bottle down atop its counter. A gust of wind peppered the window above the sink with a flurry of raindrops whilst throughout the house, radiators rattled their cast-iron bones, bringing more noise than they did warmth. She thought of Harriet, sitting alone in that awful room without enough coal to burn through the night. It was a miracle the woman had survived there for as long as she had, with no friends, no warmth, and no light to brighten her days. All she had was a cat called Tiddles. And even they weren't allowed to hang out together.

Twisting on the stiff tap spent the last of Grace's strength. A tall glass of water was gulped back and – still gasping – a second was filled immediately. Her body and mind refused to rest. Usually she only felt like this after one too many coffees on a Monday morning. The door was locked. She was safe. Grace may have been seen, but she hadn't been followed. *I look forward to talking to you soon*, is what Richard had penned in his letter. Hopefully soon meant today because, for the first time in her life, she wasn't enjoying being on her own. Grace pined for the lamplit glow of her bookshop – her sanctuary from the world, surrounded by more stories than she could ever read in a single lifetime, and more pornography than was probably necessary.

Glass of water in hand, she padded across the kitchen, deciding it best to busy herself. She could light a fire or revisit the old toys in her bedroom. There was nothing like a child's fifty-piece jigsaw to while away an evening. And who was to say what other alcoholic treasures were hiding amongst...

Grace stopped when she saw the bags.

She'd been so careful to step around each one. And yet now they were crushed and splayed across the floor as if someone had just trodden over them, tearing plastic and squeezing entrails through their ruptures. She looked to the door – to the chain still drawn across its lock, undisturbed since she'd swished it shut. No one could have come in without her knowing. Grace crept closer, struggling for an explanation, and then she smelled it: the most noxious taint in the air. A pyre of rotting flesh wouldn't have turned her stomach as that stench did now, and she had to draw her sleeve across her mouth just to keep from throwing up.

'What *is* that?' she moaned, backing into the kitchen, still glaring accusingly at the bags.

Grace's first act was to unlatch the window and throw it open, inviting the dank island air inside, as nothing could be worse than *that* smell. She looked to the whiskey bottle, recalling the last time she'd drunk it straight. That night had ended with Carrie holding back her hair while she'd emptied her stomach into a pub toilet. Not her finest hour. But unless Grace did something now, she was going to vomit anyway.

'Fine,' she muttered to herself as she reached for the bottle, surrendering to the only option that made sense in that moment.

Grace took a short sniff of the whiskey and, though her

stomach was quick to churn another notch or two, she drew it to her lips and downed as much as she could.

'Jesus fucking Christ,' she said as it set her heart aflame, 'that's foul.'

But it was better. It'd drawn the ire of her senses, which had been her masterplan all along. Grace turned and rested back against the counter, feeling no better and maybe a tad worse. With the tips of her fingers she dabbed the tears from her eyes until – with the breeze caressing her hair through the open window – she felt that same unsettling sensation. Grace looked to the open kitchen door. Though there was no one there, she knew that she was no longer alone in that house.

Grace stared at the emptiness. And she could feel it staring back.

'I know you're there,' she whispered, her body tensing as the words made it real.

The presence grew stronger, more oppressive, more alive in its acknowledgement.

'What do you want?' Grace asked, grabbing the whiskey bottle – the nearest thing at hand to defend herself – and gripping its neck like a club.

Over the wind there was the eerie sound of another's step, heel to toe, soft and serpentine. Grace swung the bottle in front of her, probing for some proof of *the other*.

But there was nothing, only empty air.

'What are you?' she whispered, imagining a body where there was none.

Whatever it was, it was now standing directly in front of her. Grace stabbed out the bottle, arm outstretched, swaying it from left to right, yielding to her instincts, refusing to believe her eyes. Something *had* followed her home.

'I saw you,' she said, lips atremble. 'You were watching me from—'

The bottle was suddenly smashed from her hand – shattered on impact – and its wet shards splashed against the wall. Grace withdrew her arm and tripped back against the counter. The pain was slow to surge above that flash of fear, but she knew her wrist had snapped, that her hand now dangled askew, its bones cracked like cheap ceramic.

'Please,' she cried, clutching it as the pain found its voice, 'leave me alone.'

Grace could sense the phantom relishing in her terror. She held her wrist as steady as possible, squeezing it tight, feeling its broken parts, wincing through the pain. All around her was still. Even the tinkling of broken glass had fallen silent. But the horror wasn't through with her yet. She heard her shin bone crack aloud before the blinding agony of it consumed her, and she collapsed, her skull clashing hard with the floor. Sticky glass embedded her skin. The kitchen was spinning now, leaving her at the mercy of whatever was hell-bent on breaking her body apart bone by bone. She tried to crawl away. But such was the anguish of her wounds that the slightest movement was unbearable. The bone had torn through the skin. Warm blood pooled over the tiles where she'd fallen. Grace screamed, hoping and praying to be heard, but there was no one to save her.

Something suddenly clasped around her ankle. She awaited another lightning strike of pain – that sickening sensation of being cracked apart like a paper doll. But instead she was dragged across the kitchen floor, laying a long red smear behind her. The terror was as maddening as the pain, for there was no one there. With her good hand, Grace gripped the doorframe. She held fast for a second or so before a violent jerk wrenched her through the bins and smashed her feet through the frosted glass of the front door. Razored shards scattered, lacerating her face and clinging like crystals to her hair as her spine cracked down on the cold concrete of the pathway. Grace felt the rain. She breathed fresh air again. Nothing in that harrowing ordeal made sense, but the elements – the cold wind and its wet droplets – she could understand, and they came as some evidence that she was still alive, still awake, and that all of this was really happening.

Her back and shoulders scratched across the ground before she was pulled into the low fog of the far field. Its uneven earth was slimy and sodden, soaking Grace from head to toe. Tall grasses swished around her as she fought to make sense of where she was being taken, and then she saw it – the hill looming ahead of her, rising closer by the second. And amidst the chaos, making their descent, she caught snap glimpses of the villagers. Grace tried to claw her fingers into the soil but the lands were too flooded and her body too weak, and her skin and clothes were too filthy now to be discerned by even the sharpest eye. And so she did all she could: she screamed. But the ruts in the ground knocked the wind out of her over and over, cracking ribs and stealing her voice when she needed it most.

A wall of rock and earth now stole the sky from view. Gritting her teeth against the pain, she twisted her body over, flinging onto her stomach, meeting the island's filth face on. The act of doing so was not without its own losses. A fresh agony chomped down on her ankle as its bones were pulverised into tiny pieces – a cruel and effortless reprimand for railing against her own ruin. In a desperate act of defiance, Grace locked her arm around a nub of rock protruding from the earth and held herself in place. She could see the villagers, maybe a hundred feet away, trudging down the path, their heads lowered, all hunched neath the cold rain. Grace screamed until her throat was stripped of sound, leaving only a desperate croak that she could barely hear herself.

'Please,' she cried, tears washing down the mud that'd caked her cheeks, 'help me!'

But no heads turned. No one had heard her.

Another almighty wrench on her crumbled ankle snapped her free.

Grace was too tired, too broken, and too defeated to fight it any longer. She was dragged like a carcass through the dirt. The pain was an indelible part of her now, amaranthine as the fear and the confusion that'd colluded so effectively to break her mind. She couldn't keep her eyes open. She was going to pass out at any moment, and in a way she welcomed it. Let there be darkness, if only because it might bring some reprieve from the agonising act of staying alive.

The hill was above her now. Life felt colder in its shadow, and the daylight was cherished for the last time before Grace was pulled into the earth. The closing sound she'd heard was not her own cries echoing through the darkness as she was dragged deeper into the abyss, but the voices of untold children, all weeping as one.

10

Robin

He'd spent the past hour sat on the altar steps, reflecting on his conversation with Tadgh Scuffel like a short stage performance, studying its every line and beat, trying to translate the man's ramblings into something more coherent. It was here, in the silence of an empty church, that Robin's mind oft performed these minor miracles – when the most hard-fought of solutions was known to magically manifest out of thin air, as if God were actually listening for once.

Though Tadgh had told his priest very little, he'd shared enough to procure his undivided attention. Those footsteps he alluded to weren't unique to his own household. That would explain why everyone had been so on edge recently, though their tenuous link to Chrissy's passing was a puzzle unto itself. It was bizarre to imagine that she was somehow caught up in all this. A creeping malaise had touched the hearts of his whole congregation – he'd suspected as much before Tadgh sought out his counsel – and Robin was determined now to find its cure.

A shadow shifted silently by the doorway.

'Brendan,' he called out, his thoughts blending back into reality, 'is that you?'

The smoky daylight remained undisturbed.

With their weekly debt delivered to the hilltop, the islanders should've already been locked up in Finnerty's at that hour. And it wouldn't have been like any one of them to squeeze in a quick prayer before their first hot whiskey. It was possible, of course, that Tadgh had split from their pack to finish the confession he'd started. That thought alone hastened Robin down the aisle, heels clipping on stone, eager for answers. When he reached the open, however, there was neither sight nor sound of the man, and for a sickening moment, Robin strained to catch his breath. A blood-warm dizziness had suddenly risen behind his eyes, skewing his balance and staggering him forward. He was stricken by the most unnerving sensation – a feeling akin to dread, though he'd never experienced anything quite like it.

And then, in the quietus of Croaghnakeela's cemetery, amidst the lank grasses and grey stone, his mind was haunted by a hundred echoes all repeating the same scream.

'Father,' Brendan called out, his gloved hand gripping a long ream of leaf and thorn, 'is everything all right?'

In his bewilderment, the priest had forgotten the man was still out there, toiling away, tearing down nature's latest harvest in the good name of God.

'It's Grace,' Robin replied, palm held flat to his heart, suffering through a dead weight that seemed to inhabit the very core of him.

Something terrible had happened, and these spiritual tremors were but its aftershocks.

Brendan cast the briars aside. 'Chrissy's daughter? What about her, Father?'

'I don't know,' he replied, gazing off, searching the sky and the heavens above it for some answer. 'But I should go and check on her.'

The islander was already pinching the fingers of his glove, slipping it above the wrist. 'I can take you. If you don't mind me saying, you're not looking the best.'

'I'd appreciate that,' Robin replied, still staring off in a daze. 'I just… I don't know. I just have this awful feeling that she's in some sort of trouble.'

'Not on my watch, Father,' Brendan said, nodding over at his car parked by the gate, its trailer brimming with what he'd torn from the wall since the others set out for the hilltop. 'Come on, I'd nearly finished here anyway.'

Brendan was no stranger to putting others before himself – a kindness the two men shared in a parish where kindness had long fallen out of favour. But no more than the rest of them, he spoke only when necessary, choosing his words like a knight mulling over an armoury of shields. Robin slouched into the passenger seat while Brendan went about releasing the trailer. With his eyes squeezed shut, waiting for that ill feeling to subside, he listened as Brendan clambered in beside him. Leather creaked. A seatbelt swished and clicked.

'Are you sure you're okay, Father? Would it not be best if I took you home?'

The priest must have looked as deathly as he felt.

He forced a dry swallow down his throat. 'No, I'll be fine, thank you.'

This was a rare opportunity for Robin to speak with one of

his parishioners in perfect privacy, far from the intimidations of Fergal Wilberforce. But it felt wrong to corner Brendan McMorrow like this – to exploit the man's goodwill when he'd relied on it most. And so, when they set out for Chrissy's home, there was a respectful, albeit uneasy, silence between them. But if the woman's death were somehow tied to these strange times, then surely it was his God-given responsibility to seek out the truth, even if that meant interrogating the only man on Croaghnakeela who he'd genuinely counted as a friend.

'Brendan,' Robin said tentatively, 'may I ask you something?'

The man's fingers flexed around the wheel. 'Of course, Father,' he replied, though his voice lacked the conviction of his words.

'I know you were very fond of Chrissy. We all were. But what can you tell me about her husband? No one around here, except maybe Fergal, ever seems to speak about him.'

Brendan's shoulders slackened. Fingers loosened their grip. He'd obviously been expecting a far more intrusive line of questioning. His loyalty to the island – as hindering as it was to Robin's needs – was admirable in many respects.

'You didn't miss much, Father,' was his reply. 'Declan O'Dwyer wasn't the kind of man you could count on for anything. Too fond of the bottle, and he'd gamble away all your worth if you gave him half a chance, the selfish bastard, if you'll excuse my French.'

'Excused,' the priest said, marking the emptiness of the hill in the distance, imagining his congregation warming themselves by Finnerty's fireplace, like sheep herded from place to place, forever on the run from some elusive wolf.

Chrissy never spoke to Robin of her late husband. Whatever

the man had done in life, it was sinful enough to make his death his one defining act worthy of remembrance.

'He was a coward, Father,' Brendan added, still frowning at the road. 'I'd hoped when they had a child that he'd change his ways. But it was worse he got. I suppose some men never know when to quit, do they? And he was an easier mark than the rest of us when—' He cut himself short, shaking his head, frustrated with himself for getting carried away. 'All I'm saying is, Father, Chrissy was better off without him.'

Absolute honesty seemed an impossible hurdle for the man.

'I believe you,' Robin said, deciding not to press him too harshly. 'In all the years I knew her, not once did she—'

Brendan slammed on the brakes, lurching them against their seatbelts.

On the road ahead, crossing from the open gate of Chrissy's home to the field opposite, both men stared at the gruesome trail of blood, freshly spilled and darkening.

'We're too late,' Robin whispered, his worst fears realised.

Brendan looked to him quizzically, wondering no doubt how his priest had known to come there, and how he'd aired his worries with such profound certainty. Their respective doors clicked and creaked, and together they edged cautiously towards the scene, unsure whether it were a crime or an accident, knowing only that it was the worst case of either.

Never was a silence so sinister. The absence of life always sounded too much like death. Robin examined the door's hollow frame from the gate. Broken glass glimmered like seashells amidst the blood; more evidence of the horror that'd visited Grace in her new home.

'It was smashed from the inside,' he said, thinking aloud to himself.

Brendan had remained on the roadside, studying the surrounding fields.

Robin stepped around the glassy shards as best he could, but there was no avoiding the blood. It'd spread in pink streams after the rainfall and washed into the grass. He peered through the door and into the hallway, unsure as to what he was searching for. Chrissy's belongings had been ripped from their bags. Trinkets and clothes, books and letters, all those precious things she'd collected in her lifetime, now somebody else's rubbish. But there was one item that drew Robin's eye above all others – a single piece of paper, carefully folded, that'd fallen free from the rest. A stray sliver of glass reflected a bead of light upon it. Such was the page's sorcerous hold over his attention, he reached in through the door to retrieve it and, still crouching, let it fall open.

> Christine,
> *I had nothing else to give him.*
> *I had no other choice.*
> *I'm sorry,*
> Declan

Glass crackled and split as Brendan passed through the gate behind him. Robin refolded the letter and pocketed it in his jacket before rising to meet him.

'Where is she, Father?' the islander asked in an uneasy whisper.

The priest stared back at him, disappointed by the man's allegiance to the others and the lies they kept sacred. 'Why don't you tell me, Brendan?'

For six years he'd tolerated their secrets. And that was long enough.

'What did this?' Robin asked.

The old man held his gaze, but through the power of sheer fucking stubbornness he gave nothing away. 'How would I know, Father?'

The priest stormed past him, his strength sparked back to life by a burning impatience. He quit where Grace's blood painted the road in a thin red carpet, and there he pointed to the wall enclosing Chrissy's home, drawing Brendan to look at the letter V scratched into its stone.

'You know what this is, don't you?' he asked him through gritted teeth.

The islander swallowed hard when his eyes fell upon it. Of course he did.

'Every home on this damned island has it,' Robin said, 'yours included.'

Something that'd lain long dormant had been disturbed by Chrissy's death. They'd all felt it, though only Tadgh Scuffel – the least likely hero amongst them – had the courage to seek out help. Robin walked to where the nearest blades of grass had been splashed crimson and looked to the hill. He knew its well went deep. But what was down there?

'Come on, Brendan,' Robin called back as he stepped off the road. 'The least you can do is help me find her.'

Wherever she'd been taken, it had to be close. If he could just track some trace of her through the marshland, there was still enough light left in the sky to guide his way. What if she were lying wounded in the open, exposed to the elements? She'd never survive the night.

'Don't, Father,' Brendan said to him. 'You'll never find her.'

Robin stopped. His shoes sank into the wet marsh as he turned his head.

'You know who did this, don't you?' he asked. 'Please, Brendan, you have to tell me. A woman's life is at stake here. How can you stand there and do nothing?'

The islander hauled his heavy feet towards him, defeated by circumstances beyond his control. Hopefully he was too good a man at heart to abandon Grace to her fate. But secrets were a coward's haven, and despite his good nature, Brendan was just as terrified as the rest of them.

'I'll tell you what you need to know, Father,' he said solemnly. 'But if you're to believe what happened here, then you'll need to hear it from everyone.'

'Brendan,' Robin pleaded with him, 'for Christ's sake, man, we don't have time. Grace is out there and—'

'There's time,' he interjected. 'We may be a simple people, Father, but there's nothing simple about what happened to us. And I reckon if anything's to be done about Chrissy's girl, you'll need to understand the truth of this island. And that's no easy truth to accept, believe me.'

Robin stepped back onto the roadside. 'Fine,' he replied, reluctantly turning towards the car after he'd stolen one last scan of the distant hillside. 'Take me to Finnerty's. But so help me, Brendan, if anything happens to that woman, God's wrath will be the least of your worries.'

11

MAGGIE

She knelt on the ash-stained rug, fanning her cold fingers over those first cracks of amber glowing between the coals; the only warmth in a house whose black mould blistered like pus-filled sores and darkened the walls of every room. Maggie had had such plans to revamp and modernise, beautifying her home by Lavelle's benefaction. She'd dreamt of building a south-facing sunroom just off the kitchen, romancing over how its terracotta tiles might have felt beneath her bare feet. The cane furniture had been picked out. And though there was no question about their cushions being blue, she never did settle on the perfect hue for them. Not that it mattered anymore. Her many colour charts and catalogues had long been packed away in the back of her wardrobe, desecrated by the same rampant damp that'd spread like a disease elsewhere.

'Don't burn too much, Margaret,' Tadgh said, standing in the doorway. 'We need to make that coal last the week.'

Her husband had finally stopped snarling. It was draining to listen to him – ranting on and on about Fergal Wilberforce as if he'd ever spit such venom if the man could hear him. Tadgh hadn't opened his mouth since they set out for the hilltop, and that same sullen silence had followed them all the way home, alone, together as always. And then, with the door locked and only his wife for an audience, he'd spoken so boldly in his condemnation of the man; all red cheeks and clenched fists, hissing like a kettle left too long on the hob.

'Did you not buy any from yesterday's delivery?' she asked him, looking to the meagre bulge in the bottom of the coal sack. 'We haven't enough to make it to next Saturday, Tadgh.'

He exhaled out his frustration in a long sigh and wiped a soft hand across his brow. 'We're not made of money, Margaret. We'll have to make do with what we have.'

'Do you want us to freeze to death?'

'Would you rather we starve?' Tadgh snapped back. 'You know times are tight right now. I don't know what you expect me to do about it.' With that he stormed off to the kitchen, his rubber-soled shoes squeaking with every step.

'Just keep on whingeing,' she muttered under her breath. 'That's all you ever do.'

Maggie thought of everyone in Finnerty's – lamplight and music, the fire ablaze – all their hands wrapped around hot whiskeys. It was one of the few pleasures she looked forward to in her week, to enjoy a glass and a chat with Sarah – the only person left on the island who could still make her laugh. The men hardly spoke to her anymore, and she was no stranger as to why. She'd overheard Wilberforce joking one time that Tadgh might as well have pissed all over her like a cat marking what was his, such was the man's neediness for her attention. And there's nothing sadder sometimes than hearing the truth spoken like slander behind your back. Her wedding ring had come with no short measure of marital shackles. Maggie's mother had warned her. But she hadn't listened, such was the hubris of youth and beauty, and the repentant wisdom of age.

No one knew how much they scrimped and saved, keeping the curtains closed to hide the poverty within, feigning the same moneyed role every day of their lives. But the others must have had their suspicions. Her husband was too quick to accept a drink and yet so slow to return it, often taking her home early to dodge his round at the bar. It was embarrassing, and she hated him for it. Maggie had seen how they ridiculed him, mocking the way Tadgh would hold on to her so tightly, worried that a better man might steal her away, God forbid. She felt like a trophy that by some cruel stroke of luck had fallen into the most undeserving hands on the island. But that was life. It doesn't always work out the way you'd hoped. Perhaps had she understood the implications of all those misdecisions, she'd have considered her options a little more carefully.

'What are we having for dinner?' Tadgh asked, having returned to the doorway, now stroking his moustache as though he were pondering over an imaginary menu.

Maggie drew her warm fingers down her face and sighed. 'Well,' she replied, making a point of keeping her eyes on the coal, 'if you hadn't insisted on us coming home, we'd be sitting in Finnerty's right now, having a drink and eating a plate of sandwiches like the rest of them.'

'Insisted?' he repeated, acting as if the very word had wounded him. 'We came home because Fergal Wilber—'

'Wilberforce!' she said, standing to her feet. 'If I hear one more word about Fergal fucking Wilberforce, I swear, Tadgh, I'll walk out that door and leave you to sit beside this miserable fire on your own.'

The man was huffing and puffing as usual, as lost for words as he was lost for a spine.

'Do you think I like living like this?' Maggie asked him, casting her arms about the squalor – threadbare furniture and unlit lamps, because light cost money. 'Everyone thinks the greatest lie we've told was to hide what we did. But it wasn't, Tadgh. It's this, pretending that we aren't the poorest family on the whole fucking island.'

Her husband stepped deeper into the room. 'It's not my fault that we're struggling, Margaret.'

'It's never your fault, is it, Tadgh?' she said. 'It's always Fergal Wilberforce or—'

The hot coals to her side suddenly went cold, startling a stillness from her lips. Wisps of smoke streamed into the white moonlight of the room as Maggie looked to her husband. The air was thick now, heavy with that same sickly stench that meant *he* was close.

'Tadgh,' she whispered, 'what's happening?'

The man didn't voice his reply. Instead, he drew a finger to his lips. Maybe he was right. Maybe it was just passing through. The house was in darkness. At that hour on a Sunday, like all those gone before it, they should have been in Finnerty's. If they stayed perfectly still, if they didn't make a sound, it might not realise they were there. They waited with their unblinking eyes locked with one another. Time crawled on. The slowest seconds imaginable eventually added up to a minute. Was that enough? And then, with the coldness still rippling across Maggie's skin, a floorboard creaked. It'd come from the doorway, from right behind her husband's back.

'Margaret,' he mouthed, guiding her with his eyes to the window, 'get out of here.'

She shook her head. She couldn't leave him. Tadgh Scuffel hadn't given her the life she'd wanted, but he'd given her all he could.

The man recoiled, as though he could feel it breathing down his neck.

'Please, Margaret, before it's too late. Run!'

12

ROBIN

Given the hour of the day, they'd all be there, warming their bones by a fire that'd be fed till last orders, the line of whiskey in the bottle lowering by the round; the same songs, the same sadness, the same secrets. Finnerty would be licking his fingers after stabbing cloves into lemon slices, pushing hot toddies as his cure-all for every ailment. After enough of them, a few might even attempt something as bold as a conversation, trite as they were. But if they thought their few coins had bought them an hour or so of peace, Robin had other plans.

Holleran drew the bow down silently by his side. And after a dampened chord or two, Tierney finally opened his eyes to see the two men standing inside the door. Wooden stools creaked and the logs crackled on, but not one amongst them offered either man a welcome, sincere or otherwise. Two novelties had just occurred. Robin was never known to land into Finnerty's so early in the day, especially on the Sabbath when the Lord was at his most needy, nor had he ever entered with another islander in tow. Intrinsic as he was to their community, spiritually speaking, the priest existed at its periphery, where his days kept true to their own lonely orbit.

He performed a quick head count, scanning for those same faces that'd stared him down with a drab disinterest only hours earlier from the pews. Tadgh and Maggie were the only absentees. It wouldn't have been unlike Wilberforce to send him home without a drink as punishment for earlier, and poor old Tadgh was just the kind of weakling who'd slink off with his tail between his legs, dragging his poor wife behind him.

'We've come from Chrissy's house,' Brendan said, slow and gruff, as though Robin held a gun to his back. 'As you all know, her daughter came back to the island yesterday. And well...' he glanced over to Robin as he cleared his throat '...she's since gone missing.'

The priest waited for him to elaborate on the grim connotations that *gone missing* really carried. But nothing came. These people had kept quiet for so many years, it was as though they no longer remembered how to speak.

'Sure she'd no reason to stay around here, had she?' Mary Malley said, looking around her for supporters. 'Maybe she went back to the mainland.'

Robin locked eyes with the widow – no more warmth, no more patience – and she practically shrank from the coldness of his gaze.

'Chrissy O'Dwyer's daughter was taken from her home,' he said, intentionally raising his voice to startle them. 'By the looks of it, I'd say she was thrown through the glass of her front door. You're welcome to follow the blood, if you wish, but I guarantee you, Mary, it doesn't lead back to the mainland.'

A roomful of eyes were seen to widen in the palpable unease that followed.

'The blood?' O'Toole's daughter whispered, looking even paler than usual.

Her father's skinny fingers clung on to her shoulders. 'Where does it lead, Father?'

'To the hill,' he replied, studying their reactions, 'and those ruins you pay tribute to every fucking week of the year.'

The fact of their priest swearing hammered the severity of their situation home even deeper. No one had partaken of a sip since Robin arrived. After his many futile reminders to give the whiskey a miss, as it turns out, fear was the only language they understood.

'You've heard him in your homes,' Brendan said, staying loyal to his priest's side. 'You know he's back. Now you're welcome to lock your doors and windows and pour out your salt, if that helps you sleep any better. But this is different. If you saw what I just did, you'd understand. This isn't like the old days. This is worse than anything we've been through, and God knows we've been through hell.'

Wilberforce was sat, scowling, on his usual high stool. 'And what exactly have you been saying to Father O'Malley, Brendan?' he said, licking around his gums. 'I hope you haven't forgotten where your loyalties lie.'

'Chrissy's girl is missing,' Brendan replied, his fists cracking as he balled them up, 'and if all you're going to do to help is sit by that bar, Wilberforce, drinking your pints and intimidating anyone with a mind to do something about it, then you can fuck off home.'

Robin stepped forward, intervening before the tension in that room got the better of them. They were such a fractured society. It was the fear – and the fear alone – that'd held them together until now, and it could just as easily tear them apart.

'Brendan hasn't told me anything,' he said. 'That's why I've come here. I want to help you. And I need you to help me find Grace. But first, we need to stop with all this secrecy.'

'*Your* help?' Wilberforce scoffed. 'You mean God's help, is it? I think he gave up on us a long time ago, Father.'

A sentiment shared across the board despite all Robin had done for them. But what if they were right? God hadn't been especially attentive to his needs either, abandoning him when his faith was at its most vulnerable.

'We've already lost everything,' Mary Malley said, hunched on her low chair beside the musicians, wiry legs coiled together, 'and I don't know about the lot of ye, but I'm sick and tired of the lies. I say we tell Father Richard the truth.'

No one argued against the widow, not even Wilberforce, who hadn't taken his stern eyes off Brendan since he'd snarled at him. Reality isn't ironclad. Spin a lie around it for long enough and eventually it'll become less clear, less credible, and less likely to survive. The deaths on Croaghnakeela had become the stuff of legend. Uncertain rumours whispered by uncertain voices, more fairy tale than fact, and only those now standing under Finnerty's roof knew what had really happened.

'John,' Robin said, looking to the publican, 'you might pour me out a brandy, would you? And see to it that everyone else has a drink too.'

Enough amongst them seemed open to relinquishing the burden, and hopefully their willingness would embolden the rest to do the same. Everyone huddled closer as Finnerty laid out the drinks. Sarah O'Toole had never looked so young nestled into her father's side – a child of thirty-nine years. Connor was blessed that his little girl had lived to grow up, and he wasn't going to let anyone take her away from him now. The musicians had laid down their instruments and dragged up two high stools. Eoin Murray followed their lead, keeping just enough distance to sit apart from them, as though the lad had an aversion to everyone and everything bar his own bitterness. Laoise Cunnane kept a hold of her husband's hand. The wine glass beside her was practically full, and there was certainly no need for Finnerty to pour her another. They were the plainest on the island, so forgettable in face and personality that it took Robin more than a few weeks of mental training just to remember their names. Wilberforce didn't budge, like a stubborn boulder wedged in place. The surly bastard didn't even acknowledge Finnerty when he'd placed a fresh pint – creamy dome and all – down in front of him. He just sat there, staring over at Brendan on the opposite end of the counter, like two rival shepherds fighting over the same flock.

'Who'd like to start?' Robin said, once everyone had settled. 'I don't mean to press you all like this. I've respected your privacy since I came to Croaghnakeela, haven't I? But Chrissy's daughter is still out there. And if we're to have any hope of finding her, then you need to tell me what's going on.'

A few lifted their eyes from the floor.

'Valentine Lavelle,' Brendan said eventually, making every syllable count.

All those in attendance looked to him, disquieted now in the company of something so innocuous as a name. It was no secret that Lavelle had done them wrong, though Robin's knowledge of the man elaborated no further than that. His name had been unceremoniously scrubbed from the church records. And whatever legacy he'd left behind, it survived only in the memories of those who'd known him.

'What did he do that made you all like this?' Robin asked.

Perhaps he could have phrased the question better, but honesty was the policy they'd each agreed upon and there wasn't time to cushion their feelings. The priest had learned in the inaugural days of his exile that the very utterance of the Lavelle name was taboo amongst the island community. Even Harriet refused to speak of the man she'd married.

'He brought out the worst in us, Father,' Brendan replied, meeting the priest in the eye as though he were the only other person in the room.

'That wasn't Lavelle anymore,' the widow said. 'If you saw the way that poor man—'

'Poor man?' Wilberforce cut across her before indulging in a false bout of belly laughter. 'Do you think he deserves our fucking sympathy now, Mary?'

'Fergal,' Robin snapped, 'I simply don't have the time to listen to you anymore.'

A frown ploughed the furrows of his brow but, surprisingly, the man didn't retaliate. As no one came to his defence, it seemed that their loyalties had finally aligned with their priest's agenda.

'Now, Brendan,' Robin said calmly, 'please, I'm listening.'

And after a steadying breath, he spoke. 'Valentine Lavelle wasn't a young man when he came here. What was he, Mary, sixtyish-odd years old?'

'Sixty-six, he was,' the widow replied. 'Tall as they come,

with a full head of white hair. Not a bad-looking creature for his age.'

'He'd been married once,' Brendan continued, visibly unimpressed by the woman's closing comment. 'But he'd no children, Father. There were complications with his wife's health. He didn't like to talk about her. But whatever it was, poor woman, it shortened her life and denied them a family. And I suppose, at that age, with no ties holding him down whether he wanted them or not, Valentine Lavelle was looking to leave some sort of legacy behind him. When he came to Croaghnakeela, he thought he'd found the makings of just that. You see, every other island on the coast was taking off around that time, tourists and the like. Hotels without a room going vacant. Full ferries travelling back and forth from coast to coast. And here were we, without a visitor in sight and nothing to offer them even if they knew we existed. It was Lavelle's grand idea to change all that. He'd come from money, you see. Wealthy fathers make wealthy sons, and apparently his father had done *very* well for himself.'

'But as you can see,' Mary Malley said spitefully, 'his plans for the island never came to much, did they? More fool were we to trust a hope.'

The woman's eagerness was appreciated, as no one else seemed so keen to speak up.

'What happened?' Robin asked.

Brendan was taking a long draw of his pint, waiting for someone else to take over. Questions were getting difficult to answer honestly already and they'd only just sat down to chew the fat.

'Lavelle met Harriet,' Finnerty said, polishing the same glass he'd held in his hand for the past five minutes. 'He fell in love.'

'That he did,' the widow agreed. 'Harriet had been engaged once when she was very young. But her fiancé drowned. It was a terrible thing. Both of them weren't even twenty at the time. And she never found love after that. Wasn't looking for it, if you ask me. And then sure, didn't Lavelle come to Croaghnakeela with his money and his charms.'

'They were wed within the year,' Brendan added, guiding their narrative to a clearer path. 'We all thought it was a great thing, didn't we?' To which everyone with the exception of Wilberforce seemed to agree. 'And not just for Harriet's sake. Lavelle had great plans for the island, and we figured these plans were more likely to come to fruition if the man had a vested interest in our community here.'

'What went wrong?' Robin asked, keen to keep the conversation flowing lest their courage dry up. 'Why didn't Lavelle follow through on his promise?'

'There were changes in him, Father,' the widow replied. 'Maybe we didn't know him well enough to notice them at first. Maybe we were blinded.'

'Blinded? By what?'

'By greed,' she replied pensively, looking at those sitting around her.

'What kind of changes do you mean, Mary?' Robin asked her directly, as she'd proven herself to be the most forthcoming speaker in the room.

But it was Brendan who answered. 'The look of him, Father. You couldn't miss it if you ever saw him. Like Mary said, Lavelle was in good health for a man in his sixties. It's true, I guess, that privilege brings more worth than just wealth. But he began to age terribly, and quickly too, as if some disease had taken hold of him.'

'It wasn't natural what happened to that man,' Finnerty added from behind the bar. 'I don't know of any disease that can change a person's face like that. Jesus Christ, it wasn't natural. It was…' The man's thoughts tailed off to silence, muted by the memories.

'And it wasn't just the way he looked either,' Sarah O'Toole said, with her father's skinny fingers still holding on to her like the claws of a hawk. 'All those plans of his, Father, changed around the same time too.'

'That wasn't Lavelle anymore,' the widow said as she locked eyes with Wilberforce, daring the man to disagree with her again. 'You know it's true.'

'In what way did his plans change, Sarah?' Robin asked, trying to draw attention away from Mary's little vendetta with Fergal Wilberforce; the man had a knack for riling up everyone on the island just by being present.

'He'd lost all interest in hotels and restaurants and holiday homes, Father,' Sarah O'Toole replied, visibly uncomfortable speaking before an audience. 'There was only one thing that man wanted to build.' She cast a gaze anxiously around the room.

'And what was that?' Robin asked.

'His orphanage, Father,' Sarah replied, lowering her eyes shamefully.

This was what the priest had been waiting for. But the truth didn't add up.

'There's no record of an orphanage on Croaghnakeela,' he said, looking to the others for some explanation.

'Lavelle kept it secret from those who might have taken an interest, Father,' Finnerty said. 'And after he was gone, we did the same.'

'But where is it?' Robin asked, baffled. 'I haven't seen any such building on the island.'

'West of the hill,' the publican replied. 'And no, you wouldn't see it unless you knew where to look, Father. We burned the damned thing, and then we buried it as best we could.'

That side of the island was of no use to anyone. The earth there was too sodden and exposed. It was a dead space of stone and marshland that none ever visited. And now, at last, Robin knew why.

'We should have burned Lavelle's body too,' Eoin Murray muttered under his breath.

'You all keep saying his name,' Wilberforce said, straightening his shoulders back, his pint emptied. 'Do you really think that's wise? Or have you all forgotten what he's capable of? Let's not forget that there's still a fucking V carved on the wall of this pub.'

'Give it a rest, Fergal, will you?' Brendan said, unimpressed.

'He could be here right now,' he parried, 'listening to you all, picking out which one of you he's going to take—'

'Stop it,' Brendan snapped, screeching back his stool as he rose to his feet. 'You're not helping, Wilberforce.'

'There's no helping any of us, Brendan, and you don't need me to tell you that. The Bodach will be looking for a new body, won't he? And we're all *old men* now. Any one of us could be next.'

Robin pressed his fingers against his eyelids, steadying himself. So much mindless bickering, and Chrissy's daughter was still out there.

'Eoin,' he said, catching the man's eye, 'you might open the window a crack, would you? I think we could all do with a little fresh air in here.'

He was up in a heartbeat, walking to the window the same way he did everything, with a darkness about his eyes and both fists clenched into boulders. Eoin couldn't let it go. He refused to. And after a lifetime of beating himself up over his brother's death, there wasn't a therapist in the world who could cure his bruises.

The air came as some reprieve when he wrenched open the window.

'But how does a man build an orphanage in secret?' Robin asked after a bracing mouthful of brandy. 'And why would he even want to? Croaghnakeela can be treacherous on the calmest day. It's no place for a child.'

That last remark seemed to stifle their eagerness to speak. But they'd already said too much to kill the conversation now. Questions had been raised, and nobody was leaving that pub until Robin had his answers.

'Lavelle couldn't have done it without us, Father,' Brendan said, squeezing around his brittle fingers. 'He preyed on us to do the Devil's work for him. The bastard came to each of us here on the island, buying our loyalty, lending us more money than we knew what to do with. No questions asked. And sure we'd nothing to our names but some land, how could we say no to him?'

'You helped him?' Robin asked, mindful of the man's honesty and how it must have pained him to support it – to finally confess to the shame that'd blighted their lives for thirty years.

'We did,' he replied, speaking to those gathered around him. 'We organised the build of that orphanage of his, and he paid us a fortune to do it too. We saw only the wealth, Father, and we took it greedily. We contacted the right people on the mainland – those who'd get the job done and not speak a word about it to anyone afterward. Lavelle was strict on that. We should have known then, I suppose, that something was off about him. But no matter our suspicions, the labourers came. Droves of them, all eager to work given how much they were earning. We even put them up ourselves. Sure, why wouldn't we? Lavelle made it worth our while. We'd plans to extend our own homes, too, when his work was done.'

'Only they weren't our homes anymore, were they?' Wilberforce added.

Brendan sighed. 'I can't recall now who noticed it first. But it wasn't long before a V was scratched into our walls. None of us cared too much about it at the time. We'd taken his coin, not realising that he was buying us, Father, and that he'd own us from that day forth.'

'The Bodach is a trickster,' Wilberforce growled. 'If it wasn't our fucking greed, then he'd find some other way to turn our fortunes against us. Sure look what happened to Declan.'

'The Bodach?' the priest repeated. 'Fergal, what *is* this word you keep saying?'

'It's a tale as old as time, Father,' he replied, his demeanour darker than Robin had ever seen it. 'A wicked thing that I'd been told about as a child. My mother, God rest her, used to use it to terrify me into behaving myself. I thought, when I got older, that it was just some make-believe – a fairy tale no more real than a changeling stealing away a newborn for the sake of replacing it. And it doesn't fucking please me to admit that I was wrong.'

Robin looked to Brendan, seeking some affirmation from

the one person whose word he'd come to trust above all others on the island, with the loose-lipped widow coming in at a close second after her performance that evening.

'Wilberforce is telling you the truth, Father,' he said sadly. 'It's real.'

'But what *is* it?' the priest asked, sitting forward, growing impatient.

'It's an old man, Father,' Wilberforce answered. 'It's always been an old man. They used to say he was a trickster who'd catch you at a crossroads and cheat you out of your last coin, as if the odds were in his favour and yours were forever at a loss. He'd come into your home, too, if you were unlucky enough, creeping down the chimney, and the only way to keep the bastard out was to lay some salt around the hearth.'

'But why?' Robin asked, struggling to believe what he was hearing. 'Why would this Bodach of yours come into someone's home?'

'To steal away their children, Father,' Wilberforce replied gravely. 'They're all he's ever wanted.'

It was then, with the cool air misting by the open window, that Robin heard it – a sound in the night where there should have been only silence.

'Can you hear that?' he whispered, rising to approach the door.

If anyone else had reacted to it, then the priest hadn't noticed. He'd never heard anything like it. Somehow, it seemed to come from the—

'Don't, Father,' Eoin said, lurching in front of him.

This truly was an evening of firsts. The islanders were in the habit of dancing around their priest whenever he approached them, not throwing themselves in front of him.

'Now is not the time to lose your faith, Eoin,' he leaned forward to whisper in his ear.

The man must have marked the steel in the young priest's voice, as he stood aside to let him pass without further contest. Robin gave his shoulder a gentle squeeze, grateful for his concerns and yet all the more curious as to what could have inspired them. The warmth and their courage were quick to slip out into the night as he pulled open the door, letting it swing all the way in. He walked, mesmerised, towards the oddity, refusing to believe what he was hearing. His hand instinctively dove into his pocket, seeking out the supporting touch of the rosary he kept there.

'That's impossible,' he whispered as the horror tightened its hold over him.

13

Tadgh

Its breath snaked down the nape of his neck, infesting the flesh, paralysing the bone, raising within him a despair that no sane mind could rationalise. The stench was so intoxicatingly putrid to swallow – so alive with impurity – that he could feel it writhing like a belly full of worms inside of him. This was the death that Tadgh had dreaded for thirty long years – it was an unhallowed invasion of the man's very soul – whereby everything he once held dear would soon be eclipsed by a cruel and sentient darkness. And yet, if that's what it took to keep his love alive – his life for hers – then he would offer it gladly.

Margaret was braver than anyone else on the island ever realised. And had he asked her to stay, Tadgh knew his wife would have done just that; she'd have run into his arms and held him tighter than those unseen tendrils now tightening around his heart.

'Please, Margaret, before it's too late. Run!'

Isn't that what he'd said? He couldn't quite remember.

Even if he'd wanted to follow her, the man's limbs were no longer his to command. The evil had cocooned him in his own skin. He'd watched Margaret hurl the lamp through the window, scattering its shards across the wilds of their garden. The sound of its shatter must have been deafening in the silence, and yet he'd hardly heard it. Tadgh's grip on his senses was loosening. Soon there'd be nothing of him left.

Never in his life did he imagine that a woman like Margaret would choose a man like him. No one else on the island could believe it either. And he reaped a certain pride from that. She'd given Tadgh the happiest years of his life. Even when the dark times came to Croaghnakeela, she was the one star that never lost its light.

A freezing fog slipped down his throat, cold and silken as long strands of hair. The man had no choice but to suffer through it – choking for air, receiving none. Death couldn't come soon enough. It felt as though a cluster of spiders were now binding his bones in reams of icy web.

Margaret glanced back to him as she'd climbed through the window frame, still desperately seeking him to join her. Tadgh could only watch as she sliced her arm on a stubborn sliver of glass that'd remained wedged in by the sill. He yearned to tend to her wounds, to hold her, to take her far from that accursed island and start their lives anew. And then, in the sharpest second, every bone in his skeleton cracked aloud and he collapsed to the floor, writhing against his will as the evil squirmed within him. Tadgh could hear his body breaking. But he felt no pain. He'd lost all touch with his physical form. He was no more than a weak flame on a wick, alone in the darkness, fading into oblivion.

Basked in silver moonlight – bloody fingers pressed to her wound – Margaret had looked back to her husband one last time, and then she was gone. He'd listened to her ragged gasps break into the night, broken-hearted, too powerless to whisper one last *I love you*.

If there was ever any light intended to soothe the passing from this world into the next, then to Tadgh Scuffel it was denied. He received only the nauseating, mind-shattering horror of being consumed by another. Until all that remained was the cold, and a darkness that fell over his life like black soil on a casket, sealed and buried where nobody would ever find him.

14

Robin

The priest stood alone, listening to the distant cry of children in the starlit darkness. There could be no doubting its source now that he'd breached the open air. It was coming from the hill, from deep within it, hundreds of voices echoing through clefts in its stone, as terrifying as it was unbelievable.

Brendan joined Robin's side, so close that their shoulders were practically touching, and for a long moment there was silence between them.

'You hear them, don't you, Father?'

All the while, that heartbreaking strain persisted.

'You mean, you can't?' the priest asked him, the lightest whisper on the wind.

The islander shook his head. 'No, I never could.'

'What is it?'

'It's not easy to put into words, Father,' Brendan replied. 'But it's something very, *very* old.'

A few of the others were now venturing outside, testing the ground with cautious steps, as if no inch of the island was safe anymore. Eoin Murray leaned back against the wall of the pub, arms crossed tight, staring at the hill. No fear tinted his expression. There was only that same anger he'd worn like a second skin since Lorcan lost his life. The widow crept over the threshold next, her body bent into a stoop, too curious a creature to stay indoors. Next came O'Toole and his daughter, moving with an urgency that was uncommon to either of them. Unlike Eoin, it would seem their fears had taken them like a strong current.

'Where are you going, Connor?' Brendan asked him. 'Don't you think it's best if we stick together tonight?'

But the man kept on going, taking his daughter deeper into the darkness and tripping clumsily over his feet to get there. 'I'm getting Sarah off this island.'

'Connor,' Brendan barked, loud enough to stop the man in his tracks. 'You know he won't let you leave. Not now. Not ever.'

'What other choice do we have?' he replied, desperation dripping from his every word. 'I'd sooner risk our lives on the water than stay another second on this godforsaken island. He's back, Brendan, and I'm not letting him anywhere near my girl.'

'Please, Connor,' Brendan said, lowering his voice. 'You were there when the Corcorans tried to leave. You know what became of them. You saw it yourself. They never stood a chance.'

Brendan's words anchored Connor to the earth. Robin recognised the name Corcoran from the church records. Five had died on a single day. A husband, a wife, and their three daughters. There were no burials. There were no bodies. There was no mention of them after.

'There's someone coming,' Eoin Murray called out, abandoning his post by the wall.

All eyes mirrored the direction of his own to seek out what

he'd seen. Though still too far to identify, there was a shape materialising in the distance as it neared the lamplit perimeter of Finnerty's pub.

'Who is it?' Sarah asked, hugging into her father's side.

'It's Maggie Scuffel,' Eoin announced with no short measure of relief.

And just when the priest thought he'd finally witnessed a smile on the man's face, Murray's earnestness was shot down by the sight of her. Robin strode over to see for himself what the trouble was, though the fact of the woman being out after dark on her lonesome was anomaly enough to raise his concerns. The woman wore no coat against the cold and – evident now as she drew closer to the light – the front of her dress was stained with blood. It'd painted her hands, too, and speckled her face like a rash where she'd dabbed her cheeks. The priest stepped closer, cautiously, as one approaches an injured animal in the wild, testing its temperament, searching for its wounds.

'Maggie,' he said, near enough now to be heard without raising his voice, 'are you hurt? Whose blood is that? Where's your husband? Where's Tadgh?'

Too many questions, but Robin couldn't help it. They were poorly equipped to treat even the basest injury.

'It took him, Father,' she replied, looking to the pub and the timid few who'd remained indoors, watching her fearfully through its open door.

'Tell me what happened?' he pressed, reaching for her shoulders.

'It was in our house,' Maggie replied as she fell into Robin's embrace, exhausted. 'I broke through the window. I ran. Tadgh told me to.'

He marked the lacerations on her bare arms – hairline slices that needed immediate attention.

'And where's Tadgh now?'

'I don't know, Father.'

Robin squeezed her tighter. 'Where was he when you last saw him, Maggie?'

'On the floor,' she replied, burying her head deeper into his chest. 'His bones were cracking, Father. I had to get out of there before it took a hold of him. He told me to, Father. I would have stayed. But he told me to run. And I didn't know where…'

The priest held his hand to her head. 'It's okay, Maggie. You're safe now.'

Nothing she had spoken made sense. But he'd guard her with his life regardless. Robin looked to those who'd lingered outside, hoping for some explanation but receiving only the same worried expression shared across all their faces. To his surprise, and much to the widow's chagrin, Fergal Wilberforce had now joined them outside too, breathing hard through his mouth as if the simple act of standing up were a challenge for the man. The bastard had been so brazen in his bullying of poor Tadgh earlier in church, and yet now he didn't look so brave.

'Where is he?' he asked nervously. 'Where's Scuffel?'

'Father,' Eoin said, anxiously staring to where Maggie had just run from, 'we should get back inside.'

That ghostly lament continued, like a symphony of doomed souls crying out to be saved, and Robin wanted nothing more than to be free of it – to hide his head in the sand like all those whose cowardice he'd condemned for six long years – but he refused to back down.

'He's right,' Maggie said, now pushing the priest towards the safety of the pub. 'He's coming, Father! He knows where we are.'

'*Who's* coming, Maggie?' he asked, holding his ground. 'Tadgh? But you just told me—'

'That's not Tadgh anymore!' she snapped, squinching her teary eyes shut. 'Please, you have to keep me safe from him!'

Robin looked back to the pub – to those who'd shunned kindness and charity in lieu of their own safekeeping. Neither musician met the priest in the eye. Gerard and Laoise were behind them, faded into the background, insignificant as ever, their hands held tight while the publican fidgeted with a sodden dishcloth. Self-centred bastards, too cowering to even—

'Get inside *now*!' Eoin shouted, waving everyone towards the door.

Robin stood against the grain of their retreat. 'Why? What's happening? What did you see?'

Murray watched the darkness as he backpedalled away from it. 'He's coming, Father.'

He'd listened to their long-overdue confessions that evening, but if Robin were to believe what he'd been told, then he needed to see it for himself. And so, stubbornly, he faced the night.

There *was* someone coming.

Whoever it was, they were throwing their body wildly across the marsh, their every breath a snap and a snarl. Robin held his ground, determined not to falter. And yet, neath that white film of moonlight, those first glimmers of its shape and size were enough to send him staggering back. It wasn't human. It couldn't have been. It was impossibly tall and thin, and those horrifying limbs – all tangled in silver strands of mist – were covering the ground with a speed that was in itself terrifying. The priest recovered his footing and fled into the safety of the pub, his courage fractured by those footsteps that'd quaked through the darkness.

The door slammed shut behind him before he collapsed to the floor. Eoin and Brendan were already dragging a tall barrel towards it as the widow went about snapping the curtains shut across every window. Finnerty had withdrawn from behind the bar, too, and was tipping salt out from a huge sack cradled in his arms, lining it along the walls, piling it thickest by the threshold.

Maggie knelt by Robin's side, offering him a comforting hand, bloody as it was. 'Whatever you do, Father,' she whispered, ignoring her own wounds, 'don't talk back to it.'

The room was silent now save for their bated breaths. They'd planned for this. They knew what was coming, and not one amongst them had thought to warn him.

A bony knuckle tapped playfully against the door.

'Mar-gar-et,' sang the voice, drawing the word like a blade through the poor woman's soul. 'I know you're in there, darling.'

It was Tadgh's voice, distorted, and deeper than was natural, his every word enmeshed in a gauze of cobweb and phlegm. There was an unearthly quality to it, like the resonance of an iron bell in an empty chamber, causing it to somehow echo around the room, making Robin fear that the damned thing was already inside.

'Won't you let me in, Margaret?' it said, chuckling through closed lips. 'Would you really leave your loving husband – the man you so adore – outside on such a cold and dark night? Be a good girl and open the door for me now, would you?'

Robin looked to her. Maggie's tear-sparkled eyes were fixed on the door – all that stood between her and the horror that'd spoken with such a cruel and sinister mischievousness, tearing fresh wounds in her already bloodied heart.

'If you only knew how much your husband loved you, Margaret. You might have been less keen to wish him dead. Forever cursing his name under your breath. Cringing from his touch whenever he lay beside you.'

She drew both hands to her face, condemned to listen to the foul thing's every word. There was nothing anyone could do for her. They were, each of them, at its mercy.

'Don't think I haven't seen how you look at him, Margaret. The pity. The shame. The hate. Poor Tadgh, so worried that his darling wife wants to fuck every other man on the island. But he isn't wrong, is he?' The laughter exploded in a spine-chilling cackle. 'It's all you dream about, isn't it, Margaret? Legs spread before an orderly queue, and the pleasure would be all the greater knowing the pain it would cause him. The man who ruined your life. The man who even your own mother despised. The man who—'

'Please,' she whimpered, so softly that the thing couldn't possibly have heard her, and yet somehow it had, 'make it stop.'

'You want to make it stop, Margaret,' it said, all humour discarded, 'then all you have to do is open this door and let me—'

'Leave her alone, you bastard!' Fergal Wilberforce roared, sweat streaming his brow, eyes bulging from their sockets, helpless as the rest of them. 'Be gone from this place!'

More giggling permeated through the door, like an airborne virus seeking out its next victim. Robin felt sick just knowing that such horrors could exist. He'd never felt a presence like it. Such malevolence wasn't of this world. Even mankind's most wicked soul was angelic in comparison to that which now taunted them from behind that door.

'I've been watching you too, Fergal,' the voice returned. 'Shivering alone in your bed at night, wondering why no one has ever loved you, masturbating over your favourite little fantasies of Margaret Scuffel. And yet you've never had the balls to speak to her, have you? And so what do you do? You taunt her husband. You belittle the man who has everything that you never will. You hide behind all that hatred when deep down you're just a lonely little boy who cries himself to sleep at night.'

'Lies!' Wilberforce spat before glancing embarrassedly at those around him. 'You can't trust a word the trickster says.'

'Poor old Tadgh,' it said, almost musically, enjoying its audience. 'No wonder he was so easy to take. Do you know what his last wish was, before I strangled the soul out of him? It was that *you* should suffer too, Fergal. That you feel the same disgrace you brought upon him, and that you never lay one of your filthy fingers on that beloved whore he called a wife. But I'm going to go one better. I'm going to mutilate you in the most exquisite ways imaginable and dress your fat around the rafters of every home.'

'Don't listen to it, Fergal,' Brendan whispered over to him. 'Don't let it get to you.'

'*Don't let it get to you?*' it repeated mockingly. 'Your dear daddy's madness must be in your blood too if you've forgotten our little agreement, Brendan. I own you. Never forget that. Every single one of you belongs to me.'

Robin lifted himself back onto his feet, unable to endure

its wicked tirade any longer. If the Bodach had the means to enter and follow through on its threats, then why hadn't it done so already?

'Whatever claim you think you have over these people,' he shouted, lurching a step closer to the door, 'Grace has nothing to do with—'

Brendan seized Robin by the sleeve, urging him not to talk back.

'The priest?' it said amusedly. 'Our hero of blind and beautiful faith. Such a waste of a man. But you have my gratitude. Without you, I wouldn't be here now, would I?'

Everyone looked to Robin, their expressions as baffled as his own.

'Your fate will be the same as theirs, *Father*,' the voice added with a chilling calmness. 'Once all of your bones are piled together, nobody will know you were any different.'

The lamplight around the room flickered. Robin looked to those who'd fallen back from the door, each one more terrified than the other. Breaths now fogged around open mouths as a creeping coldness fastened to their skin like a light frost. Through some ungodly artifice, the fire's flames no longer brought any warmth. A bulb suddenly exploded neath a corner lampshade when the Bodach clubbed its knuckles against the door. It was so perfectly in sync; one could have sworn it'd smashed it with its own hand. Amidst the gasps and stifled shrieks, everyone herded closer to the fireplace, allying their lives to its light.

'Step away from the door, Father!' the widow shrieked.

Another knock shook Finnerty's walls. Another light was lost. The damned thing was feeding off their fears like its favourite fucking meal. One by one, with each hammer of its hand, every bulb in the room was reduced to broken glass and the darkness grew bolder, its shadows laying steady siege to the light. The fire was all that remained. Robin was never so grateful for Finnerty's fascination with keeping it fed. But his relief was short-lived. The flames themselves now began to falter. He watched in helpless disbelief as they shrank into the grate, leaving a dark that was terrifyingly absolute and a silence more sinister than any voice.

Despite Mary's warnings, Robin had stayed by the door, and there he now discerned the crick and crack of broken bones on the breeze.

'John,' Brendan said in a hoarse whisper, 'didn't I tell you to ready a torch for this? Damn it, man, get us some light!'

A chair screeched across the floor as the publican blundered blindly into it.

'Hang on,' Finnerty replied, distraught, 'it's behind the bar. I know where I put it.'

Robin crept closer to the curtained window. With his hand atremble, he peeled it back. The moonlight leaked in a thin pool across the surrounding fields. There was no sign of the other – no fiend to meet him beyond the glass. But he knew it was out there still. He could feel its presence smouldering crimson in the black.

Finnerty was heard fumbling his way to the back of the bar, stumbling into all that furniture they'd shifted around earlier in the evening, cursing under his breath with every collision.

'It's okay,' Robin said, trying to subdue their panic, though he himself had to wrap his lips around every word to keep them steady. 'We're safe so long as we—'

That eerie clicking sound returned, louder now, closer, as if it were inside the room.

And then came the scream.

Everyone scattered throughout the room as Sarah O'Toole howled with a sick and sirenic desperation. Her voice filled the darkness, fattening it with a fear that couldn't be contained. If she'd spoken some word amidst the madness, then it was lost in the chaos that ensued.

'Sarah!' her father roared, but the man was blind as the rest of them to his daughter's plight.

Nobody knew what was happening.

'Finnerty!' Brendan bawled, his voice rising above the bedlam. 'Turn that fucking light on!'

A tray of glasses smashed to the floor.

'I'm trying, for Christ's sake!' the publican called back to him.

He was tearing through the shelves, casting their contents about him, his hands fumbling for the torch he'd stashed there.

'Help!' Connor shrieked. 'For the love of God, someone help me! It has her!'

The priest ran to the sound of his voice but clacked his knee off a low stool that sent him floundering forward. 'John! What's going on? Where are you?'

The ceiling was suddenly awash with light. Finnerty quickly lowered its beam towards the commotion, and there they all saw it – the monstrous arm that'd reached down the chimney. Its bones had torn through the skin as they'd thinned and elongated, mutilating their form in order to capture its prize. Sarah fought to free herself, but the Bodach's hand had clamped around her waist, fingers cracking from their joints to trap her, and it was wrenching the woman towards the firepit, seeking to steal her away.

Her father's hands were locked with hers, battling against it, refusing to let go. But Connor hadn't the strength. Every violent tug sent him skidding forward, and no one made any move to help him.

'John!' Robin roared, dashing to the man still hiding behind the bar. 'A knife! Give me a fucking knife!'

The light was lowered, descending the room back into darkness as the publican reached behind the counter and passed him the closest knife at hand – the long, serrated one with a red handle that he used to cut up his damn lemons. It was the best Robin could have hoped for. Sarah – with her arms at full reach, holding on to her father – had wedged her feet into the hearth, but the Bodach was tightening its grip around her ribcage. If it couldn't have her, it was going to split her in two.

Bounding across the room, Robin drew the knife upon its wrist. Shadows danced riotously in the torchlight as he sawed it back and forth, over and over, across the exposed bone. Deeper hewed the blade. Sarah's screams – and the pains of being crushed alive – intensified. And yet, even when the priest had scratched through to the very marrow, still the Bodach refused to relinquish her. But he kept on going, forcing the blade's teeth down with all his strength until finally the bone tore apart and Sarah crashed into her father's embrace. The arm retreated back into the darkness of the flue, where the echo of its bones faded out of earshot. On the floor, the dissevered hand grabbed at nothing, twitching mindlessly until its fingers gnarled up like the legs of some petrified insect.

Robin collapsed to his knees, exhausted. The knife slipped from his hand and clamoured on the floor. He looked over to

Finnerty, squinting against the light still trained on his face, and waved the man over towards the chimney, infuriated by their fecklessness but too drained to do very much about it.

'Salt,' he said, breathless, 'and seal it up!'

Connor O'Toole was holding his weeping daughter in his arms.

'Thank you, Father,' he said, sniffing back the tears.

Robin was still trying to breathe. 'Is she okay?'

Connor nodded. 'She is, because of you.'

The priest staggered back onto his feet. He couldn't tear his attention away from that hand, the size of it, how it no longer resembled anything remotely human. Even the nails – yellowed and thick now – had curved into the most ghastly claws.

'What was that thing?' Robin asked, his skin burning despite the lingering cold.

More than a few of them looked to Brendan as he picked Finnerty's knife up from the floor.

'At first light, Father,' he replied, pocketing it inside his jacket. 'I'll try my best to show you. It's time you knew what we're dealing with.'

15

Harriet

Valentine Lavelle died long before they buried his body. Harriet had mourned him in her own private way: imprisoned, forgotten, abandoned by those whom she'd once counted on to care for her. If anyone suspected the cruelty that came to define her life – the bruises, the tears, the terror – then no one did anything about it. But Harriet didn't blame them. How were they to know that *her* Valentine was no longer the same man who double-locked that door behind him each night, pocketing its key, sealing his wife inside like his favourite treasure.

She was sat by the fireplace as that all too familiar darkness gathered around her. The woman's gaze fell sadly upon the empty windowsill, wishing that Tiddles were there now to keep her company. But her best friend – clever little girl that she was – would have sought out some shelter from the cold elsewhere, as anywhere on Croaghnakeela was warmer than that room, in the home that Harriet's husband had built for her, back when he was still the same man she'd fallen in love with.

He had been so handsome when they'd met. And that's how

she remembered him, freshly doused in a splash of cologne and clean-shaven as a matter of principle, gladly showing off that pointy chin of his, which – like that subtle bump on the bridge of his nose and that half-smile he wore come rain or shine – made the man so distinctive, so flush with charm and character. His snow-white hair had thawed slightly on the brow, but elsewhere it was long and soft to the touch, flaring light as cotton in the breeze. Truthfully, the man had aged better than the best leather. Faint wrinkles broke from his eyes like the veins of a leaf, cracking deepest around his lips. But he wore these laughter lines as proudly as a crown, like any good man should.

Harriet still brooded over the day she lost him. Such was the heartache that followed – and indeed, the horrors that persisted into the very present – that it was far too easy to dwell on the many *what-ifs*, though they too sired their own disappointments. How different her life could have been had they not ventured down to the coast that day. But it'd been so clement and so beautifully out of character for the season that Valentine insisted they make the most of it, and so a walk was decided upon.

'Fresh sea air and sunshine, my love,' he'd declared, inhaling deeply. 'What more can one ask for in this life?'

They'd ambled down to the shoreline on the western side, a part of the island that even Harriet – who'd lived on Croaghnakeela all her life – was mostly unfamiliar with. Aside from there being nothing in the way of novelty or attraction to invite any visitors, people generally avoided it for reasons that, much like the lives who recall them, had been forgotten over time. Regardless, together, hand in hand, they'd clambered over the rocks as Valentine led her to the island's edge. The man had a gift for making her feel young again, convincing her without argument that their brightest days were yet to come, and she was so in love that she'd believed him. *That* was one feeling Harriet would never forget.

'Such untouched beauty,' he said, squeezing her hand tighter. '*This* is Croaghnakeela's greatest asset, my darling. Trust me, in a few years it'll be the talk of the country.'

The shore was a ragged, misshapen shelf of stone, and one far too treacherous to navigate by water, even for a boatman as skilled as Colman McMorrow. Great chunks of it had fallen to the ocean floor, cutting caves into its side and yet, despite the risks, Valentine was far too young at heart to turn back. If anything, the dangers therein probably held their own allure for the man.

'A few more feet, darling,' he said, his white hair lifting high in the wind. 'I see a hole or something up ahead. I just want to have a quick look. Who's to say what treasures have washed up here over the years. You can wait here, if you like. I shan't be long.'

Harriet could only titter at the man's enthusiasm and bade him to hurry back. Valentine had a magpie's eye, so easily drawn to shiny and curious things. And the fact that this hole of his was encircled by four tall stones – hand-carved ones at that – must have made its investigation all the more irresistible. She'd watched the man battle against the wind, skipping like a child over cracks in the stone. Perhaps if she'd been brave enough to follow him, none of this horror would have come to pass. Another *what-if* – another pain to endure.

Valentine had waved back at her excitedly. He'd found something, apparently, in the exact crevice that he'd made a beeline toward, as though some dark fate had taken his hand from hers and carried him towards it. He held up two fingers, requesting just two minutes to investigate his discovery deeper. Pleasant a day as it was, Harriet's cheeks were beginning to ache in the wind, and yet she mirrored his gesture. Two minutes. If that's all it took to please him, then who was she to deny the man?

She'd watched as he lowered himself carefully into the ground, pleading with him to be careful, whispering every prayer she knew to keep him safe. Two minutes passed silently and slowly and without dire event. And then two more, and still there was no sign of her husband's return. Harriet couldn't tell how long she stood there with the worry of losing him worming its way around her thoughts. But eventually a hand rose above the rocky surface and Valentine was clambering into the daylight, weaker than she'd ever seen him.

'Where did you go?' she asked.

'I... thought I heard someone,' he replied, dazed and distant.

Harriet couldn't believe that to be true, not down there of all places.

'And was there someone, darling?' she asked him, humouring the man's obvious mistake, thinking it kinder to let him correct it himself.

He shook his head as he stared off into space, squinting against the daylight. 'No,' he said, 'I don't think so. I don't know. I... can't really remember.'

Harriet looped her arm through his and leaned into her husband's side. 'Come on,' she said with a smile and a shiver, 'let's get you home.'

Valentine was out of sorts on that walk – uncannily sullen,

and quieter than his usual chatty self. She'd assumed that his exertions had gotten the best of him; a credible explanation considering his vintage. It was all well and good behaving like a younger man, but that didn't mean the body was always so keen to play along. And their evening wasn't all that dissimilar to those gone before it, though Valentine kept mostly to himself – captivated by his own private musings – and retired to bed early, blaming some dizziness for which Harriet knew he'd no one but himself to blame. Too much excitement for one day. Rest was all he needed to recoup, and when she'd sidled in beside him, the man was already sound asleep.

That night, however, whatever late hour it was when Harriet awoke, her husband was gone. Dismally wet were those moonlit hours, and yet the islanders came out in number to help find the man – a testament to how indebted they'd become to Valentine's beneficence in the short time they'd known him. It was close to sunrise when he was discovered on the western shore, distraught and soaked through to the skin, not far from where he and Harriet had visited that afternoon. And it wasn't long before the sinister implications of his ordeal came to reveal themselves. The wicked voice that'd spoken to him from the darkness had drawn the man back. And it had taken from him everything, his wife included.

Harriet looked to the Bible atop the hearth. Father O'Malley must have left it behind him again, though he probably had more than a few, like a collector seeking out different editions of their favourite book. Maybe he'd meant it as a gift for her. But Harriet had given up on prayer. She'd asked God to save her too many times by now, and nothing ever seemed to change. If there was some higher power, out of sight above the clouds, then it could neither see nor hear her pleas on that island. The evil kept it hidden.

Harriet knew that the man who'd returned to her wasn't the Valentine she married. And yet, owing to the oddity of it all, she'd kept her suspicions to herself. The clues were subtle at first. But these became more conspicuous as the days rolled on. A mean glint in the eye. A shortness of temper. A flagrant lack of interest in all but his own selfish needs. And there was the sickening crack of bone that came to score his every movement. The evil endeavoured to keep its presence hidden, and only Harriet knew her husband well enough to see through the veil of its disguise. The islanders remained oblivious to the man's sudden twist of temperament. But even they must have marked the physical changes over time – those deformities that gradually warped him into something horrid.

Whatever had seized control of Valentine's body struggled to hold his appearance intact, like a large hand squeezed into too small a glove, bursting at its seams. It was first evident in his fingers. They'd stretched so hideously long, to twice their original length, with thick nails that resembled more animal than man. The affliction affected his limbs too, though in much slower increments. He soon came to stagger about with a stoop, concealing his newfound height as all those brittle bones creaked and split with every step.

But it was the face that tormented Harriet most of all. She'd watched in quiet terror as it twisted into a repulsive caricature of the man she had loved. What remained of Valentine Lavelle was no more than a mask, and the devil behind it was pressing against his dead skin, causing his features to protrude in ways that defied disease and injury. His white hair had withered, and those eyes that scrutinised Harriet's every movement – like a jailor obsessed with its only inmate – paled to a creamy white, holding a devilish crimson pupil in their centre, visible only when denied any natural light. If there was such a thing as pure evil in this world, then it was in those eyes.

The poor woman had vowed her loyalty and love to the man Valentine Lavelle, binding her to his body and soul, though the latter was lost many years ago. And so all she could do now was sit beside her lightless hearth and wait, sifting through the ash of a life that had dragged on for far too long. Harriet's bright eyes returned to the window. The night was going to be a cold one, and she hoped that Tiddles was somewhere warm.

16

Robin

A murky soup of grey air swirled in the headlights. Morning was still too young to bring any meaningful light, but Brendan knew those roads well enough to drive blind. The soulful agonies of the night before still echoed in the silence between them, and neither man had spoken since they'd set out for the home of Brendan's late father – where those answers he'd alluded to could best be explained. He drove with his side window slightly ajar, keeping one ear trained outside as the cold air snaked in around them, his speed hinting at a threat that was far from over.

Finnerty's door had been edged open with the paling of the sky, and together they'd listened for a long time – testing the dead air for a pulse – before making a break for it. Robin never could explain the eerie silence of a sunrise on Croaghnakeela, nor why the birds deemed it undeserving of their songs. But he finally understood. If he were gifted wings, knowing now the evil that cursed its shores, he'd have flown far from that island too.

'Brendan,' Robin said, watching the fog roll against the windshield, 'that… thing that attacked us last night, I can't shake something Maggie told me. She said that it was *inside* him. Inside Tadgh, I mean. Am I right in saying that whatever took a hold of Valentine Lavelle is now... inside Tadgh Scuffel?'

Brendan took his time, choosing his words to best soften the hard truth. 'The Bodach infests the bodies of old men, Father,' he replied grimly. 'Never the young, only the old, and don't ask me why. That's just the way of it. It can hide beneath their skin without you ever realising. Or it can twist them into the most nightmarish of things, as you saw yourself last night. But whatever remains of poor old Tadgh, the man's no more than a puppet now – a hollowed-out body with a devil inside it. And you'd be wise to remember that.'

Of all the vile entities condemned by his Christian teachings, nothing compared to the horror that Robin had found on Croaghnakeela. Could *this* be God's calling? Had he been sent to the island for this very reason? To somehow save it?

'You knew this thing was here all along, didn't you?' he asked.

Brendan's eyes didn't stray from the road ahead. 'I knew.'

'Why didn't you tell me?'

Perhaps there was something the priest could have done to prevent all this. Any precaution would have been better than nothing at all.

'Because, Father, it's been thirty years since we buried Lavelle's body in the earth, and that's the only flesh and blood the Bodach had ever taken. We paid the bastard back what we could, throwing our fortunes down that fucking well, thinking we were reclaiming what was ours. But sure, after he was gone we'd nothing left to our names. And do you know what we did, Father? We picked apart whatever was left. Like vultures we were, breaking into the homes of the dead, scraping together what we could find of Lavelle's fortune just to keep ourselves alive for these past thirty years. But as poor and hopeless as we may be, at least we thought we'd seen the worst of it. How were we to know that it'd come back? Are we so doomed that we can't still cling to a hope?'

Robin's congregation never struck him as the hopeful sort.

'Why didn't you just leave?' he asked.

The question seemed to cast a sullen cloud over the man. 'We can't, Father. No more than the Bodach can. The bastard may have a weakness to the salt in the water, but he's able to work the waves to his will regardless. The Corcorans were the first to try it, but they weren't the last. And after seeing enough of them fail, we knew that none of us were ever getting off this rock alive.'

Robin ran a hand down his tired face, doubting if this weren't some awful dream he'd yet to awaken from. The night had been a sleepless one, fraught with ancient horrors fresh only to him. The islanders had chosen to keep their priest safe by keeping him in the dark. And now that darkness was all he knew. Every soul under Finnerty's roof had remained on their guard as they awaited the dawn, dreading the Bodach's return, and Robin cared for them too much to speak of it again, to invite it back into the moment when the past still rang so loudly in the air. Tall wax candles kept the lights on. The chimney had been sealed with wood cracked from Finnerty's furniture, and the hand entombed within it.

'When Tadgh came to me yesterday,' Robin said, still panning the past for answers, 'he mentioned footsteps in his home. He said he'd first heard them the night Chrissy died.

Does that make any sense to you? What could her death have to do with all this?'

'I couldn't say, Father,' Brendan replied, shaking those dark thoughts around his skull. 'But I heard the same steps, just like in the old days when we traded all we had for Lavelle's coin. Our homes. Our belongings. Our... families, God save us. We didn't know at the time what we were agreeing to, and the bastard never thought to tell us. But we gave it all back, Father. We made amends as best we could. It was the only way to keep the damned thing defeated. The Bodach thrives on offerings, whether it be our wealth or the life of some poor child. And by giving it nothing, it received no power in return.'

'Offerings?' Robin repeated thoughtfully, dwelling on the word as he rooted in the pocket of his jacket.

He peeled open the letter he'd found on the floor of Chrissy's home and read it aloud.

'Christine, I had nothing else to give him. I had no other choice. I'm sorry, Declan.'

Brendan blanched beside him. He'd clearly drawn more sense from the dead man's words than Robin had.

'*He* did it. He sold out his family to the Bodach, Father. Declan's the reason why it's come back to—' The old man stopped himself just as his voice rose. 'When we realised what was happening,' he continued, quieter now, 'when we knew that our debt to Lavelle was the cause of him entering our homes and taking away our young, we paid back all we could to keep the bastard out. But Declan had nothing left to give, Father. He'd squandered it all away, drinking and gambling, as if the poor fucker could ever win with that trickster running the odds. The man dug his own grave. And there was nothing any of us could do to get him out of it. We needed whatever we had left to protect our own. Why should we have jeopardised our families to save the likes of Declan O'Dwyer?'

'And what happened to him?' Robin asked, trying – despite his weariness – to take in all that Brendan was telling him.

'I don't know, Father,' Brendan replied sullenly, embittered by the man's betrayal of his own kin. 'That night, when the Bodach was due to visit him, he disappeared. There was never a trace of Declan after that. We just knew that the lad's luck had finally run dry and that death was the last hand he'd been dealt.'

The priest looked down at the letter, to those desperate words that Grace's father had penned before his death. 'He offered the Bodach his family to save himself?'

Brendan's sore fingers squeezed tight around the steering wheel. 'The fucking coward did just that, Father. He gave up Chrissy and his little girl to that thing.'

'But I don't understand,' Robin said, refolding the letter, 'why didn't the Bodach take them then? Why wait thirty years?'

'Because Lavelle was killed, Father, and we'd given back what was owed before the first shovel of earth dashed his coffin. The Bodach's sway over us was weakened. It couldn't do fuck all to us anymore. And so it'd no choice but to wait until Chrissy died to claim what was owed to him. The poor woman, she knew what Declan had done. That must have been why she sent little Gracie off to the mainland. It all makes sense now. When she passed away, that was the night we first heard his footsteps in our homes again. Some of the Bodach's power must have returned. And then...'

Brendan paused, as if the truth were too painful to speak.

'And then *what?*' Robin asked, though he already knew the answer.

'And then it took Declan's daughter – the only other soul that'd been offered to it.'

Robin had gone against Chrissy's dying wish. In doing what he thought was right, he'd brought her daughter back within the Bodach's grasp.

She must never step onto Croaghnakeela. It's best, Father, if she doesn't know the cursed thing exists.

'It's my fault,' he whispered, weakened by the realisation, one he knew would haunt him for the rest of his days, no matter God's forgiveness.

'None of this is your doing, Father,' Brendan said comfortingly. 'This tragedy was set in motion long before you ever came to the island.'

Robin couldn't bring himself to tell the old man the truth. He'd become no better than those they'd left behind in Finnerty's that morning, smothering their shame with silence, denying the trail of sins that'd led them to their spiritual bankruptcy.

'No,' he said, refusing to abide by the lie, 'you don't understand, Brendan. Before Chrissy died she asked me to—'

'Quiet,' the man snapped, looking anxiously to the rearview mirror.

The priest matched the terror in the man's eyes. 'What is it?'

Robin was pinned back in his seat as Brendan forced his foot down on the accelerator, hurtling them faster through the fog as the engine roared. Even through the clamour of the car clipping over potholes in the road, there was no mistaking the thunder of the Bodach's footsteps. It had found them.

Robin scanned every direction, twisting and turning, but the mist was too disorientating to discern its whereabouts. He imagined its spindly body tearing towards them with those same monstrous strides he'd beheld the night before. Capture seemed inevitable. The hammer of its steps was getting closer and closer and it was a miracle that Brendan hadn't already ploughed the car into the ditch. The road they followed was no more than a gutter of dirt, with deep trenches of marsh running along both sides, steep enough to tip them over should a single wheel have strayed too close.

'Hold on, Father,' Brendan growled. 'We're nearly there. But we're going to have to open the gate ourselves.'

'Gate?' Robin repeated, sweaty hands held to the dashboard. 'What gate?'

It came at them so quickly, there was no time to anticipate the impact, and before the priest could brace himself, the car smashed through its iron, exploding both headlights as it swung inward. Robin narrowly avoided crashing his skull off the windshield, and he immediately turned in his seat, expecting to see Tadgh Scuffel's distorted bones reaching out from the fog. They'd lost their momentum, but Brendan was sure to recover their speed before it was—

'What are you doing?' the priest shouted, as the man brought the car to a standstill.

The handbrake was wrenched up. The key was turned in the ignition. And then, with only Robin's anxious breathing to break the silence, they listened. Those footsteps that'd shaken the very earth only seconds earlier were nowhere to be heard.

'Where is it?' Robin whispered, still searching, still dreading their discovery.

Brendan relaxed back in his seat and unclipped his belt. 'It can't get us here, Father.'

'Here?' he repeated, squinting outside. 'Where is *here* exactly?'

The fog still filled the air with a palpable sense of nothingness.

'This land belonged to Colman McMorrow. He knew more about the horrors on this island than anyone else. And he knew how to keep them out.'

'The fucking gate is gone, Brendan,' Robin said, running a hand through his hair.

'Father, my old man dug a trench around the entire boundary of his land. At the time there were those who thought he'd lost it, and more than a few of them were fairly vocal in dragging his good name through the dirt. But he wasn't mad. He was cautious. He lined the earth with rock salt. It runs along the wall *and* across that open gate that we just took from its hinges.'

'So we're safe?'

'In a way,' Brendan replied as he clicked open his door. 'But I know myself that I'll be a lot happier once we're indoors. Follow me, Father, there's a lot you need to see if you're to understand what I'm about to tell you.'

17

Brendan

Those lonely days of sweeping the western shore were behind him. He'd held on for as long as he could, knowing full well that age would eventually pry the responsibility from his aching fingers. But there were so few left on the island anymore, and none ever visited that side of it, not since Lavelle was found weeping by a low tide with no memory of how he got there. This was the only life Brendan had ever known, and he'd seen too much to abandon his post now – to gamble what time he'd left on something better. Besides, the nightmares would follow him wherever he went. Maybe something worse. But he'd been careful. He had lived to be an old man for that very reason. Every new dawn was a new day, and he was grateful that after all these years they still kept on coming.

The wind was ripping through the worst of the fog, and though it'd abide inland throughout the day, the coastline would soon be clear of it. That was important.

'Let's get you inside and out of the chill, Father.'

It'd been his own home once, back when he was just a boy and his mother was still living, short a time as she'd been given, poor girl. Losses like that leave a deep scoop in a heart. But at least she'd passed on peacefully. It was his father's death that'd turned the house against him. The smell of its rooms alone stirred a mind full of memories like rancid meat in a broth, ugly morsels that Brendan now had no choice but to choke down again. He closed the front door behind them and turned its key. Judging by the wide eyes on Father Richard, the man had been expecting more. A slew of steel locks perhaps, or some trap above their heads primed to douse any unwanted caller with a heavy pinch of salt. If only he knew. Doors worked wonders on a draught, but they were never much good at keeping the really bad things out – another wisdom the old man had shared with him before he'd died.

'Don't worry, Father,' Brendan said as that familiar mustiness filled his nostrils, 'the Bodach won't come knocking here.'

The young priest's restlessness needed to be addressed if he were to be in any fit state to listen. Even in the dim light of the hallway, a slight sparkle drew Father Richard's curiosity to the wall. From the floor to the ceiling it glittered like the night's sky, and the sight of the salt looked to come as some relief to him.

'Is that…?' he asked, looking hopefully to Brendan.

'Aye,' he replied, grinning at the old man's handiwork. 'The whole house is coated in the stuff. Like I said, Father, Colman McMorrow wasn't mad. But he *was* cautious. This way,' he said, turning towards the back room, 'let me show you why I brought you here.'

Brendan always was fond of Father Richard. He'd come to the island with a wonderfully coy way about him, shy as a fox taking a treat from your hand, as though his own faith in the Lord Almighty hadn't long taken down its scaffolding. And that was more welcome than some maverick priest prying into their past and quoting lines that they'd already heard a thousand times over. The Father did all that was needed of him. He'd respected their privacy. But he also gave everyone his time as if he didn't need any for himself, and that was appreciated more than he'd probably ever know. Maybe they could've shared their secrets with him sooner. It might have made a difference. But it'd have been bad form on their parts to sully the lad's innocence with the same shameful dirt they'd been trying to shake off for thirty years.

Brendan paused at the door. The observatory was what his old man had coined it, enjoying the word for its fanciness, as if Colman McMorrow were ever anything more than a boatman.

'How well versed are you in the old lore, Father?' he asked. 'You know, superstitions and folk tales and the like.'

The priest shook his head nervously. He didn't quite seem to understand the question nor the reasoning behind it, and that was fair. Nothing he was about to hear ever occupied a line of space in the Bible, and he'd have to suspend a few of those Christian beliefs if he'd any chance of learning some new ones.

'Not to worry,' Brendan said before pushing the door open. 'Let's see if we can fix that.'

This was the room where Colman McMorrow had whiled away the last years the Lord gave him. But it was also where it all began, where the fog first became a fascination to the man. Brendan still remembered being called over to that window as a child. On its glass his father had drawn a small outline in black pen. He'd held his only son by the shoulders, positioning him in front of it.

'Look through that, Bren,' he had said excitedly, 'and tell me what you see.'

The sky was clear that day – an unbroken horizon of blue above an ocean sparkling. And yet, where Brendan was staring at his father's behest, there remained a thick bank of fog. It fit perfectly inside the frame that he'd drawn on the glass.

'Do you see it?' the old man pressed, squeezing him tighter. 'It's been in that exact same spot for weeks now, Bren. The fog,' he whispered in his ear, 'it never moves.'

That was his father's first discovery, and no matter how long Colman McMorrow watched it after that day, neither extremity ever waxed or waned. The way it sank into the horizon, anchored to that one spot, Brendan thought even then that it resembled an island, or the ghost of one. But if the latter were true, then why did it look so *alive*?

'Make yourself at home, Father,' he said now, gesturing the priest inside.

The priest's shoes sank into the carpet as he took in the room around him, his bemusement on par with Brendan's expectations. Regardless of the oddity that effected its renovation, the observatory was a curiosity in its own right. A long rectangular pane ran the length of the west-facing wall. It presented a living landscape of the open Atlantic, its white waves stirring to life in the dawn light. That's where his father's chair and desk were set. His instruments and journals had been laid out neatly in its centre, and Brendan still pictured the old man peering through that telescope of his. On the floor beside it was a sizeable wooden chest, too heavy for one man to shift about without injuring himself.

That remained locked at all times. The northern wall held a miscellany of maps, each one preserved behind a thin sheet of glass. Their hues and the style of each cartographer varied between them, but there was one commonality that linked the collection together – the world at large had been omitted. Colman McMorrow had cared only for Ireland and one particular island off its west coast. Brendan watched Father Richard as he examined them more closely. He'd failed to spot the peculiarity right in front of him. But it was probably best if he saw it with his own eyes first.

'What is all this, Brendan?' he asked, none the wiser as to the maps' significance.

'Maybe that's a good place to start, Father,' he replied, guiding the priest's attention to the telescope.

It was a one-of-a-kind piece, locked in place and immovable. After the old man had it installed, there was no need to keep those black pen stains on the window anymore. Father Richard considered the instrument with the same mystification he'd applied to the rest of the room. Maybe he assumed that Colman McMorrow had a fondness for gazing longingly out to sea, dreaming of America and all its fancied opportunities. But there was only one thing the old man ever had an interest in staring at.

'May I?' he asked, leaning in closer to it.

'By all means,' Brendan replied, waving him ahead, imagining that this was how his father must have felt when he'd propped him down in front of that same window.

The priest squinted through the telescope's eyepiece. It had been aligned perfectly with the fog. Even now, with the early morning mist still haunting the air between them, it roiled darker than the surrounding sky, and Brendan didn't doubt that the priest had identified the strangeness of it all. Only when he tried to alter the instrument's direction, however, did he realise that *this* was what he'd been brought to see.

'What is it?' he asked, taking a step back from the window.

'That, Father, is the reason why Croaghnakeela is the way that it is.'

He'd never shared his own discoveries with the rest of the islanders. After the way they'd turned on his old man, disregarding his well-intended warnings as madness, Brendan didn't think them deserving of the truth. But he still kept them safe as best he could despite their wicked tongues.

Father Richard glanced back to the ocean. 'How long has it been there?'

Now he was asking the right questions.

Brendan turned to the northern wall. 'The oldest chart dates back to 1325, Father. It's the work of an Italian-Majorcan cartographer by the name of Dulcert. There's a Venetian one, too, from 1436, and the next oldest would probably be the Catalan, which was drawn up around 1480, if my memory still serves me.'

It was probably best if he broached the anomaly with broad strokes to begin with – nothing too detailed in case he should make the poor lad dizzy. Brendan gave the priest a moment to re-examine the maps with a fresh perspective, pinpointing what he'd missed on his maiden run.

'As you can see, Father,' he continued, 'the Isle of Hy-Brasil appears on every one of them. Granted, its location differs slightly in each case but given the tools at their disposal, I'm sure we can forgive the mapmakers a few inaccuracies.'

'Hy-Brasil?' Father Richard repeated, wearily scratching around his beard.

'Aye, the Phantom Island is what they called it.'

'But what I saw through the telescope didn't look like an island,' the priest said, and he wasn't wrong. 'It just looked like fog.'

'Looks can be deceiving, Father. I take it you're not familiar with the stories surrounding it then, are you?'

The priest shook his head embarrassedly. 'I've never heard of Hy-Brasil, Brendan.'

Delivering the lore was straightforward enough. Accepting it was the tricky part. But after what Father Richard had experienced the night before, hopefully he'd left his scepticism amidst the broken straw on Finnerty's floor.

'It was said that you could only see the island for one day in every seven years,' Brendan explained. 'The rest of the time, Father, as you've seen yourself, it's kept hidden by the fog.'

'So the island is real?'

Brendan had learned through hard trial that questions are the weeds some men can't tame. They grow wild and spread beneath the skin, tangling around even the purest thoughts, and Colman McMorrow's mind had been rampant with them. At least he'd left some answers behind him.

'If you were to delve deeper into the lore, like my father did, then you'd learn that there's always been something odd out there on the ocean. I wouldn't necessarily call it an island. The old stories say it's where Tír na nÓg can be found. The land of eternal youth and beauty, where the Tuatha Dé Danann came from way back when. There are those who refer to it as the Otherworld, where souls are forever exchanged back and forth with the world that we know, reborn after death in some kind of never-ending loop. What I'm trying to say is,

Father, that fog has been out there since before any Irishman ever caught sight of it.'

'I see,' the priest said distantly, his mouth hanging open after the words were spoken. 'And all these cartographers, they saw this... *island* for themselves?'

'Maybe,' Brendan replied, frowning down at the telescope. 'Maybe not. Who's to say? They could have heard the stories about it, Father, and in the interest of not omitting something as important as an island, they might have opted to add it in. That would explain why its location differs slightly between maps.'

'So... is it real?'

The questions were getting more complex to answer simply.

'Colman McMorrow certainly thought so, Father. So, too, did the old pagans who'd made a home for themselves on this island. And as you can probably tell, I'm of a mind to believe it myself. But there's one thing you need to understand. It's something that, unlike everything else I've just told you, isn't so commonly known.'

Brendan gave the young priest a second or two to prepare himself.

'And what's that?' he asked, glancing towards the fog, seeing it differently now.

'It's not an island,' Brendan replied, deciding that now was the time to throw Father Richard in the deep end. 'It's a portal. And when it opens, that's when the bad things tend to land ashore here on Croaghnakeela. Though, that being said, some do creep through in the time between. That's why the pagans settled here, to make a point of keeping them safe.'

It was enough to sap what ailing strength the priest had left in him. Brendan drew out his father's chair and guided him to sit down, which he did, working his body like a man twice his age. And no sooner had he sat than his eyes were lured back to the telescope, revisiting the memory it'd imprinted on his mind – that fog, unmoving, its silver threads of mist swirling like silkworms in a jar.

'But there are no records of these pagans anywhere,' Father Richard said, 'if that's even what they were. The remains on the hilltop are so few. And there's no other trace of them on the island. How can you be so sure that they knew about Hy-Brasil?'

It was healthy for the priest to challenge what he'd been told.

'Have you seen the etches around the well, Father?' Brendan asked him.

'Yes,' he replied with a short nod, 'I have actually. There are three hundred and sixty-five on it. I counted. So I'm guessing whatever they were doing up there must have been some sort of annual ritual. But that doesn't mean they believed in a phantom island.'

'Those etchings aren't days, Father.'

'They're not?' the priest said, cocking an eyebrow in disbelief.

'No,' Brendan replied. 'Each one is a week.'

'Three hundred and sixty-five weeks? And how many years is that?'

The McMorrows never were great at the numbers, and it took the old man long enough to realise the well's significance. But when he did, that was the last piece of the puzzle.

'It's exactly seven years, Father.'

Father Richard slumped back in the chair. The long shadow of scepticism that so often followed intelligent men was finally being lifted.

'So this Bodach came through a portal,' he said, 'out there on the ocean? Brendan, it's almost too much to take in.'

But the lad, to be fair to him, was doing a fine job so far.

'Not just the Bodach, Father. All those horrors that live in the Irish psyche like some nightmare we can't forget. Your banshees and your changelings, these aren't just some folk tales used to scare the little ones. They're real, Father, and that,' he said, pointing out towards the fog, 'is where they all came from.'

The priest perched both elbows on his knees and held his head in his hands. 'But how?' he asked eventually, rubbing the tiredness around his eyes. 'If these things have been washing up on our shore, then shouldn't the island be teeming with them?'

Another good question, and if Brendan was to make a decent case for his argument, then he'd want to back it up with some proof.

'These horrors aren't entering our world in the ways you might think, Father,' he replied, slipping an old pair of gloves from his pocket. 'Look, it's probably easiest if I just show you.'

Brendan knelt beside the chest, grimacing through the sharp pain that attacked his knees. They felt no stronger than his hands these days. He flexed his fingers – trying to work some feeling back into them – before reaching for its clasps. And then he paused, primed to open it, though he'd promised himself he never would again. Even the hardest rules broke like brittle bones when the situation was this dire.

'I don't want you touching anything in here, Father,' he said, looking to the priest. 'Do you understand me?'

Father Richard sat back straight, his restlessness renewed. 'Of course.'

After a resounding click, Brendan lifted the chest's lid, taking care to withdraw his hands to safety before it fell back completely. Its wooden interior wore a thick layer of salt, so white as to make the contents appear all the darker. Inside were the iron tongs that Colman McMorrow had forged specially, essential for retrieving whatever may have washed in with the tide. Strangest thing a father and son ever did – pinching relics from the sand like cockles and putting them where they could cause no harm. Any disbelief on Father Richard's part was understandable, but hopefully this was evidence enough. Like every other soul on Croaghnakeela, he'd probably learned to fear the standards – disease, injury, loss, hunger, even the cruelty of man and beast. But few knew to be wary of what lay before him now. Within the chest there were six pieces of black wood, each one no larger than a rotten cake of soap. With the salt shimmering in the daylight, their symbolic etchings were easy to spot without having to lean in too close. And beside them, fallen in the chest's corner, was a comb carved from bone, though there was no telling what living thing it'd been cut from.

'What are they?' Father Richard asked, so quietly that the islander barely heard him.

No man alive could explain with any accuracy what the young priest was staring at now. But Brendan thought he'd give it a stab regardless, if only to prove that Colman McMorrow's death hadn't been for nought.

'*This* is how the bad things get through, Father. That's why the old tongs there are the only way to handle them. If you were to touch one of these, then the entity would latch itself onto you. *That's* how they get out. It happened to Valentine Lavelle. And it happened to my old man too.'

'He *touched* one of these things?'

Brendan had hoped the conversation wouldn't lead them there. But, as he'd learned that day, keeping secrets does a fine job of keeping no one safe.

'Not one of these in particular. But he touched something, Father. It'd got caught up in his net when he was out on the boat. He didn't realise what it was until he held it in his hand. And sure by then it was too late. The old lad should have been more cautious. He knew the risks. Fat lot of good that knowledge did him in the end.'

Colman McMorrow had tried to carry on as if nothing had happened. But denial is a weak old shield to hide behind, and he knew soon enough that he'd picked up something that no doctor or priest was ever going to cure. Any other man alive would have deemed himself mad, but old Colman knew better. And Brendan still couldn't decide which was worse.

'Why don't you destroy them?' Father Richard asked.

'Don't think we didn't try, Father,' Brendan replied. 'They don't break. They don't burn. The fucking things are indestructible, if you'll excuse my language.'

'Excused,' Father Richard said sheepishly. 'I'm sure it's not easy to talk about, and I hate to ask, but what happened to your father after he came into contact with it?'

'*She* began to follow him.'

Colman McMorrow never saw the woman move. But she was always watching him from a distance, skin pale as the sand, and not a scrap of clothing to cover her naked skin, no matter the weather. Her hair was a lightless black and hung sodden wet down to her feet. It looked like a human. But no human alive ever had eyes that glowed like hers.

'We don't know *who* she was,' Brendan continued, 'or *what* she was. But she wouldn't leave him be, Father. No matter where he looked, she was there, haunting him, following him everywhere he went. It was enough for the poor lad to call it a life. And I hope now that he's at peace, somewhere that fucking woman won't ever find him.'

Brendan slammed the chest shut. Its latches were locked, one after the other.

'These *things* that the pagans were keeping safe,' Father Richard said, 'they stored them somewhere in the hill, didn't they?'

The priest, God love him, was smart enough to draw his own conclusions. If only the rest of the island were ever as sharp as he was, they might have had a chance of saving themselves.

'Aye,' Brendan replied, guessing where the priest was taking this thought of his. 'They're in there somewhere, Father. I've no doubt about that.'

'That's where the Bodach has taken Grace,' Father Richard said, jumping to his feet. 'It has to be. You saw the trail of blood for yourself, Brendan. If she's still alive, then that's where we'll find her.'

'I know what I saw, Father. But surely you can't think—'

'Is there somewhere that we can enter it?' he interjected excitedly. 'Some passage, perhaps, that the pagans once used. I know that the well is too deep to descend through, but there has to be another way.'

Brendan hadn't expected this. He had hoped that the

horrors he'd just shared would be sufficient enough warning to keep the young priest from pursuing Chrissy's daughter any further. But Father Richard O'Malley was a good man. Everyone said it, even when they couldn't bring themselves to say anything else. And so the lad's courage should have probably come as no surprise given his nature – kind without need for a cause.

'Father,' Brendan said, slowly, patiently, silently pleading with the man to pay attention to what he was about to say. 'Colman McMorrow knew Croaghnakeela better than any man and even he never discovered a way into that place. Some things that enter this world are too sacred to be touched by the common man. They're meant to be kept safe and worshipped for—'

'But Valentine Lavelle found a way, didn't he?' the priest cut across him.

The lad wasn't going to let it go.

'He did, Father,' Brendan replied with a sigh, 'but his secrets were lost with him. There's not a soul on this island who knows his movements on that day.'

There was a warm spark in the priest's eye that the islander knew meant trouble.

'Not necessarily,' he said, proving Brendan's suspicions right. 'I know someone who might be able to help us.'

18

Fergal

Good riddance to Brendan and that doe-eyed priest he'd adopted, trading the island's secrets for the sake of his own atonement, and to what end? He must have a head full of his father's madness in him if he thought Chrissy's girl was still alive out there. Not that Fergal cared. Let them off! Croaghnakeela didn't need the likes of McMorrow, disturbing the quiet when the quiet was all that'd kept them safe these thirty years gone.

'The bastard Bodach,' Wilberforce grumbled under his breath.

His blood had been on the boil since it'd said all that shite about him pulling himself and fantasising about Maggie fucking Scuffel. Fergal couldn't decide which was worse – the fact that the Bodach had been watching him or that everyone now knew what he was at. But he had warned them enough times by now that the trickster's word couldn't be trusted, and he'd deny it till his dying breath if any fucking one of them dared to mention it again.

'Bastards,' he muttered, rebalancing himself on his stool, feeling the effects of too many pints and too few of Finnerty's paper-thin sandwiches.

Looking around him, with his fat arms folded on the candlelit countertop, leering over the dregs of a stout, he noticed nobody was paying any heed to him. Better off. He'd no time for them anyway, miserable shower of bastards. Not one of them had budged since Brendan and Father fucking Richard took off together like Bonnie and Clyde. Fergal wished they'd all just leave him be to enjoy his pint in peace. Well, maybe not Maggie. He wouldn't be complaining if she'd stayed back to keep him company. There was the chance that the Bodach had been speaking truthfully about her too: mad to fuck every lad on the island was what it'd said. But Fergal knew she wasn't like that. Maggie was a lady – the best of them, and the only one he'd ever make any time for when it came down to it.

'Bastards,' he repeated, though no one was listening.

Any friends he'd once had were all dead and gone. Good men like Dec O'Dwyer, and more than a few good women. And yet, like some cruel fucking joke, Brendan and the widow Malley remained. It's true what they say, you can't kill a bad thing, and that bitch was the worst of them, forever whispering lies behind his back and disagreeing with him just because she'd nothing fucking better to be at. She never was the same since her Jackie disappeared. Three of the best lads lost in a single night, and for once the bastard Bodach had played no hand in it.

Fergal knew Lavelle was bad news from day one. He'd called it when no one else had, and he took some pride in the fact that he'd taken the bastard's money without doing a tap in return for it. Not like some of the others, his fucking accomplices, ferrying all those children across the bay and then working in that orphanage of his, pretending they were doing some good instead of the Devil's work, as if a few fucking happy kids were going to turn the island's fortunes around. It didn't make sense all those years ago and it made even less sense now. But then, that'd be the greed. It does what it has to do to get what it wants.

All Fergal ever cared about was his own pocket, and Lavelle had done a fine job of keeping that full. He hit the drink hard when that first windfall came in. He'd gotten fat too. Sure, why wouldn't he? There was nought to be doing for a man of wealth on Croaghnakeela but eating and drinking. And Fergal was more than content to sit at that bar until he'd drained Lavelle's private treasury down to its last coin. All he had to do was keep his mouth shut. That's all any of them had to do.

There was a time when he'd considered abandoning Croaghnakeela altogether and setting up on the mainland as a man of substance, telling no one where his wealth came from. He'd even had the enterprise to invest in a boat for himself – top of the range, the kind that never rusts, or so he was told. It had been tied up in a cove not far from the pier for three decades now. If only he'd had the moxie to make use of it before he got all old and shapeless, he might have met a woman like Maggie Scuffel. Who knows, he might have even taken her away with him, leaving her mutt of a husband whining on the shoreline.

Fergal stole a glance over at her, sleeping by the fireplace, a widow herself now. If he hadn't squandered all that money, he might have been in a position to finally make a move on her. But then, after a lifetime of idleness, it wouldn't have been like him to take some action for himself. Especially not when the pints were going down this smoothly.

When the children first started to go missing, he did nothing. The little ones weren't his concern, nor were they his responsibility. Besides, there were plenty others who were genuinely invested in that fucking orphanage Lavelle had built for them. It was their job and nobody else's. Even when his own niece was taken, still Fergal stayed at that bar, supping his stout. It was always easier to do nothing. And now, here he was again, thirty years later, doing the exact same thing – *nothing*.

'Another pint?' John asked him, his jaded eyes at half-rest.

Fergal looked over to Maggie, wondering if she'd care for him at all if he ever stopped drinking. Would anybody, for that matter, ever care for such a selfish bastard?

'Go on,' he replied, clearing the phlegm from his throat, 'sure we've nothing else to be doing.'

19

ROBIN

Grace was alive. To abandon hope now went against everything he believed in. And if God *had* brought Robin to Croaghnakeela for a reason, then maybe it was to stay true to his faith, even as those around him abandoned theirs, to hold that flame aloft against the impossible darkness rising on the horizon.

Whereas the shoreline and its rocky hinterland had cleared as the morning hours rolled on, nothing had yet disturbed the silvern mists that clung to the Lavelle estate. It carpeted the cold earth in a low haze and spun through the breeze in fat, flossy threads, keeping secret Robin's surroundings and any threat that lurked therein. The echo of the Bodach's step still tolled through his thoughts as he crunched down the gravel path, keeping him vigilant even though nothing could keep him safe, not where he was going.

Robin had been fiddling with the key to Harriet's home since he'd closed the car door behind him – walking at a pace that belied his angst – and he now looked back to Brendan's rear lights glowing red in the fog. The priest had told him to drive on, to get somewhere safe, but the stubborn bastard wasn't having any of it.

'The Bodach may well prey on the bodies of old men,' Brendan had said, gruff as a bear standing over its cub, 'but it has no qualms in killing the young ones either. So, if you don't mind, Father, I'll be staying put, if only to keep an eye out. And here,' he added, taking a torch from his wax jacket, 'whatever it is you're looking for in there, this might help you find it.'

No more dawdling on the doorstep. It wasn't a case of *if* the Bodach would find them, but *when*, and Robin had wasted enough time already.

'Harriet,' he called out as he jerked the key around inside its lock, 'it's just me – Father O'Malley. I'm coming in, okay? Don't be alarmed.'

There was no knowing who was waiting on the other side of that door. But in spite of the fears that'd attached to him these past twenty-four hours, Grace was still out there, and only Harriet knew her husband's movements that day on the western shore. But this house was where the damned thing had lived, dressed up in the dead man's skin. Why shouldn't it be at home now, poised like a spider, waiting in silence and in secrecy for its next victim to walk into its web.

The door's old hinges squealed aloud as he eased it inward – a pithy cry that sharpened every soft part of him – but the silence elsewhere remained unscathed. No bones creaked. No godless voice greeted him from the shadows. Robin dashed his palms together as he stepped into a room colder than the morning mist he'd travelled through to get there. Poor Harriet, condemned to inhabit such a place, in fear and reclusion. He padded quietly over to the dead ash of the hearth, taking count of the firelighters and the last dregs of the coal bag. Even if the Bodach were to return home in that instant and catch him on his knees, Robin's last act would be for Harriet's well-being – the old woman who needed light and warmth now more than ever. And a hot fire was a good place to start.

'I'm sorry it's been so long since I visited you,' Robin called out as he crouched by the hearth, tipping out whatever coal remained. 'A young woman came to see you yesterday.' He strook a match alight and held it out. 'Her name was Grace.' Thankfully, the firelighter caught despite the air of dampness beleaguering it. 'Chrissy O'Dwyer's daughter. I told her it might be nice if you two got to know each other.' Robin groaned as he straightened up, suffering the thorns from what had been a terribly restless night. 'She was only meant to stay here for a week,' he said, kneading both hands into his lower back, 'but I'm afraid she—'

He turned to find the woman standing in the kitchen doorway. 'Harriet,' Robin whispered, startled by the sudden sight of her, but relieved all the same. 'Sorry, I let myself in and thought I might get a fire going.'

She looked to those young flames breaking the black with their faint splashes of gold, and then she offered Robin that same sad smile he'd come to expect from her.

'Are we alone?' he asked, his voice lowered to near silence.

'Yes, Father,' she replied in kind with the gladdest insinuation. 'He's not here.'

Robin had been dreading this conversation since the day they'd met. It broke the very rules he'd forged for himself over the years, but Grace's life depended on it. And should anything have happened to him, there would be no one left to tell the old woman the truth. For all he knew, it was now or never. And *never* was a long time indeed.

'Can we sit awhile, Harriet?' Robin said, looking to the

Bible by his feet, untouched since he'd left it there. 'I have something I need to talk to you about and it's very important. That lovely woman who came to see you – Grace was her name – she needs our help. And we don't have much time. She's in a lot of trouble.'

Harriet's confusion pressed the slightest frown upon her brow. 'Grace?' she repeated as though the sound of it were new to her.

'That's right,' Robin replied, sitting down in his usual chair and guiding her to join him.

The woman, still perplexed by the name she'd spoken, accepted his invitation. Robin gave her a moment to adjust to his company, concealing his restlessness as best he could, and together they sat, gazing at the flames like two house cats at peace.

'How have you been, Harriet?' he asked, drawing her attention away from the fire.

The woman's hands were laid on her lap, their fingers fidgeting. 'I've been okay, Father.'

Nothing could be further from the truth. But he pressed on…

'Is Tiddles still coming to see you?'

'Oh yes,' Harriet replied earnestly, 'she comes to see me all the time, Father, always on the same sill. I just wish that I could bring her indoors,' she added sadly. 'I wouldn't like her to get sick.'

If God *had* heard Robin's prayers, then now was the time for the Almighty to act on them.

'I know you don't like to speak of Valentine, Harriet,' he began, softly, slowly, listening out for the creak of a floorboard in one of the rooms above. 'But I understand why now.

I know that the man who made your life a misery was no longer your husband. It wasn't a man at all. It was something else. Something very ancient and very evil, Harriet, and I'm sorry. I didn't realise.'

The woman blinked away her sorrow and held Robin's gaze in silence.

'Brendan McMorrow told me about that night, Harriet,' he continued, 'when they found Valentine near the western shore and brought him back to you. But only you know where he went. You were with him that day, weren't you? Can you remember? Please, Harriet, it's very important.'

She sat back rigidly, discomforted by the memories as the past came into focus. 'Four stones,' she replied as though she were staring at them in that same moment. 'There were four tall stones. My Valentine found an opening in the centre of them, a hole in the ground. And that's where he went. He said he'd heard voices. Something called to him from the darkness, Father. And once he'd entered that place, it never let him go.'

'These four stones,' Robin said keenly, 'where are they?'

'They're very near the edge, Father,' Harriet replied dreamily, 'where the island drops down into the ocean and its waves splash the sky. You'll find them. They're tall. Each one is identical to the other. I know that my Valentine was too curious a man to ever walk away from them. It wasn't God who laid those stones there. They were cut by human hands. Bad people, Father, who knew this island was a bad place long before our families ever settled here.'

Brendan knew the island better than anyone. Hopefully, he'd know of the site. And if he didn't, then Robin wouldn't rest until he had found it for himself.

'Thank you, Harriet,' he said, letting his shoulders relax for the first time that day. 'I'll do all I can to put an end to this; you have my word. There has to be a way. There just has to be.'

The woman studied him, examining more closely the flecks of grey in his beard and those first faint wrinkles.

'Are *you* okay, Father?' she asked, her pale skin aglow in the firelight. 'I'm worried about you. You look very sickly these days. Have you been taking good care of yourself?'

He'd put it off for as long as possible, hoping that she'd discover the truth on her own terms. But maybe this was the release she needed after all.

'I'm not sick, Harriet. I've gotten older. You don't realise it but I've been visiting you for six years now, and I suppose I'm not ageing as gracefully as I might like.'

'Six years?' the woman repeated, her vacant eyes seeking out some solace in the flames.

'That's right,' he said patiently, letting the fact sink in. 'Time can be a tricky thing to hold on to. Trust me, I know. It's not as straightforward as people would have you think. But tell me this, do you remember how your husband died?'

Robin needed to know how much she'd forgotten, like sorting through the missing jigsaw pieces of her mind.

'I killed him, Father,' she replied with an eerie nonchalance. 'I had to. I poisoned his broth and I watched him eat it. Because that *thing* wasn't my husband. And I refused to live with it any longer.'

If only the other islanders had been so brave.

'I know,' Robin said sympathetically, 'and everyone is glad that you did. He wasn't your Valentine anymore, Harriet, and we all know that. So, too, does God. But how well do you remember that day? I need you to remember, Harriet.'

The woman closed her eyes, accepting the memory back into the moment. 'I prepared him a bowl, Father,' she replied. 'He didn't know what I'd done. But he was always suspicious of me. He knew how much I loathed the very sight of him. He made me sit down at the table with him while he ate it, as close as you and I are now. I can still remember the smell of him, like burning, like death, like something that'd crawled out of the fiery pit, Father, and had no place on this earth.'

'Is that all he did, Harriet?' Robin asked. 'Did he not make you eat the same broth?'

The woman's head tilted as the thought weighed in on her mind. Her lips parted aquiver when she finally recalled the reality of that last meal.

'He did, Father,' she replied, her eyes widening at the realisation. 'He made me make a bowl for myself. I ate it, if only so that he would too. But how can that be? How come the same poison didn't kill me?'

Even now, with those final moments alive in her mind, Harriet's death eluded her.

Robin sat forward. 'It did, Harriet. You died that same day.'

It was his gift and his curse, and he knew that Grace shared it too, even though she'd seemed so unaware of it when they'd spoken. That afternoon, when they had stood by her mother's grave, she'd watched Bridie pass through the cemetery – Bridie, the poor woman who'd slipped on the stairs six months earlier and lost her life.

'But... how, Father?' Harriet whispered, more afraid

than he'd ever seen her, and it broke his heart to be the one responsible.

Robin reached forward a hand and passed it slowly through hers – a simple, silent show more harrowing than stabbing a blade through the woman's heart.

'I'm sorry, Harriet,' he said, 'but I'm here for you. And maybe now you can move on. You've no reason to stay here any longer. You deserve peace more than anyone.'

The woman withdrew her hands and scanned the room around them as though seeing it for the first time, taking in each dismally dark corner before her eyes settled on the window and the world beyond it – that which had changed so much since her passing – where Tiddles the cat sometimes peered in curiously at the old woman who never stepped outside, wondering perhaps, for all her kindness, why she never thought to feed her. If only she could.

'He won't let me, Father. He'll never let me go.'

For years he'd wondered what it was that held her there, lost in limbo, haunting that sad space for all eternity. Could it be that the Bodach—

Robin jolted back as a flurry of knocks thrummed against the door.

Harriet didn't react to it. But then, the woman's soul was encased in its own bubble, clouding more than the mere passing of time. The priest listened out for Brendan's voice. When nothing came, he walked warily over to the door.

'Brendan,' he whispered, 'is that you?'

Though he may have imagined it, Robin thought he'd heard the flighty patter of feet scrunching down the gravel path. But such childish pursuits were unknown on Croaghnakeela. He hadn't laid eyes on a child since he'd landed there. Edging the door open a notch, he peered outside. There was no one there. Even Brendan was nowhere to be seen – a reasonable cause for concern in its own right. Surely he would have blared the car's horn if he'd marked the Bodach's approach. Or perhaps, given the time that'd lapsed, he had deemed his priest a lost cause. Robin hadn't shared his reasons for visiting Lavelle's old home, though Brendan probably would have shouldered the truth better than most. But now wasn't the time. People acted differently towards Robin once they knew of his gift. Everyone who'd lived to a ripe age had lost someone they loved. Death was one of life's unmerciful absolutes – a one-way journey from which none returned, and it was dangerous to disrupt that rule. If Brendan thought he could see his father one last time, then that'd only distract from the task at hand. And Grace was all Robin cared about now.

'I'll visit you again soon, Harriet,' he said as he surveyed the misty estate for movement. 'We'll bring Tiddles inside this time, okay? I'll make a fire, just for the three of us. I promise, you'll never be alone so...'

But when he looked back to the woman's chair, she was gone.

'...so long as I'm here.'

20

CONNOR

As it was before, when the island was purged of all its youth and innocence, their houses were no longer homes. The Bodach could come and go between them as it pleased, slipping like a cold draught through every room, picking them off one by one until all that remained of Croaghnakeela's people were bare bones and bloody whispers of what they'd done. Tadgh Scuffel was only the beginning – the first in a short line of dominoes destined to fall – and there was no telling who would be next. Connor hadn't taken his eyes off his daughter for that very reason. She was dozing on a corner couch at the back of the pub, safely apart from the others. He knew what they were capable of, and so none could be trusted.

Sarah was the youngest of them, the purest, and the only one under that roof worth saving, and how Connor wished her mother were still alive to see the woman she'd become. It was Orla who'd openly championed Lavelle's sudden change of heart; just like her daughter, kind as she was clever. She'd cared nothing for the financial boons of his initial proposal: all those hotels and restaurants, serving the wealthy and those who'd need for nothing but more. And when the orphanage was built, it was Orla who'd first volunteered to guide all those children across those precarious stepping stones towards their new lives.

She was also the first to suspect that the orphanage's mission followed a far more insidious agenda than what they'd been sold. Connor was too quick to dismiss his wife's concerns. And he'd never forgiven himself for letting his faith in Lavelle twist his loyalties against the woman he loved. It was another shame he'd no choice but to live with, even though that past version of himself felt like a stranger to him now – a money-grubbing wretch just like the rest of them, enslaved and bound by the evil's promise.

Unlike the others under Lavelle's employ, Orla refused to abide by the man's questionable standards of secrecy. Paperwork was strictly forbidden unless Lavelle were its sole possessor, and no records ever linked those children to the island. Any trace of their existence was erased on arrival. No aspect of the orphanage's administration made sense. How were those kids supposed to have a future when they no longer had a past? Orla had tried to warn everyone of what was happening, but nobody wanted to listen. And it was these accusations that inevitably brought about her death – tragic an accident as it was, falling from the orphanage's top floor like that. It was all the more tragic knowing now that it wasn't an accident at all. Orla was killed because she knew too much. And still Connor had done nothing about it. Too weak. Too selfish. Too scared. But he wouldn't make that mistake again.

If he could just keep Sarah safe until Saturday, the ferryman might be able to provide them passage to the far shore. Connor had heard Brendan grumbling about him whenever he returned with their week's delivery – damaged goods and extortionate prices and the like – but the fact of the man surviving the journey back and forth after all these years meant he must have known something they didn't. And if money were his weakness, then Connor would trade every coin he'd left to his name to get his daughter onto the mainland and out from under the Bodach's shadow.

'Sarah,' he whispered, crouching down closer to her, 'do you remember the name of the lad who does our deliveries?'

Her eyes blinked awake as she sat up, and it took her a slow moment to register the question.

'I think it's Maloney, isn't it?' she replied as she shifted painfully into a seated position.

He'd never erase the mental image of the Bodach's fingers clamped around her, striving to steal his little girl away from him. But she was alive. And he'd only Father Richard's courage to thank for that.

'That's what I thought,' Connor said with a lie and a nod. 'I'm hoping that maybe he could take us with him when he comes back here on Saturday. It's worth a shot, isn't it?'

'I don't know, Dad,' Sarah replied, suppressing a yawn. 'Brendan says that he never steps off his boat. I reckon he's heard all the stories about this place and wants nothing to do with us but our money.'

She was so much like Orla. Rarely were the harmonies of a mother and daughter as pitch-perfect as theirs. Her voice even carried that same delicate crackle when she was freshly awakened.

'Well then, that's what I'll give him,' Connor said firmly, giving her thigh a gentle squeeze. 'And we'll get on that boat of his, even if he doesn't want us, okay? We can't stay here.

It's too dangerous, and I can't let anything happen to you. Your mother would never forgive me.'

He'd spoken too loudly, but no one around him seemed to notice, or else they simply didn't care. Everyone was content to keep to themselves, offering no support and seeking out even less. Perhaps they were each planning their own escape. There might even be a queue on the pier come Saturday afternoon to pay the ferryman, like a day trip for the doomed. Most of them looked half asleep, clustered around the fireplace, using coats as blankets, waiting for time to decide their fates. Wilberforce was still hunched over his usual spot at the bar, facing what little remained of his pint, staring at its creamy streaks as though the stout were writing a message across the glass for him.

'You can't all stay here,' Finnerty announced, breaking Fergal out of his trance. 'I've paid the Bodach more than most of ye, and I won't have you bringing it back to my door. I think I've been kind enough to you all already.'

The room stirred awake, all creaking wood and rustling blankets. Its many foggy faces turned towards the publican, who it would seem had finally tired of their patronage. Sad times had a nasty habit of turning people to the drink, and John Finnerty had made quite the pretty penny for himself. It was no surprise that he could pay back more than the rest of them. Connor had helped filled the coward's pocket too, dulling the nightmares with the only medicine he could afford.

'You all have your own homes to go to,' Finnerty said, hands planted on the counter if only to keep them steady. 'So, if you don't mind, I think it's time you left.'

In Brendan's absence they were adrift without an anchor, lacking anyone brave enough to challenge the publican's demands. Connor himself was slow to speak up, worried that drawing Finnerty's ire would put his daughter's life in more jeopardy. Wilberforce glanced coyly over at Maggie Scuffel, still ensconced by the fire, and then – though Connor may have imagined it – the man looked over to Sarah, airing a concern that was wholly unexpected.

'No one's going anywhere, John,' he said gruffly, sliding his glass forward. 'You know as well as any of us that this is the safest place on this fucking island, and we're not leaving.'

Finnerty snatched the glass away. 'We have to do something, Fergal.'

All the publican cared about was himself, and the fact of them taking refuge under his roof combatted those priorities. If he were a rat on a sinking ship, he'd be throwing the other vermin overboard in the hope of keeping it afloat.

'What would you have us do, John?' the widow snapped at him. 'If you've got some grand scheme to save us, then I'm sure we'd all like to hear it.'

Wilberforce hadn't glowered at her. For once he seemed to approve of what she'd said. Connor sat down by Sarah's side and roped his arm around her. There was nothing any of them could do. They'd given the Bodach all they had, and still the horror lingered like a black poison in their blood. Finnerty should have known better than to disrupt what little peace they'd fostered for themselves by his fire. There was nothing to be gained by upsetting everyone. They just had to survive until Saturday.

'We all know what it wants,' the publican replied with a noticeable tremor to his voice. 'Am I the only one who's willing to say it?'

The rumours surrounding Croaghnakeela's grim depopulation had reached far and wide, and the truth had been stretched thin with every mile. There were still those who spoke of suicide – that the islanders, crushed by the dual weights of isolation and depression, had taken their own lives. But the secret they'd sworn to take to their graves was far worse than any fabrication the mainlanders could turn against them. And if Orla had been alive to see it, Connor knew it would have broken her heart in ways that no husband could ever fix – to realise the unspeakable horrors that *these* people were truly capable of.

'Those days are in the past, John,' Wilberforce said, speaking with a sober softness that was unlike him. 'You should know better than to speak of them. We did what we had to do.'

'And it's what we have to do again!' Finnerty declared, causing Connor's fingers to close around his daughter's shoulder. 'It's the only way, Fergal, and you know it.'

Eoin Murray rose up and strode to the fireplace. There he scratched out a shovel of coal and poured it out, splashing embers onto the hearth and drawing the eyes of all those still too lost to find their voices.

'Who would you have us sacrifice this time, John?' he asked, turning to face the man who was now cowering behind the beer taps. 'Because I'd love to see you try to throw me down that fucking well.'

Everyone knew what answer was coming. Connor did too.

'It wants the children who got away, Eoin,' Finnerty replied, struggling to get the words out. 'That's why it took Chrissy's daughter. It doesn't matter if they're adults now. He still wants them.' He looked to Sarah as these last words were spoken.

Connor's arm tightened all the stronger around her.

The island truly was cursed. So, too, were its people. His wife had tried to warn him.

21

Robin

No hour, no minute, no dismal second of that mist-veiled daylight could be taken for granted. So rarely had Robin walked the western shore – and so unacquainted was he with its raw and rocky topography – there was no telling how long it would take him to discover the site of the four stones. Brendan's knowledge of the island was more crucial now than ever before. And yet the journey on foot to his father's home or Finnerty's – wherever he'd fled to – would squander too much of what little light remained. Should darkness have fallen before Grace was found, all hope would be forfeit. And so he set off alone, traipsing neath the shadow of the very thing whose ancient secrets he sought to expose.

'Well, *Richard*,' he muttered wryly to himself, 'the bishop isn't going to like this, is he?'

Much like Croaghnakeela, Robin's first and only other parish had its secrets too. It'd kept itself mostly hidden from the country at large until he put it on the map, and not for the right kind of reasons. The village itself was so far removed from any main roads that it was seldom seen by any who didn't have a home there. Like similarly small communities elsewhere, it'd farmed the same blood for countless generations and thus came with its own back catalogue of quirks, none of which seemed all that wholesome in hindsight. The seasons were counted to the day. But the year was just a number, and nothing ever changed there. Even the names remained the same, handed down like heirlooms alongside the same accents, the same clothes, the same beliefs. Its only notable aspect, or so Robin thought when he'd arrived, was its insignificance.

The land was its life source, and all trade there was founded around farming, offering little else in the way of pastime or distraction. But its people were stalwart in their faith; Robin had to give them that. Mass, without fail, drew full attendance every Sunday, and families fought over his time like hagglers in a market, inviting him into their homes on a whim and treating him like royalty whenever they crossed his path. It was how Robin imagined Ireland must have been decades earlier, when Catholicism was common as a hard rain and just as oppressive. They were God-fearing people and so, for the sake of their immortal souls, the sins they confessed to were barely sins at all really: the occasional impure thought or accidental utterance of the Lord's name in vain, and that was about the extent of it. Robin couldn't have asked for a more docile group of worshippers for his parochial debut. But wherever there was light, as he would learn, so too must there always exist an element of darkness.

The hilltop still stole the southern sky, denying Robin any warmth from the low sun as he traipsed towards the shore. Legs had stiffened fast in the cold, and he hauled his feet along the path like two concrete blocks. Slight as the breeze may have been, it brushed his cheeks with a light powdering of ice that'd seeped through his entire body by now. Should the Bodach have made another dash at him, it would catch the priest before he'd even remembered how to run. Waves crashed off in the distance as he trudged onward, head bowed, promising himself that should he survive past this day, then the church collection basket would afford him a new coat before the winter rolled around again. Besides, there was no telling where the bishop would send him after this. Not that it would make a world of difference. Whether the church wanted to accept it or not, the dead were everywhere. And it was by the dubious grace of God that Robin could commune with them. That's exactly what had rubbed the bishop up the wrong way in the first place. Past sins, buried secrets, and one naive fucking priest who thought he could make a difference.

Partial as Robin was to the acoustics and airy atmosphere of a good Christian church, his old parishioners held true to a bygone tradition – one that'd fallen out of fashion long before he'd even entered the seminary. And so, once a month, whether their priest approved or not, Mass had to be held in one of their homes. It was like taking the holy sacrament on tour to smaller and far less suitable venues with questionable catering. But, if anything, it offered Robin a chance to step behind the curtain and see the backstage of their lives as opposed to the usual Sunday best they put forward like an unconvincing lie whenever the church bells summoned them together. And in the spirit of honest one-upmanship, with every house he visited the mound of sandwiches grew taller and taller, as if the mark of a good host was how much sliced pan they were willing to waste upon a single evening.

One such ceremony came to pass in the cottage of a

pair of brothers – odd as two left shoes, old ones at that, weatherworn and unwanted by all who knew them. Each man was grey as the other – skinny, wild-looking creatures – with a very particular ugliness that betrayed their common ancestry. Neither had spoken more than a word that their priest could translate, so garbled and absurdly cryptical were their accents. Their clothes were borrowed from a different time and habitually smoked from the turf fire they burned throughout the year. Robin had caught sight of them a few times whipping their terrier with a stick when they thought no one was looking. Cruelty came naturally to some men, and he'd only ever seen them smiling when that poor dog was in pain.

They'd lived on the outskirts of the village all their lives, the closest home to the main road, though civilisation was still a way off. The other parishioners tolerated these men, as was their Christian protocol, but that didn't necessarily mean they liked them, and it was probably for everyone's benefit that the brothers kept mostly to themselves. Eventually, however, after every other family had held their Mass, the time finally came to take the sacrament in their home. Robin expected a full turnout, but he couldn't imagine many would brave a sandwich from the brothers' plate.

Theirs was the dingiest cottage in the village and less than a quarter the size of their barn out in the back field – a worrying testament to the men's priorities. Unsurprisingly, nothing within its four walls had been updated for decades. And in that time, Robin suspected, not once had either man made any attempt to clean it. Just standing under its roof was enough to make his skin itch all over, whilst the strong stench of a flooded septic tank made everyone in attendance terribly nauseous. Blackened pots hung by the hearth – their rims lined with the congealed run-offs of meals gone by – and every piece of furniture and soiled inch of carpet was tattered and torn. No effort had been made to make it remotely welcoming, and with nowhere to sit in so cramped a space, his congregation – the very young and the elderly included – had to stand shoulder to shoulder as he powered through his prayer book, determined to get everyone out of there before the reeking drains and fumes from the fire did their health a disservice. There was a *feeling* to that house that troubled Robin more than the smell, however, and as was often the case, his intuition would eventually be proven right. Beneath the filth and the squalor, there was hidden something far darker.

He had come to care for these people since joining their community. Midlands Ireland wasn't without its eccentricities, but their moral compass overall seemed to hold its north without much prodding. Every welcoming face had a name, and each one now evinced that same infectious revulsion at having to visit this hovel that the two brothers somehow called a home. And yet, on that crisp autumnal evening, as they huddled together in communal disgust, there was a woman unfamiliar to Robin's eyes standing at the back of the room. She was staring at him with the most lost expression – as if she'd sleep-walked into the cottage and only just woken up, baffled as to her whereabouts and how she'd come to be there. Robin knew immediately that she was one of the dead, so incongruent was she in that society, so beautiful and perfectly out of place. Straight blonde hair hung just below her ears, and she was young, probably still in her late teens, with a kindly roundness to her face that the years never got a chance to sharpen. Only her shoulders were visible across the crowded room. But she was wearing a baby-blue T-shirt, which led Robin to presume that it wasn't winter when she'd died.

He acknowledged her in his own subtle way and, though she didn't react, she remained there throughout the ceremony, watching him like a child too young to understand what was going on around her. And by the hour that Mass concluded, when Robin searched for her, the woman was gone, leaving no trace that she was ever there.

Once his Bible was pocketed and the last *amen* recited with no short sigh of relief, their many bodies were quick to flood outside, funnelling impatiently through the narrow door, all gasping for fresh air and the chance to breathe again. The priest couldn't blame them. He'd have to give his clothes and vestments a hot wash once he got home, and it'd take more than a few glasses of brandy to cleanse that awful taste from his palate. So keen were the parishioners to distance themselves from the brothers' cottage that few hung around to make idle talk with their priest.

Had they each been jostling for his attention as they usually did, then Robin might not have caught sight of the woman again. She was standing by the open door of the brothers' barn, in near-perfect dark, visible only because her skin was so white and exposed. She'd watched the priest as though she were urging him to follow her. And Robin, despite his own trepidations and reluctance to draw attention to his God-given gift, did just that. He ambled across the field, making vague apologies to those he was abandoning, determined to meet with the woman, even after she dissolved into the darkness of the doorway.

'Hello,' he'd called out upon reaching the barn, drawing a hand to his nose as another smell accosted his senses, 'are you still there?'

The stench was unlike the broken septic tank of earlier, and somehow even more sickening to breathe through. It filled that barn like a gas leak – thick as black smoke around his nostrils – and Robin dreaded to imagine what foulness ran beneath him through those drains. Luckily, on that night, given how late those particular gatherings tended to run, he'd pocketed a torch before leaving home. And it was this lone beam that now pierced the blackness of the barn as he searched for the stray apparition who'd led him there for reasons still unknown to him. Not to cast aspersions on the attractiveness of his parishioners, but it was obvious from her beauty that she wasn't born of that village. But no matter where she'd come from, it was there that she had died. The spirits never strayed too far from their final resting place.

'My name is Robin,' he'd said, panning his torchlight across the emptiness, hazy white on black, disturbing the ghostly shapes of old and abandoned tools. 'I'm the priest in this village. I don't mean you any harm. I just want to talk to—'

With the word half formed on the tip of his tongue, the light grazed her face like a porcelain mask afloat in the darkness, pale as the moon itself. She was standing in the centre of the barn now, wearing shorts and strappy sandals whilst Robin's fingers ached from the cold air misting around his torchlight. One bare arm pointed down to the floor by her feet, and those same soulful eyes pleaded with him to come to her.

'Would you like to show me something?' he asked nervously. 'Is that what you want?'

He'd encountered bad ones in the past, those poor bitter souls who'd forgotten themselves over too much time, forced in death to dwell on the horrors they'd suffered in life – twisted, spiteful things beyond redemption, smouldering with an unslakable malevolence. They were deserving of Robin's sympathy, of course, for it wasn't by their own free will that these spirits had been left on earth to fester. But they were the dead that'd once terrorised him as a child, and hauntings like that aren't so easily forgotten.

This woman, however, meant Robin no harm. He was sure of that. There was a peacefulness about her, an innocence that she'd retained in the afterlife. He stepped closer, braver now. On the floor where she directed him to look there was a wooden hatch. Someone had tried to cover it with a light scattering of hay, but so poorly done was the job that they obviously didn't expect anyone – especially not their priest – to come snooping around with a torch in his hand, guided by the dead to find it.

'Is this what you want to show me?' Robin whispered, steadying his light as best as he could, seeing up close just how young she truly was.

She finally acknowledged him with a nod, though the vacancy of her expression remained unaltered. There was always a coldness about them, a mystifying detachment that held them somewhere between life and death, and this poor soul was no exception. It was unlikely that she recalled the exact circumstances of how she died, as there were no visible wounds on her body that Robin could see. Sometimes, so traumatising are those final moments that the dead simply choose to forget. It was a kindness, in a way, though he was more than acquainted with its mixed results.

Harriet remembered everything but the last meal that'd been forced upon her. And yet that was enough to deny the woman the truth of her passing, like the missing final chapter in the story of her life. She'd recycled the same motions – pacing back and forth between the fireplace and the kitchen, constantly clicking on the kettle and resettling herself in that chair, watching the world through the grime of her window, waiting for some friend to visit her though none ever came, lost as to the hour, the day, the year, and the curious space she inhabited between this life and the next.

Robin knelt on the barn floor and, dashing the straw aside, discovered an iron handle by his feet. Whatever it was that lay hidden beneath him, he knew it wasn't good. And he didn't need his gift to draw that grim conclusion. The malodour slipping up into the air was all the proof he needed. Before his courage had chance to falter, he hauled the wooden panel open and let it crash down on the floor. The woman who'd stood over him an instant earlier had disappeared – gone in the blink of an eye – leaving Robin to crouch alone above the opening, and it took all of his resolve to keep from throwing up as the whole barn was suddenly consumed with the unmistakable stench of death – rotted corpses, old and many, all of them piled into that pit beneath the brothers' barn. And as he shone his torchlight across their myriad vacant eyes, his heart twisting at the sight of each and every one of them, Robin knew that the beautiful young woman who'd led him to discovering that horror was buried down there somewhere too.

For years the brothers had been preying on those who'd lost their way, those innocently seeking out directions or some help from the first house they found. But the two men had been selective in choosing their victims, reaping the most pleasure from the young and the pretty, maiming and killing, and burying their bodies where no one would ever find them.

The sun finally broke around the hillside as Robin neared the western shore. He swallowed back another lungful of cold air and blinked the tears away. The wild Atlantic wind was worsening, blinding his eyes, chilling every painful breath that passed his lips, making that final stretch a battle that he felt unprepared for. But he was close enough now to mark the coastline, where the mist had cleared to an overcast sky. To Robin's surprise, Brendan's car was parked on the roadside, where the horizon led off to a plateau of knobbly stone and the land was traversable only by careful steps.

Had he not abandoned Harriet's front gate for fear of the Bodach? Or perhaps Robin had been too hasty in assuming the man's motives. He squinted against the gathering gale, trying to make some sense of the shore, where the waves crashed in clouds of white, and there he saw someone – a lone body amidst all that grey. It could only have been Brendan. No one else had been brave enough to follow them out of Finnerty's that morning. The priest's past experiences in humanity's more secretive and less humane agendas had groomed the cynic in him, and something about the circumstances of this reunion just felt wrong.

The Catholic Church had been less concerned about the victims and those whose sisters and daughters had been identified mostly by their teeth. Rather, they cared more for how the gruesome affair had further brutalised their reputation. Controversies like that were bad for business. This was, after all, one of the last few devout communities left in the country, still abiding by the old standards set out by their so-called *good book*. The church's questionable legacy was dragged through the dirt once again. And, of course, there was Robin's role in the whole tragic affair – the priest who'd spoken to the dead, as he'd confessed to doing when the Guards interviewed him. Suffice to say, the bishop was none too pleased when that little headline made the papers. There was morality and there was sin, as there had always been a Heaven and a Hell. And aside from the Holy Ghost himself, the church couldn't condone the existence of such apparitions, even the ones who went out of their way to aid the living.

In doing what he thought was right, Robin had invited the choler of the clergy's upper echelons, and they weren't as forgiving as they'd have the faithful believe. It was decided – without great argument or debate – that Father Robin Thompson had to disappear. New name. New parish. Same shit all over again. Death didn't just follow the priest. It embraced him with open arms wherever he went.

Brendan had been waiting for him, standing between the four stones curiously at home amongst them. Any other man might have welcomed the sight of him, but Robin's gut told him to postpone any such celebrations. The islander had denied all knowledge of Valentine Lavelle's movements on that day, and yet there he was, occupying the very space where the man descended to his doom. He'd saved Robin the trouble of finding the site for himself, but the mean glint in Brendan's eye now invited its own complications.

'Father,' he said in a tone that was far from welcoming.

Robin stepped cautiously within the square of stones.

Harriet had been right. Each of the four was carven into a pillar, imperfect only because time never did like perfect things.

'You told me you didn't know how to get into the hill,' Robin said, peering down at the circular hole cut into the ground, that which Valentine's curiosity couldn't let go of.

'Aye,' Brendan replied with a nod, 'that I did, Father. But I had my reasons.'

Every lying bastard had his reasons. Twenty-four hours had passed since Grace was taken from her home. Wherever she was, she was alone, she was wounded, and this son of a bitch couldn't bring himself to help Robin find her. He'd thought Brendan was the best of them, the one man on the island whom he could trust.

'I take it that saving Chrissy's daughter isn't one of those reasons, is it?' he asked, biting around his cold lower lip, prepping himself for bad news.

Brendan shook his head. 'I'm afraid not, Father.'

Robin edged closer, forcing his legs against a gale that skimmed like ice across the stones. Everything for miles was hard and cruel and hostile – and the old man standing in front of him fitted seamlessly within that tapestry.

'I was hoping, Father,' Brendan said, his tone cool as the wind, 'that you'd come to understand the importance of this island. The others are too narrow-minded to grasp what Croaghnakeela really is, and I'm not the young man I used to be. The arthritis, Father, it's breaking every part of me. I can't keep doing this for the rest of my life. I need someone else to take on the responsibility. You're young. You're smart. Not that I'm exactly overrun with candidates, but I thought you might be the best man for the job.'

'And what exactly have you been doing here?' Robin asked him, his patience freezing up in the cold. 'I don't have time for this.'

Brendan gazed out towards the distant fog. 'You believed what I told you, didn't you, Father?' he asked, softer now, almost fatherly. 'I know you did. I could see it in your eyes. It's hard to turn away from the truth once you've met it.'

'Get to the fucking point, Brendan.'

'There's no proof of God,' he replied, unfazed. 'I know that, and you know it too, Father, despite that collar you wear around your neck. Your kind may have sung about his son for over two thousand years but it's all bullshit at the end of the day, isn't it? If this God of yours is so omniscient and invested in our best interests, then why doesn't he do something? No prayers are ever answered. No miracles make our lives any easier, do they? But *that*,' he said, pointing out to the ocean, 'is proof of something far greater than you or I. What comes through that portal needs to be worshipped for what they are. Even the old pagans knew that, Father. That's why they settled here. If ever there were any real gods in this world, then that's where they'd have come from.'

Robin's fond take on the man had coloured his judgement. Brendan hadn't condemned the phantom island for corrupting Croaghnakeela's people, he'd been exalting the fucking thing.

'Gods?' Robin echoed, faltering a step back, wary now as to why the islander had been waiting for him. 'These aren't gods, Brendan. You've seen what the Bodach did here. This island is in ruins. Your lives are in ruins. It took everything it wanted and left you with nothing.'

How long had the old lad been staring at that fog, mooning

over its unearthly possibilities, forging – in the silence of his father's observatory – his own unhinged philosophies?

'Well now, that *is* a shame,' Brendan said disappointedly, shaking his head. '*You've seen what the Bodach did here*,' he repeated with a sneer. 'You really don't get it, do you? I know exactly what it did. It exposed us for what we really were, Father. The greed. The selfishness. We were weak. And the Bodach made us stronger. It made us better people than we ever were. And that's more than your god has ever done.'

Is this what faith had become? Had the world strayed so far from the Lord that they now sought out the sanctity of devils?

'And what about Grace?' Robin asked, hoping to reach the good man who'd once pruned his churchyard and offered aid to all who needed it. 'If the Bodach *has* made you better, Brendan, then won't you help me find her? That's all I ask of you. She has nothing to do with this.'

'Chrissy's girl is with the rest of them now, Father,' he replied solemnly, looking back to the hill. 'She was dead soon as she stepped onto Croaghnakeela, and there was never anything you could do about it.'

Robin refused to believe him, and if the old bastard tried to stand in his way, then those brittle bones of his would be a long time healing. He stepped into the centre of the four stones, where the daylight drained through the entranceway. The priest had expected to find a cave or some crude opening hacked out by the basest tools. But instead there were steps – a narrow stairwell that coiled down into the darkness.

'Grace is alive,' Robin said assertively, 'and I'm going to find her, with or without you.'

Brendan mocked the priest with a deriding chuckle. 'By all means, Father, you do whatever you want. The Bodach will be more than pleased to see you. But I won't be there to save you this time.'

'I think you should focus on saving your own soul,' Robin replied before turning his back.

If there was any good left on the Isle of Croaghnakeela, then it wasn't to be found in the hearts of men like Brendan McMorrow. Robin inspected the entrance more closely, secretly dreading the journey downward. He pawed around his pocket until his cold fingers found the torch that the islander had given him. If Lavelle – a man in his sixties – could find his way to the bottom and back up again, then surely the feat wasn't beyond Robin's abilities, though he felt a shadow of his former self. Too little sleep. Too many secrets. And there wasn't a soul alive on that damned rock that he could trust. The dead had proven themselves better company than the living once again.

Robin gazed out to the ocean, letting its elements instil every part of him, invigorating his body for the last stretch of that impossible journey. There was always light to be found, no matter how all-ruling the darkness may have seemed. And wherever there was light, there was hope. It was with this thought in mind that he reached his foot out to catch the first step. But Robin hesitated, still unsure of the man standing at his back.

'Should I be worried about you, Brendan?' he asked grimly. 'You're not going to do anything stupid now, are you?'

The old man grinned as he shook his head. 'You've far worse things than me to worry about, Father. Jesus Christ himself can't follow you where you're going.'

Robin knew better than to trust him, but there wasn't time to assess the threat of his duplicity. And so, with no other choice, he steeled himself with a lungful of sea air and began his descent, leaving the wind and the daylight behind him. He stabbed his torch's white beam into the black below, but the sharp bend in the stairwell revealed only that same endless spiral of worn stone steps. Memories of the brothers' barn returned to him. Absent was the stench of rotted flesh, and gone was his heavenly guide in her baby-blue T-shirt. And yet it was the same feeling Robin suffered whenever he drew closer to the dead, as if he could sense their eyes opening in anticipation of him. With each step that carried him deeper into the unknown, every fibre of his being urged him to return to the surface, but Robin charged on, ever faithful, and ever determined to bring Grace back into the light.

Brendan's boots were suddenly heard stomping above him, and before Robin had chance to turn around, the islander's body had blocked out that thin sliver of daylight above his head.

'Brendan,' he roared up, 'what are you doing?'

He was coming down. Robin aimed his torchlight up as the steady trudge of feet scratched into the stairwell. He'd prayed the man had had a change of heart and come to aid his search. But those hopes were quickly dashed as Brendan rounded the corner and Robin saw the knife in his hand – the same red-handled one that he'd used to cut Sarah free. He retreated down the stairs, holding on to the walls for support, trying to put as much distance between them as possible.

'This is a sacred place, Father,' Brendan called down. 'It's not meant for the likes of you.'

The man's grunts and groans and the scrape of his boots

echoed down the passage's stony throat. Robin delved deeper, searching desperately for its end, but the stairs just kept on coming. They were so perilously steep, he had to study each one just to keep his footing. But it was this diligence that suddenly skidded him to a stop, scattering a spray of stony particles into the black depths below. A section of three steps or more had crumbled away, and he'd been but a short stride away from plunging his leg into nothing. He glanced back to where the dark above him remained unchanged. Brendan must have entered without a light. Robin, stealing the chance to gain some advantage, went about lowering himself down to safety. The break in the stairwell was deeper than he'd expected, but his feet touched safely down on solid stone.

He turned off his torch and rested against the wall, his motives muddled. He thought to call out Brendan's name – to speak some sense into the man or warn him of the pitfall that he was thundering towards – but a fearful indecision held the words hostage, and then it was too late to act either way. A short, explosive scream signalled Brendan's undoing as his foot sank into the emptiness and he tumbled forward in a boulder of bone and flesh. In such a narrow space, there was nothing Robin could do to avoid him, and he hadn't the strength to stand his ground. Brendan's body collided with his own, and the force of the islander's fall carried both men down the stairwell, their limbs and fates entwined as that unfathomable darkness devoured them.

22

Eoin

He'd stayed by the fireplace, steady as a gargoyle welded into its hearth, watching the hot coals smoulder, content to let the others hash it out amongst themselves. The time would come to speak – to tip the scales, if that's what it took – but not yet. Not until he'd sussed out their allegiances. Finnerty was right in what he'd said, and that's what had spooked them. They knew what the Bodach craved more than anything else. It was the sole reason Lavelle had built that fucking orphanage of his. But the publican was grossly mistaken if he thought he'd sacrificed more than the rest of them.

'Why should we all have to die?' John asked, seeking out those whose loyalties he could count upon. 'We did it before. Why shouldn't it work again now?'

The two musicians practically lived under Finnerty's roof, stealing his heat to save on their own and taking pints over payment, though the money would have gone to the same cause regardless. Neither man was blessed with a note of thought that wasn't lifted from the music sheet, and their sway to the publican's side was never in any doubt.

Three votes out of eleven wasn't a bad start.

'Think about it,' John carried on, wringing that dirty dishcloth of his like a neck. 'One more sacrifice, and the rest of us live through this. That's all we have to do.'

Gerard and Laoise Cunnane – loyal to none but each other – would leave no mark or memory after they were gone. And without a voice between them, they'd roll in line with Finnerty's agenda without anyone even noticing.

Two more makes five.

Considering that Connor and his daughter stood on the wrong side of the firing squad, their votes hardly counted. And with nine other bodies in the room, the pendulum of public opinion had swung in Finnerty's favour.

'You know it makes sense,' the publican added, growing more anxious by the moment, looking at everyone bar the family he was victimising. 'I'm sorry but it has to be done. There's no other way.'

That was about as much as any loving father could stand to listen to.

'*No other way?*' Connor shouted, jumping up to shield his daughter despite being half the size of her. 'You can't be serious? No one is touching my little girl. Do you hear me? No one!'

John's bitterness wasn't without its legs. He'd stood to gain more than anyone when Lavelle came to Croaghnakeela with all those notions of his. Finnerty's was the only pub on the island, and no matter how many others found their foundations there, it'd always be the oldest, and that was tempting enough for any tourist with a mind for emptying their pocket. And, of course, there was Annie and the two boys. No man could ever be the same person he was after a loss like that. But sure, they'd all lost something. None who'd survived that time came through it without their own share of regrets. And Eoin Murray was no different.

Lorcan died less than a week before Lavelle ate a feed of his wife's poison. Only two years Eoin's minor but smaller in every way imaginable. Soon as he learned to walk he was chasing his big brother around the island, always happiest in his shadow. Their father passed on shortly after he was born. Too little to do and too fond of the bottle, it was a miracle he lived long as he did. And it was Eoin who'd inherited his brother's unconditional adoration after that.

Whereas the youngest Murray had a heart of gold and grew up to be the most honest fool on the island, Eoin was born with a dark streak in him. He'd learned to keep to himself at an early age, avoiding others more for their sake than his own. And so, understandably, when Lorcan lost his life, everyone on the island gave Eoin the widest berth they could. Fury like that wasn't safe to be around. They knew as well as he did that it was no accident. But what they didn't know was that Lavelle wasn't the sole recipient of all the rage that followed his brother's wake. It was that stupid bitch wife of his: Harriet. The one who took away everything that was owed to him.

Not a day had passed in thirty years that he hadn't revisited *that* night. It must have been the smell that'd awoken him. He recognised Lavelle's tall, gangly silhouette standing before the lace-curtained window of his bedroom, his snow-white hair like mist in the moonlight. Eoin thought he was dreaming till the bastard spoke to him, his voice so deep and warm you'd swear every word had been dragged from the hot gates of Hell.

'What is it that you dream of when you lie in the dark,

Eoin?' he'd asked, as though he'd been pondering the question all his life.

How many nights had he stood by his bed, watching him as he'd slept?

'I don't want anything from *you*,' Eoin had whispered back. 'I never did.'

Though that wasn't the whole truth.

'Every man wants something,' Lavelle said, chuckling amusedly to himself. 'If you give me what *I* want, Eoin, I can give *you* everything you've ever dreamt of.'

There weren't too many men alive who could resist a deal like that.

Connor loved that girl of his. But as much as the wind and the cold and the fucking guilt were a part of Croaghnakeela, so too were the sacrifices. It was a terrible thing, and yet if the majority approved, the rest would follow. In any case, O'Toole was too meek a man in mind and body to do very much about it. The votes had been cast, some by word, others by their silence. And that was enough for Eoin to act.

'John's right,' he said, finally turning to face the room. 'There's no other way. We're all dead unless we do something about it. Sarah's the youngest who survived, isn't she? If there's one person in this room that the Bodach wants… then it's her. Sure didn't we see it last night? It could've grabbed any one of us. But it didn't. All it wanted was Sarah.'

'Eoin?' Connor said disbelievingly, his eyes welling up. 'Please, you can't do this to me. We're friends. Jesus Christ, man, we've known each other all our lives. We grew up together.'

Much like the rest of them, he obviously had no idea what Eoin Murray was capable of.

Few had tested the water since the Corcorans were mangled on the rocks. Dangerous as the land may have been, stepping off it was certain death. Lorcan knew that too, despite his innocence. And yet, such was his faith in his big brother that he'd followed him down to the shore regardless, ever eager to be by his side.

'I want to show you something,' was all Eoin had said, and that was enough.

Rarely did he invite his brother to join him when he did anything, so sick had he grown of his constant devotion, and it was sad in a way to see how excited Lorcan was at the prospect of spending some time together. They'd ambled over the stones, out to the very edge of the island where the ocean and earth collide. The drop down from that particular spot wasn't all that severe, but that hardly mattered. It wasn't the swell that made the waters around Croaghnakeela so treacherous.

Eoin glanced over his shoulder. There he saw Valentine Lavelle in the distance, watching and waiting for what'd been promised to him.

'Have a look down there, Lorcan,' Eoin had said, pointing towards the cliffside. 'You won't believe your eyes when you see it. I had to show you before anybody else.'

With absolute trust in his brother, Lorcan crept out. 'What is it, Eoin? What did you find?'

Wealth, women, power, everything that only the Bodach could give him.

Had Eoin asked his little brother to sacrifice himself, he probably would have gone through with it. He would have done anything to make him happy. As it turned out, all he had to do was die, and Eoin didn't need Lorcan's consent for that.

He hit the water hard when he'd pushed him, all flailing limbs and gracelessness. He was the better swimmer out of the two of them, and that was the worst part of it: when he broke back above the surface and looked up at him, heartbroken, betrayed by his favourite person in the whole wide world. And that was the last Eoin ever saw of his brother before he was wrenched down into the cold depths of the ocean. Another sacrifice. Another life lost. And the waves crashed on.

He'd given the Bodach what it wanted. That was the deal. And no one suspected that Eoin had played any part in it. But the anger he would carry for the rest of his life was sired a few days later, when Lavelle was poisoned by his own wife and promptly buried in an unmarked grave. The whole island was grateful for what she'd done. All except for Eoin. Because of Harriet, he'd killed his only family for nothing.

'This isn't right,' Wilberforce said, scratching around that filthy beard of his.

'And when did you start caring about right and wrong, Fergal?' the barman hissed at him. 'You've done nothing but sit on your fucking arse and drink since Lavelle threw you a few coins.'

'That's all any of us have done,' the widow put in, unexpectedly coming to Wilberforce's defence. 'And sure aren't you the one pouring the fucking drink, you lousy hypocrite. Do you realise what you're asking us to do, John?'

Nobody wanted to play the role of executioner. For Eoin, however, taking a life was nothing new. And if he could kill the only other person who'd ever loved him, then sacrificing the likes of Sarah O'Toole wouldn't faze him in the least. It might do his fortunes a favour to remind the Bodach what he was capable of. Their deal still stood, after all. And Eoin had waited these thirty long years to collect what was owed to him.

'Fine,' Finnerty said, throwing down his dishcloth, 'have it your way. But don't any of you come knocking on my door ever again, do you hear me?'

Fergal shook his head in disgust. 'What happened to you, John? When did the Bodach kill the good man inside you?'

Connor hoisted his daughter up by the hand. 'Come on, Sarah,' he said, his panic rising. 'We're leaving.'

With Finnerty wedged in behind the bar and no one else so committed as to take any action, Eoin did what had to be done. He strode over to the door and put his back against it. Connor must have hoped that he was a better man than the lies he'd sold them.

'Please,' he said, gripping his daughter's hand all the harder, 'you don't have to do this.'

'I know, Connor,' Eoin replied, staring through the tears in Sarah's eyes. 'But I want to.'

23

ROBIN

'Wake up!'

A snap seizure wrought him back. Gasping, choking, blinking frantically in the black, he gleaned only molten shapes from the blood rushing in rivers behind his eyes. Without some standing in time or space, there was no solid memory to anchor Robin to the moment. A dreamlike suspension held him in its orbit, swinging his subconscious through a thousand thoughts and a thousand dreams, none of which were so focused as to shed a bead of light on the here and now. There was only a pained feeling of cold. And then, in that perplexing dark, the agony of Robin's wounds swelled across his entire being, too many to isolate. Bruised flesh. Fractured bone... but by some divine miracle he was still alive.

The vaguest impression of a voice still lingered in the air.

'Brendan,' he whispered, groping around him, 'where are you? Are you okay?'

The fear of being alone was more pressing than any threat the old man could wage against him. Robin patted his hands across the floor, searching for his torch – anything tangible to hold on to – and then he felt the stiff wax of the islander's jacket.

'Brendan,' he repeated hopefully, gently nudging him.

But the old man was dead.

Strong as his beliefs may have been, Brendan's arthritic bones must have shattered like hollow glass during that downward spiral. For six years he'd been a friend, and Robin refused to let a lone act of madness tarnish his memories of him. No man was perfect, after all. And Croaghnakeela had a cruel habit of leading the best of them astray.

Every tender motion was an agony to absorb as he clambered back to his feet. Robin stared bleary-eyed around him, blind to his surroundings. And then, amidst that unearthly silence, he heard a knocking. It was the same rhythmic pattern that'd played against Harriet's door – an eerie consonance that enlivened its own unease. So disorientating was the dark, it was impossible to place where it'd come from. But there must have been a passageway close by. How else could its sound have travelled to him so directly?

'Hello,' Robin called out, his voice repeating far into the unfathomable distance.

He could barely summon the strength to stand, and yet somehow he would have to walk. With his torch lost and most likely broken in the fall, Robin staggered towards where the echo of those knocks had rung loudest, ignoring the many horrors his mind was now conjuring in the black. Hands outstretched, he flinched back when his fingers touched a wall, almost doubting it to be real, such was the overriding sense of emptiness that ruled that darkness.

'Okay, Rob,' he whispered, trying to measure each breath. 'Just because we can't see a way out, it doesn't mean there isn't one.'

He used the wall to guide himself through the unknown,

shuffling slowly, wary as one lost behind enemy lines. Nature wasn't renowned for its straight lines and flat surfaces, and yet the stone felt curiously smooth to his touch. Pawing along it like a blind man in a maze, Robin's hand finally felt a corner. It was cut so sharply that it could only have been manmade. And around it, in the distance, though his eyes disbelieved what he was seeing, he found light.

Before him lay a narrow passage, illumed by unseen flames burrowed deep into its walls. There was no end in sight. The lights just went on and on, like a bridge reaching out over some bottomless abyss. And though the priest may have lost his bearings in the fall, he knew it had to lead east, where Grace and the wakeful dead were waiting for him.

Firelight lapped overhead in waves of shadow as he forced himself onward, ignoring his wounds and the surrealness of his surroundings. The stone amped up every sound – the scuffle of his feet, the low grumble of the flames, and every groan and gasp too pained to contain in a body so worn. There was an unnerving, almost purgatorial, feeling to that journey. The glowing hollows in the walls were identical in form, with a measured distance between each one, tricking him into imagining that he was repeating the same few feet over and over. Robin was desperate to be free of it, but his sore legs could only carry him so fast.

He stopped a moment, choking back as much of that musty air as he could suffer through. And somewhere, amidst the strained rhythm of his lungs, there was another sound – one not of the priest's making. He turned, certain that it'd come from where he had just travelled. The tunnel behind him bore a perfect likeness to what lay ahead. Robin blinked the sweat from his eyes. But they were too weary to focus with all that damned firelight coursing across the walls, and their shadows were just as hindering. Again he heard it – a shuffling, as if something were being dragged across the ground towards him, and he knew that he was no longer alone.

Robin held his breath and listened. A bone cracked. One at first, and then another, and then more. The most guttural scream suddenly surged through the tunnel, tremoring through its walls, and he watched on in horror as Brendan's twisted body materialised from the darkness.

The man's right leg had split at the knee, and yet still he threw himself forward, his every exertion lame and jagged, and so terrifyingly swift. Robin staggered backwards, unsure in the wavering light if this was an apparition or whether the Bodach had somehow reanimated the dead man's body into pursuing him. No inkling of humanity remained. The rage in the islander's eyes was insatiable, more fiend than fellow man. And with his face ravaged from the fall, he scrambled through the tunnel like some mindless creature hell-bent on tearing the priest apart.

Sapped of sinew, the fear willed Robin to keep on going. It was fight or flight, and neither option carried a great deal of promise. Between the flames he ran, fumbling his hands across the walls to stay his balance, terribly aware of the bones cracking louder and louder behind him as the dead man's screams raced past his ear. The thirst was unbearable. The pain, even more so. Robin's injuries had flared up from their exertions. No fevered whipping on his part could keep his legs from faltering, and he crumpled to the ground, his body no longer yielding to his command.

A pure and undistilled despair seized Robin when he

beheld Brendan's crooked remains in all their horror. More bones had snapped in the chase, crumbling within him like chalky honeycomb, and yet still he kept on coming. The priest closed his eyes just as the old man was on the cusp of falling upon him, yielding to his inevitable death in that darkest of places. And though he whispered to God for deliverance, it was his memories of Father Macken that he clung to like a talisman.

But a sudden silence snapped over the corridor, leaving no echo, no evidence of any sound that'd come before it. The pendulum that'd counted down to Robin's oblivion now hung steady, frozen in time as he was frozen in fear. He peeled open an eye, doubting if he himself still counted amongst the living.

The passage was empty. Brendan's spirit was gone.

'Holy fuck,' he whispered, lying back, resting his head and shoulders on the floor.

The fear had bested him, just like it used to. Robin should have known better, but the line dividing this existence and the next felt so faint amidst the firelight. He reflected breathlessly on those closing seconds, when death seemed the only certainty in life, and how Father Macken had stood centre stage in his mind. It'd been so long since he thought of him. And that alone was a sin in itself.

Robin had often been alone as a child. His mother and father cared for him in their own perfunctory way, but they were parents strictly by name and not by nature. In the Thompson household it was better to be out of sight than in the way, and the surest way to safeguard the peace was to disappear completely. Solitude became the template from which all childhood activities followed. His father, especially, disdained his son's so-called *sensitivity*. If Robin's parents suspected that some malady of the mind were responsible for his chronic angst and bouts of terror, then neither had cared enough to do anything about it. In their eyes he was troubled, and the trouble was none of their concern. More pity them for receiving a child so broken at birth, so easily upset by figments of an overactive imagination. Perhaps they wouldn't have been so quick to condemn his tears had they seen the horrors for themselves.

Some were indistinguishable from the living. To Robin's innocent eyes as a boy, the nice ones were similar to any stranger on the street, and most of them were too wrapped up in their own sorrow to even notice him. Others were more upsetting – those who'd carried their wounds into the afterlife. Often bloodied. Always distressed. No child should ever have seen such things. And then there were the bad ones. Robin took great care to never make eye contact with those.

His parents were faithless as they come. God caused trouble, they used to say. And, historically speaking, they weren't wrong. Robin had never set foot inside a church until the day he met Father Macken. Who knows what darkness might have taken him had he not found some light to believe in. He'd been walking home from school, alone as usual, his backpack of books weighing his tiny shoulders into a stoop. The journey wasn't far, but it had its obstacles. There was one house in particular, terraced and abandoned, that Robin habitually crossed the road to avoid. In the corner of his eye he'd seen something in there: a dark shape behind the glass, watching the world go by, ignored and unacknowledged since the day it'd died. Robin knew not to look at it directly.

Even then, before he truly understood the nature of his gift, he'd had a bad feeling about that house. He knew something awful had happened there – the kind of awful that'd kept any prospective homeowners from ever moving in after the fact.

And on that afternoon, he abided by the same rules: keep moving, focus on the pavement, don't look up. All was going according to plan until he bumbled into a woman twice his height and in just as much of a rush. Between the apologies and the embarrassment, Robin – with the pages of his rulebook momentarily scattered – glanced back over his shoulder.

His eyes locked at once with the old man smiling back at him.

'Are you okay?' the woman had asked, marking his sudden distress, worried that she were the cause of it.

If only she knew what he'd seen, the dear girl would have run away just as quickly.

The man's naked body was skeletally thin and grey-skinned – a wire model of limbs and black bubbling sores. Robin knew that the good ones retained some sense of themselves in the in-between. This thing was too far gone, too debased to even remember who it'd once been in life. His skull was hairless save for a few long white strands hanging behind his ears, and the face was so gaunt, it looked almost fleshless. But it was the eyes that haunted Robin's dreams for years to come. They seemed to glow in the dimness of that room – a red fire in a fog of murky glass – and they'd stared upon him with a chilling obsession, as if they'd finally found what they'd spent an eternity searching for: some innocence to feast upon, as the darkness swallows the light.

Robin's home was too far to reach at a single sprint, but he had to try. He would have tossed his backpack to the ground had he not known the terrible trouble he'd be in when his parents found out. The woman whom he'd collided with must have been perfectly confused. Maybe she still remembered him. Maybe not. It's strange sometimes what people take with them. When he'd covered as much ground as he could, he looked back, seeking to quell his fears with the sight of an empty street. The dead rarely moved; that much he'd worked out for himself. They seemed to haunt the same places, trapped in some spiritual perimeter; that's how he'd learned to evade them. But not this one. The old man was standing on the pavement, staring at him with that same smile, those same eyes.

Robin would never make it home. And even if he could, the bad one would know where he lived. Whatever peace he'd made for himself there would be obsolete, and his father's cruelty would thrive in its absence. Nothing accentuated his loneliness quite like the fear. It was the one ruling element of his life that he couldn't share, and the only one he wanted no part of. Robin checked his surroundings, spiralling wildly on the pavement, hoping to find somewhere safe to hide, where there were people. They may not have understood the nature of his plight, but their presence might have deterred the old man from hurting him. But as fate would have it – if providence were a word worthy of its meaning – Robin had tarried outside a church. It was little taller than the houses around it, with a thick bed of white chippings leading to its door. Not every path to God is gilded, and that's the one that Robin took as a child.

He paced up the aisle, aghast at the emptiness, more fearful than before in a space so unfamiliar to every sense but his soul. But he kept on, hunched under his backpack, head twitching all about him, awaiting some adult to pounce on him for trespassing. Robin reached the altar steps. Even that short ascent felt like climbing out of harm's way. He had to arch back his head just to take in the colossal cross that rose above him, and though its significance was lost on a child unversed in Christianity's teachings, he slipped the backpack from his shoulders and sat beneath it, watching the open door like a Spartan at the hot gates.

'Hello, my boy,' came a voice behind him.

An elderly man dressed all in black groaned under his breath as he settled on the step beside him. His stance and manner mirrored Robin's so perfectly, like two old souls reunited after an eternity apart. He didn't speak for a long time. He just sat, watching the same door, breathing in rhythm with the boy's unease until both lungs seemed to steady.

'Are we expecting company?' the priest asked eventually, sharing a smile.

There was a peacefulness between them in that moment that Robin had never forgotten. If there was a clock somewhere in that church, its tick and its tock didn't matter. Sitting on the altar steps, side by side, they had all the time in the world.

'There's someone out there,' Robin replied, politely as he could, but the fear crept through regardless. 'One of the bad ones. They were following me.'

The priest sat back straight. He'd listened. He'd understood.

'Okay,' he said, nodding his head. 'Well, if they're bad, then they can't come in here. This is a safe place. So long as you're *in here*, then you've no need to worry about anything *out there*.'

★

Dashing the dirt from his sleeves, Robin picked himself back up onto his feet and squinted against the endless reams of firelight reaching to the east.

More broken than before and just as stubborn, he walked.

24

Mary

It wasn't the fear of the Bodach that bound their tongues on that journey to the hilltop, it was the fear of each other – the realisation that the devil they'd buried six feet under had made devils of themselves. Finnerty may have singled out Connor's daughter for her youth. But he could have just so easily turned his wicked eye on the elderly. The man didn't recognise friend or foe anymore. He saw only offerings. And no matter how many innocent lives that well swallowed up, Mary knew that it'd always be hungry for more. The peace that they'd so wretchedly clung to for thirty-odd years was a lie – proof enough now, scraping through the mud, climbing high as they could just to drop back into the same depraved old ways.

Connor, God love him, was still trying to writhe himself free. 'Get your hands off me,' he growled for the umpteenth time since they'd set out.

Beautiful to see it, a father's love for his child; shame it couldn't make a spit of difference. The fiddler and that tone-deaf guitarist of his held him on either side, their arms locked tighter than a straitjacket. And without a muscle on him, sure

Connor hadn't a hope of doing anything about it. Even when he'd dug in his heels, they hoisted him up like a child with his skinny legs kicking above the dirt.

'It's going to be okay, Dad,' his daughter called out from behind him.

But the widow had her doubts.

It was Eoin who gripped Sarah by the arm, volunteering his services to bully the poor woman up that hill. Strong as he was bitter, that one, like a pot of cold black coffee. Mary had always known it. She'd seen the way he moved, restless as a shark, forever brooding over some mischief, his dark eyes looking anywhere but the light. Whatever lean sympathies he'd once had for his own kind died alongside his brother all those years ago. Poor Lorcan, harmless a creature as they come. He wouldn't have borrowed a coin from Lavelle's pocket if the bastard had forced it into his hand, and yet he'd fallen foul of the evil regardless. And now, just like old times, even the good ones weren't safe.

'Come on,' Finnerty shouted back to them, 'we're almost there.'

No one was allowed to stay behind. It was the publican's way of doling out the guilt, making each of them his accomplices, though Mary knew it was him and Eoin who'd be leaving that hill with the heftiest share of it. The path they followed had deepened into a trough over the years. On the wettest days the rain raced through it in a brown stream, ankle deep and so cold it'd numb Mary's bones from the waist down. She'd memorised every bend and miserable scrap of stone on that walk, and she knew now without lifting her head that they weren't far from the top. But whereas the others trekked up that hill upon a Sunday to pay back the Bodach, exonerating their sins with a few fistfuls of coin, Mary had her own reasons, and they were hers alone.

She wasn't born a widow. No poor woman ever was.

Married as he may have been to the open sea, Jackie Malley pledged his love to Mary after only a month's courtship. The way his warm hand would hold on to hers, there was never any question that they were the right fit for each other. And he wasn't the kind of fisherman who'd let a catch like that slip through his net. Though not an islander by birth, he'd settled on Croaghnakeela so that they could make a go at a life together. It seemed like a grand plan at the time, such is the hopeful ignorance when youth and love collaborate on a dream.

And yet all Mary had now were nightmares – dark imaginings of Jackie's final moments, of an ocean alive and insane: rising, crashing, devouring. It was always the same, all those sweaty, heady episodes when she'd see it play out: the capsize, the fight, the fear, the pain. Too much water. Too little air.

There'd been no distress signal, and no explanation other than the lone survivor's ramblings: a young lad called Reilly, still a child in Jackie's eyes. The old hands, Doyle and Heery, were both lost at sea, with neither body ever finding their way ashore. Reilly only lived through the night because Jackie wouldn't let him on that deck unless he were wearing a lifejacket. And that's how they found him, afloat on the ocean, his belly and lungs bulging from so much saltwater it was a miracle the sea level hadn't dropped. Rescue teams searched the coast like gulls that'd lost a nestling, but no part of Jackie's trawler was ever found.

The general consensus was that missing meant dead. But

Mary never bought into that. It felt like some sick conspiracy to forget that he'd ever existed. Everyone was in on it, turning a blind eye to that empty stool at the bar and refusing to speak Jackie's name for fear someone might raise the mystery of what'd happened to him. But the cruellest thing any of them did to Mary Malley was to christen her *the widow* – that daily reminder that she'd lost the man she loved, leaving her to cherish in her lonely moments a life that had a beginning, a middle, and nothing else. Not even a goodbye.

The hillside was steepening. They now slipped between great slabs of rock where the wind howled loudest overhead. This final test was the most gruelling, when Mary's years and all their pain combined seemed to concentrate solely around her old legs.

'Sarah!' Connor shrieked, causing her to look up.

One of the musicians had slipped in the mud, loosening his hold just enough to liberate him. Useless bastards, the pair of them, but Mary was finally glad of the fact. Connor was trundling down, holding the stones on either side to keep him from toppling forward, his course set on Eoin Murray, who'd stood his ground, clearly enjoying the anticipation of what was to come. He twisted Sarah's arm and planted the woman down on her knees. Clever fucker, making sure she couldn't help her father should it come to blows.

'Take your hand off my daughter,' Connor spat, standing just beyond his reach.

'Why don't *you* take it off her?' Eoin replied tauntingly, wrenching her arm even tighter so that Sarah cried out in pain.

Connor was a slight man, scrawny as they come. His anger may have made him fearless to any foe who'd lay a finger on his daughter, but Mary knew it wouldn't do the lad any favours. If someone were to come to his aid, he might have stood half a chance. But none did. They couldn't even bring themselves to look at him. He strode forward, too focused on Sarah's distress to consider the threat of the one holding her hostage. And before he'd thought to raise a fist, Eoin Murray headbutted him square in the nose. Mary heard the dull crack of bone on bone, and Connor went tumbling back into the dirt, blood streaming down his lips, barely holding on to consciousness.

It was Donal who'd descended first, leaving the other feckless piece behind him to wipe the filth from his jeans. He looked to Eoin, wondering perhaps if it was best they just left O'Toole where he was.

'What'll we do with him?' the fiddler asked, looking down at Connor, who was still squirming on his back, too stunned to even open his eyes.

'Get him up,' Murray barked as he hoisted Sarah onto her feet. 'There's no point in putting him to waste, is there? He'll follow his daughter down the same fucking hole.'

The worst of men always were in their element at the worst of times. The good ones, bless them, didn't fare so well.

Reilly never was the same after that night. The boy was delirious when they'd picked him up. Sedation was the only way to keep him calm. And even in the days after, when he'd stare off into space with a pitiable peace about him, the touch of another could send the poor lad into hysterics. He was in no state of mind to speak clearly of what'd happened. And so everyone just assumed that a storm had swallowed her Jackie right up and spat his most useless crewman back out to sea. But Mary knew it wasn't some storm that'd taken her husband from her. And if it hadn't been for Colman McMorrow, she might never have learned the truth.

Reilly became a resident in one of those homes for the fragile-minded on the mainland, where everyone wore white and they either screamed or said nothing at all. He was definitely in the quiet camp, though he was so heavily drugged when Mary visited him, it was unlikely the boy could scream if he wanted to. She'd sat with him for an hour or so before he found his voice. Reilly began repeating her husband's name over and over, massaging his temples as if he were trying to knead his memories of the man back into a shape he could recognise. Odd it was, especially considering it'd been less than a month since they were together, and the two men had worked side by side for three seasons before that.

'I liked Jackie,' he whispered eventually, as if he were reminding himself of the fact. 'He was nice to me, wasn't he?'

Mary felt the sorrow welling up within her like a burst pipe. It was a wonderful thing just to hear someone speak his name again.

'How long was I in there for?' Reilly asked, his drowsy eyes finally seeing the widow beside him.

She didn't understand the question. Had no one told the boy how long he'd been at sea before they'd saved him from it? He must have lost consciousness. Or maybe whatever medication they'd been feeding him had darkened all those days gone since. Mary felt so sorry for the boy, the least she could do was answer honestly.

'They found you not long after the dawn,' she replied, cushioning every word as best she could. 'And they say the boat went down sometime around midnight. They think that's when its GPS tracker stopped working, though no one really knows what happened. Well,' she added, bracing herself, 'no one, that is, except for you.'

'How long?' he pressed impatiently.

Mary did the maths. 'Around eight or nine hours, I suppose. It can't have been much longer than that.'

Reilly shook his head violently, rejecting what she'd told him.

'Whatever's the matter with you?' she asked, sitting forward.

'Time's different in there,' he whispered, examining his own hands, stretching his fingers apart, like a newborn making sense of them for the first time.

Mary had to drag her chair in closer to hear him. 'What do you mean?' she asked.

'I don't even know where I was,' he replied vacantly. 'The fog was too thick to see anything. It was all so... white. After a while my thoughts just kind of went quiet. I stopped thinking. And I floated there, on my own, for hundreds of years, maybe thousands. There was just... the water and the fog and the silence. But look,' he said, holding up his hand for Mary to see. 'I didn't age at all.'

Whereas Reilly's face was clean-skinned and even younger-looking than his years, his eyes were some of the oldest Mary had ever seen. *Hundreds of years, maybe thousands*, and she knew to believe him. Whatever had held him captive out there for all that time, it'd taken her Jackie too, preserving him as he was in her memories, imprisoned in some unearthly limbo.

'Keep going, all of you!' Finnerty roared down at them from the hilltop now. 'Best we get this done before the Bodach comes looking for us.'

Connor's dead weight had been hauled up by the two

musicians, his arms draped around their necks, two feet dragging tracks in the mud behind them. There hadn't been a peep out of his daughter since Eoin nutted him. And Mary knew there was no stronger despair than the silent kind – that's when you knew the end was all there was. They bunched together when they'd reached the summit, aching from the trials of climbing that fucking hill twice in as many days. Wilberforce was bent over, barely breathing. Fat bastard, his belly was as big as a boulder and to think he'd carried that weight with him all the way. Gerard and Laoise were seen to study him with a morbid eye, wondering perhaps if the first casualty of the day were to come before they'd even reached the well. Maggie Scuffel kept her gaze pinned firmly to her feet, all set now to inherit the title of widow when Mary's time was up.

Years after she'd lost her Jackie, Colman McMorrow came to Finnerty's, sober in every way a man could be, pleading with them to hear him out. It was no secret on the island that he'd been acting strangely, occupying himself with interests that only his son was privy to. But no one expected what was to come. He'd spoken so vehemently of myths and monsters, it was too easy for them to brand it all as madness. Between their smirks and side glances they'd listened – and Mary didn't doubt that a few believed him – but the majority's vote sided with ignorance, as it often did on that fucking island. All the man was trying to do was keep them safe. And yet denying the truth always made it easier to pretend, and that's all those cowards were good for.

However, despite mocking Colie's warnings and sending a good man home in tears, Mary noticed how they all looked at the fog out there in the west differently after that day.

Maybe they were waiting for it to move, even just a little, to prove themselves right. But it never did. And the more they stared at it, the harder it came to pretend.

That's why she climbed that hilltop every Sunday, come rain or shine, in sickness and in health, till death, if that's what it took. Its western side gave her a full bird's eye view of that dark bank of fog that'd taken her Jackie. Mary would scan the entire ocean, searching for the man she loved, hoping that someday he'd be returned to her.

Patience takes time.

She wasn't born a widow. Maybe she didn't have to die as one.

25

ROBIN

The passageway became a suffocating tomb of shadow and light, forever teasing an escape that never came. It'd taken him an hour or less to walk from Harriet's home to the site of the four stones. And surely this journey – given his haste, ungainly as it was – should have taken half that time. Robin now feared that the corridor hadn't led east as the optimist in him had presumed. Could it have burrowed under the very ocean itself, leading him deeper into the depths of nowhere? What if this hell was all he had left – the same shadows, the same lights, over and over until that final darkness overcame him.

Robin's mind was a lawless land where rationality and reason had been overrun. He felt like a rat spinning on a wheel, chasing the false illusion of freedom. The panic pervaded every part of him now, corrupting his courage like a cancer. His skin burned in some patches and chilled him in others, and everywhere his body was tormented by a thousand isolated injuries, all allied in some cruel campaign to drag him to his knees. He needed to keep his faith, for Grace's sake if not his own. But God seemed so indifferent to the trials set out against him. Robin's prayers were never answered. No miracles ever made sense of the sacrifices he'd made. What if Brendan had been right after all? He slipped his fingers into his pocket and touched the rosary that Father Macken had given him – a memento of a more faithful time, when the Lord's allegiance was never in any doubt.

The church was Robin's refuge from the world – a safe port he could depend upon no matter the storm – and another secret he'd guarded long into adolescence. His parents used to quiz him occasionally on his whereabouts, but he never once told them where he went during those surreptitious hours outside of school. Their presence only added to the myriad shadows he was trying to escape in life. And their open disapproval of all things church-related would have nipped his blossoming faith in the bud before it'd had chance to grow.

Father Macken must have been in his seventies when Robin met him, possibly older. Children, in all their innocence, tend to lack an appreciation of age, mortality, and the drawbacks of one too many birthdays. He was a sallow-skinned man with a curly head of greying hair, and there was a warmth about him that could put the most anguished soul at ease. It was remarkable really, how nothing ever seemed to faze him, and Robin had gleaned a profound comfort from that, fancying back then that the old man's faith made him invincible, like a superpower divined from the Almighty.

The old priest had cared for him like a grandson in many regards – always making a point of hearing about his day and asking the perfect questions to get the young boy talking. This genuine interest in his life was altogether new to Robin, and it was through Father Macken that he learned the importance of giving everyone his time, especially the very shy – those whom he knew in his heart needed it the most, for they hadn't the courage to ask for it.

Despite the rapport that'd ripened so naturally between them, however, Robin was reluctant to share the secret of his gift. Not that he didn't want to, of course. But given how his parents had reacted, he worried that such a confession might ruin what little happiness he'd found in Father Macken's company. For all Robin knew, the church frowned upon such people, and he hadn't studied enough of the Bible by then to know otherwise. But unbeknownst to him, the priest was playing a long game with the nervous child who followed him around his church like a stray cat. He was but biding his time, slowly building a bridge of trust in the hope that the truth might someday pass over it. And eventually that day came.

'Can I ask you a question, Father?'

They'd been sitting in the pews, watching the sunlight sear through the stained glass.

'Of course you can,' the priest replied cheerfully, and though he hadn't turned his head, Robin detected the slightest hint of a smile – the satisfaction of having his patience rewarded.

'On the street around the corner, there's an empty house. It's the only one. I don't think anyone has lived there for years. Do you know it?'

Robin noticed how a slight frown settled above Father Macken's eyes. 'I know the one, yes. Why do you ask?'

He shifted in a little closer to the priest's side. 'Who was the old man that used to live there?'

'Oh, that was a long time ago, Robin. And I think men like that are definitely best forgotten. He wasn't very nice, is what I mean. Whoever told you about him?'

The boy glanced back over his shoulder, checking that they were still alone. 'No one,' he replied quietly. 'Do you remember when you said the *bad ones* can't come in here?'

Father Macken nodded. 'I do.'

Robin had been so nervous. How many times had he parted his lips only for them to snap shut again?

'Can the *good ones* come to church?' he asked eventually.

The priest looked to him, seemingly surprised. 'The good ones are always welcome here, Robin. You know that.'

He'd expected as much. But it was still nice to hear it. Asking questions was always easier when he guessed he would like the answers.

'But why don't they all go to Heaven?' Robin said, staring at the cross atop the altar, having since come to admire its significance. 'I don't understand why they stay here when they all look so sad all the time. Maybe you could show them how to get there.'

Father Macken's mirth was replaced by an expression bordering on concern, but his smile wasn't absent for long. It never was. He placed his hand on the boy's shoulder, squeezing it proudly, as if Robin had passed a test he didn't realise he was sitting.

'You see them, don't you?' he asked.

There was no need to say what they were. Robin nodded nervously, and though he wasn't sure why at the time, he cried. The tears just poured out of him. All his life he'd kept his gift a secret, and without Father Macken he may never have found the courage to share it with another. He didn't feel odd in the priest's company. On the contrary, he finally felt understood.

'You're a very special boy, aren't you?' Father Macken said. 'And I think God has a very special purpose in mind for you.'

If the old man had been right and God had given Robin his gift for a reason, then this was it. For Grace, for Harriet, and for all those lost children who'd wept neath the stars. Fate had carried him into Father Macken's friendship that day, and the same fate had brought him here, to this very moment. Committed, he peered up the corridor, expecting the same never-ending gauntlet that'd feasted so greedily on his faith and body. And yet, though he'd distrusted his own eyes at first, something *had* changed. Beyond the last of the firelight there was… *nothing*. It was as though the passage simply ceased to exist, leaving a vast and empty expanse of black.

Robin walked to where the light abruptly ended. He reached his hand forward and watched it disappear at the wrist. Swallowing down his fears, he immersed himself deeper in the darkness. That relentless trial of firelight may have scored its golden scars across his eyes, but its absence now ushered in a new league of hardships. The dark, he'd learned through hard experience, had a nasty habit of doing that. Robin imagined the worst of the dead – those twisted, wrathful souls he'd run from as a child – all forgathered in silence around him. But still he dragged his feet forward, resolved on bringing that journey to an end. He glanced back over his shoulder, where the lights he'd abandoned now looked impossibly far away. Time and space had never seemed so unstable. And then, finally, Robin's fingers graced the corridor's end.

How different his life might have been had he not found Father Macken's church that day. Without a friend to confide in, the fear and loneliness may have bested him as it did to those on Croaghnakeela, paring down the most sacred parts of him – the kindness, the honesty, and the goodness that the old priest had taken such care to cultivate. Or perhaps, given the singularity of his affliction, his sanity would have been called into question. Robin had often pondered if others had shared his gift over the centuries, and how many had been declared mad because of it. No miracles. No rosaries. Just padded rooms and chains, and a God who seemingly couldn't care less.

With Father Macken's guidance, the uncertainty that'd tainted Robin's youth was exchanged for a far more favourable course of enlightenment. He became a teacher, a protector, and, most importantly, a friend. The old man must have been fascinated by the spiritual ramifications of such a gift, and yet he never let his own curiosity take precedence over the boy's well-being. Ancient as the world may have been, it was still too young to understand. The concept alone of communicating with the dead had been long discredited by clairvoyant charlatans and opportunists, and regardless of Robin's authenticity, it was decided – as would eventually be proven true – that secrecy was paramount if he were to have some shot at a normal life, albeit one disposed to do God's work in ways that the faithless could only dream of. Given his mixed results thus far – a pissed-off bishop and six years of idle exile – maybe this was his chance to finally make his old friend proud.

In the darkness, the door felt so cold to Robin's touch. He tapped his knuckles against it, recognising at once the hollow ring of iron. Since setting out from the stairwell, he'd hoped and prayed for a way out. And now that he'd found it, if any more miracles remained on God's heavenly table, all he wanted was for that door to open. It had to. Returning back the way he'd come was no longer an option. Robin hadn't the strength to repeat it.

He forced his shoulder against the door and, through the clamour of its metal screech, the first drips of light trickled into the passageway. Heartened by the sight, he hammered his body into the door harder, ignoring all those pains reawakening inside of him, until he finally wedged it open just far enough to fall through. Robin collapsed to the floor, and there he lay, cognisant only of the cold air now fastening itself to his skin and an eerie feeling of emptiness. But he was no longer alone.

'I knew you'd find me.'

It was the same voice that'd snapped him awake.

26

John

He loathed the air up there, how it clung to the throat, tainting his tastebuds for days afterwards, like a spoilt oyster tucked under his tongue; whiskey was the only force of nature strong enough to cleanse it. The fog was known to clear around the island's shore on a fine day, what with the wind and the waves forever whipping at it. But atop the hill it rarely lightened long enough to see the summit, even passing for snow in the wintry seasons. If the island were alive, like old Colman had tried to warn them, then the damned thing was of a mind to keep those ruins hidden. Nothing was without its secrets on Croaghnakeela, even its fucking stones.

'Go on ahead there,' John said to his fiddler, trusting Donal to do what he was told, as the publican had no notion of walking first into that fog without knowing what was in there.

Connor O'Toole looked to be regaining some sense of himself – groaning louder than he had since Eoin put him on his back – but the musicians still had to prop the poor bastard up for that final stretch to the well. John was secretly glad to see it, though. If the Bodach were to turn on them despite their offerings, then what the publican lacked in strength, he more than made up for in speed. And he'd abandon the rest of them without a second's thought. John owed them nothing. He knew all their dirty secrets, dropping eaves from behind his bar, always polishing a glass with one ear trained to listen. He'd watched their fortunes in life wax and wane long before they were eclipsed. Selfish fuckers, the whole score of them, crying about their misfortune when they'd no clue what true loss really did to a—

'Aren't you joining us, John?' Eoin asked with a mean little smirk. 'Let's not be forgetting, this was *your* idea, wasn't it? Now come on,' he added, forcing Sarah ahead of him, 'this one hasn't got all day.'

Croaghnakeela had long been an island of broken hearts. All anyone cared about was their own suffering, and selfishness can be a hard sin to shake off once you get a feel for it.

John's own life changed the night Declan O'Dwyer came knocking on his door. So long ago now, and yet it didn't feel like the past anymore, more a recurring nightmare that'd worn him down like a nub of chalk scratching out the same horror over and over. They'd all made the decision to cloister themselves away, keeping their young close and under constant supervision. Every household had laid their lines of salt across any weaknesses – windows and doors and the like – and John's family were no different. He was slow to trust their safety to such superstitions, but the pub was more secure than any home on the island, with walls thick as a fortress. *And* he'd paid Lavelle his share.

Maybe it was that arrogance that'd drawn the evil to him, the hubris in fancying that he was better off than most. He'd only opened the door a crack, just enough to send Declan off on his way. But what if that's how the Bodach got in? The wind might have swept the salt from his threshold, or maybe he'd dragged his foot through it without even realising. One mistake, that's all it took. And yet, Chrissy and little Gracie survived the night just fine. It didn't seem fair, not then, not now, not ever.

John didn't care much for money back then. With Annie and the two boys, he was rich in other ways. And if Lavelle had demanded the publican's livelihood in return for his family's safekeeping, then he'd have handed over the deeds in a heartbeat. But that was never what the fucking thing wanted. Bricks and mortar were poor substitutes for flesh and blood in the evil's eyes.

Their sons were four and six. Ronnie was the eldest, tall for his age, full of stories, and bold as his mother when the mood took him. Dara was more like his father and left a beautiful mess after him wherever he went. Annie was convinced he'd have made an artist someday, splashing around paint like he did his bowl of porridge in the morning. Both boys were so different, and each one was as perfect as John's memories of them.

The rooms above the pub had been their bedrooms once, always bustling with light and laughter, the way a happy home should be. Rare was the night when the boys would be let into bed with them. But so long as the Bodach was doing his rounds, they weren't leaving their father's sight. And once they were held tightly enough in their parents' arms, there was more than enough space for the lot of them to sleep soundly. And sleep soundly they did… for a while at least.

The dawn couldn't have been far off when he'd awoken. He had left a candle burning on the bedside locker; it'd melted down to a stub since he'd dozed off. John scanned his eyes about the room. Its shadows were empty. The door was locked. All was well, or so it seemed, until he heard those footsteps pacing across the floor downstairs. He squeezed his son tighter and listened. A bottle was heard to slide from a shelf. It was placed down hard on the bar counter. John could picture it all as though he were down there, serving the drink himself. But who was it? Lavelle cared only for the little ones, and he wasn't in the habit of stealing away a man's whiskey. Had Declan O'Dwyer returned, deranged by the drink to die by the same well that'd poisoned him?

With his nightgown fastened around his waist, John crept down the stairs, flexing both knuckles around the old golf club that he'd left by his bedside. Again he heard the glass bottle slam down. Whoever it was, they were having more than a quick nightcap for themselves. It had to be O'Dwyer. The publican was sure of that as he picked up his pace, enraged that the lad would put his family's lives in jeopardy for the sake of drowning his sorrows, though he couldn't understand how he might have gotten in.

'Declan,' he snapped in a shrill whisper as he pushed open the door, 'what the fuck do you...'

'John,' Lavelle said, sitting by the counter, whiskey in hand. 'How good of you to join me.'

The publican almost collapsed on the spot. His first thought was for his family, asleep upstairs, oblivious, vulnerable, a few short stairs away from death. The Bodach brandished a shark smile of rotted teeth as he watched John's fingers tighten around the golf club.

'Come to play, have we?' He chuckled to himself. 'Be a good lad and leave it by the door, would you? We don't want to wake the two boys now, do we?'

John could feel his heart thrashing about inside his chest like a caged animal as he rested the club against the wall.

'Please,' Lavelle said, gesturing to the high stool beside him, 'sit.'

John knew better than to deny the Bodach. He glanced hopelessly back to the stairs, regretting that he hadn't locked the bedroom door behind him. Lavelle placed another tumbler down and poured out a full glass, flooding it to the very brim. It was true what they said about him: the man's face had much changed. Though its bones overall had forsaken their old form, his nose and chin protruded most prominently, like some grotesque goblin in a Grimm fairy tale. The man's hair had thinned like torn cobweb, and his skin was a flaky grey, withered and stippled with spots, as if the body – that fleshly shell the Bodach had crawled into – was already starting to rot from the inside. But it was those red eyes that made Lavelle resemble something truly devilish, sowing fear across all those who met them.

The publican did as he was told and sat up beside him. 'What do you want from me?' he whispered. 'Tell me what it is and you can have it. Just, please, don't hurt my—'

'Drink,' Lavelle said, frowning down at the whiskey he'd prepared for him.

John's hand wouldn't still itself, and he had to grip the glass with both just to draw it to his lips. A sip was managed before the urge to vomit wormed its way up his throat.

'All of it,' Lavelle said to him sternly. 'Drink every drop, or I'll kill your entire family this instant and make you drink their blood instead.'

John did what the Bodach asked of him. He swallowed back the whole glass, his throat contracting as he fought to keep from throwing it back up. The whiskey engulfed his senses, spraying out his nose, wringing streams of tears from his eyes, and when the last drop was gone, the force of it knocked him from his stool and he emptied his stomach across the floor. It burned through every terrified part of him, igniting his chest like a stove. On his hands and knees, struggling to breathe, he heard Lavelle gigging to himself, alive with the most sadistic joy.

'Come now, John,' he said, guiding him back to his stool, 'on your feet.'

'Please,' he whispered, 'I don't want anything from you.'

The Bodach looked up to the ceiling and smiled. 'That's where you're mistaken, John. You see, everybody wants something. It simply depends on whether or not I want to give it to them.'

Despite the fog, John knew the way well enough to reach the ruins with his eyes closed. So, too, did the others; those half-seen bodies haunting his periphery, like lost souls walking somewhere between life and death, unsure as to which side of the line they'd rather be on. It was as if they were trudging towards some gallows with a neatly tied noose swaying in the wind for each of their necks. Maybe that'd have been for the best – one last cull to put an end to them once and for all. They'd strayed so far from God's path, John knew that even if the fog cleared, they'd never find their way back to it.

The dark shape of Eoin Murray was stalking in front of him, dragging Sarah by his side. It was then that the thought occurred to him: *what if that'd been his own child?* If Ronnie or Dara had lived, they'd be of a similar age to Connor's daughter. A cold sickness seemed to permeate through his skin as he imagined his boys as men, being delivered to their deaths.

Wilberforce, who'd been a few steps behind, now stopped by his side.

'This isn't who you are, John,' he grumbled, keeping his voice out of Eoin's earshot. 'Don't let the Bodach take away what little good we've left in us.'

And with his message delivered, he walked on, abandoning the publican to the company of his own guilty conscience.

One night – that's all it takes to break a man.

Even if he'd come down the stairs swinging, just to buy Annie enough time to slip the boys out the back door, where would they have run to? Croaghnakeela's coast might as well have been the edge of the world, and there wasn't a family on the island back then who'd have taken them in.

'I know what you're thinking, John,' Lavelle said casually, tinkering with his glass. 'You're wondering why old Val is in your home when Declan O'Dwyer's debt is so great. You thought he was next, didn't you? He came to your door. He asked you for your help. Of all the friends he had on this island, Declan honestly thought that you were the best of them. But you were never his friend, were you? You poisoned the man with drink and watched him waste his life away, and then you sent him off to die when all he needed was a little charity to buy himself another day.'

John tried not to react. Anything he said would only be twisted and used against him.

'Well,' Lavelle continued, cracking his neck to one side, 'Declan and I have come to an arrangement. He offered me something that few men ever have – a wife and a daughter, can you believe that? I considered taking them tonight, of course, but then I thought of you, John, the very man who made all this happen.' He raised his glass. 'It wouldn't be right now, would it, if I were to celebrate with anyone else.'

It was toying with him. There was a single reason why the Bodach trespassed in someone's home, and John had two of them upstairs.

'I'll give you whatever you want,' he said, 'but please, leave my family be. They're all I have left.'

Lavelle sat back straight, smiling more menacingly than before. *'They're all you have left,'* he said musingly. 'That's an interesting way to phrase it. By that reasoning, John, your family is the only possession of yours that I can take. And, not to be constantly picking your pocket, but your debt is far from—'

'No,' John shrieked, 'you can have anything else. The pub! Take the pub! It's all yours. Take all the money I've left. Take me, for Christ's sake! But don't take my boys!'

Lavelle swirled the last spit of whiskey thoughtfully around his glass.

'Pick one,' he said, licking that black tongue around his lips.

John shook his head, dizzy with disbelief. 'I don't understand,' he whispered, though that was a lie.

'I think you do,' Lavelle said with a smirk. 'Pick one of your boys as payment. Otherwise I'll take them both.'

'No,' John cried, standing from his stool, 'I beg of you, please, don't—'

Lavelle's whole skeleton cracked aloud as his body stretched to its true terrifying height, and he towered over John like a praying mantis primed to devour him.

'I own you,' he rasped, 'and your family.'

The publican fell to his knees, pleading with the Bodach for mercy.

'Did you kiss them one last time before you came downstairs?' Lavelle asked him.

Clutching tearfully to the man's coat, John shook his head.

'Too bad,' the Bodach said before his hand clamped around the publican's neck.

He closed his eyes and awaited the snap of bone. It would all be over soon. And the pain would only last for a second. The Bodach hadn't taken Declan's family. John had every reason to hope that Annie and the—

'Dad?'

Ronnie had come downstairs in his pyjamas and was standing barefoot by the door. John stared into his son's eyes, but no words came. Not even one last *I love you*.

'If only you'd picked one of them,' Lavelle said with a long sigh of satisfaction, 'there might still be something left for you.'

John's skull was cast against the wooden counter, and the night went dark.

The well was close now. If there was ever some hope of a heaven – some happiness in the life after – then that's where Annie and the boys were waiting for him. And to see this atrocity through – to sacrifice Connor's daughter to the very thing that'd taken John's family from him – would seal God's golden gates for good.

Panicked now, he peered through the fog, searching despairingly for some movement in the grey.

'Eoin,' he roared, his bearings mislaid in the pursuit, 'where are you?'

Was he too late? Had the foul deed already been carried

out in his name, damning his soul to an eternity without those he loved? It felt as though he were losing his family all over again.

'What's going on, John?' Eoin snapped, appearing behind him, one hand still clamped around Sarah's arm.

He was relieved to see her alive, but his gladness was short-lived as he beheld the fresh bruise swelling around her eye.

'What have you done?' he said, stepping forward to comfort her.

But Eoin barged in front of him. 'Are you fucking kidding me?' he said, flaunting his incredulity. 'You're the one who wanted to kill her, John.'

'I was wrong,' the publican said, stumbling over his words. 'I let the Bodach get the better of me. We can't do this, Eoin. It's not right.'

Murray had a wolfish glint to his eyes as he peered around him, probably looking for some audience to witness whatever he was planning. But the fog was all either man could see. Regardless of how many bodies had climbed the hill, in that moment there were only three.

'Let her go, Eoin,' John said, though his voice sounded meek as he felt.

Murray shook his head in disgust. 'I always knew you were a—'

Sarah sunk her teeth into the man's hand, clamping her jaw around it. Eoin roared as he wrestled himself free of her, and by the second he'd swung his fist at the woman, she'd already found her feet and escaped into the fog.

'Dad,' she screamed. 'Dad, where are you?'

More voices called out from nowhere. It was done. Sarah was safe.

Blood seeped between Eoin's fingers as he gripped his wound, and John knew what was coming. The full force of the man's rage had been unleashed, and he stormed towards him with more fire in his eyes than the whole of hell itself. The publican backpedalled quickly as he could, clenching his fists for what good they'd do him. But he froze, his eyes widening at the shadowy shape growing behind Murray's back. It was twice his height, with its long monstrous arms enveloping him from both sides. Eoin looked to John, and for the first time in all the years he'd known him, the publican saw fear in the man's eyes. Murray knew what was coming before the Bodach's fingers clamped around his neck, cracking it like a thin bundle of straw and wrenching his dead body into the fog.

It could have just as easily taken John too, but it didn't. Once again it'd left him alive – a shameful reflection of the man he'd once been, a coward and a killer, and a father who'd failed to keep his family safe.

Daylight was gleaming through the pub window when he'd finally stirred back to life that morning. For a benighted moment, the pain was all John knew as he peeled himself up from his own vomit. A bruise had risen like a tumour by his right eye, too sore to grace with even the lightest touch. And then, like a siren in his subconscious, that closing memory materialised in his mind, and he looked to the stairs.

'Annie!' John screamed as he crawled back onto his feet.

He ran up to her, tripping and stumbling, his worst fears rolling against him like an avalanche. They had to be alive. There was nothing else without them. But whatever fragile hopes he'd carried to their bedroom died the instant he reached its door. John's mind refused to accept the meaning behind the emptiness. He still imagined the room as he'd left it, with those he loved lying asleep, warm and safe and his to hold upon his return. There were no signs of a struggle, only their heartbreaking absence. The duvet had been neatly folded back, as was Annie's way, forever keeping some order amidst the chaos. He noticed a stain on the bedsheets where one of the boys must have wet themselves – the only clue as to the terror they'd suffered while John was passed out on the floor downstairs.

He would never know the true horror of his family's final moments, though his nightmares had certainly been creative over the years. Perhaps had he sacrificed one of his sons to the Bodach, some shred of happiness might have survived past that night. But having mulled over the same agonising question a thousand times over for thirty years, John still couldn't *pick one.*

He'd lost everything he ever loved that night. But a man can lose his wife and still remain her husband. He can even lose the two most precious boys in the whole world and still call himself their dad.

'Eoin!' he heard someone call out. 'Where the fuck are you, lad?'

John turned in the direction of their voice and set off into the fog.

27

Robin

She was exactly as he remembered her, and that's how Robin knew she was dead. There were no wounds that he could see. No blood. No pain had been carried over from her final moments. She was as beautiful in death as she'd been in life. Her hair even retained that same curly bounce that'd gifted it such life in the chill breeze of the cemetery when first and last they'd spoken.

'Grace,' he said, heartbroken, struggling to speak above his swelling sorrow. 'I'm... I'm so sorry. I should never have brought you here. I... I didn't know.'

She drew a finger to her lips and whispered, 'You need to keep your voice down.'

Robin glanced nervously around him, spellbound by the sheer vastness of the room. It was too mystifying for the eye to openly welcome into its reality. He'd expected a cavern, an empty space of rock and earth, ragged and timeworn as the hill above it. But the priest now knelt on a raised aisle, its stone reaching like a bridge over the misty shadows swirling on either side of him despite the stillness of the air. And cut into the ceiling, beguiling his gaze like a shiny lure in the darkest ocean, the daylight fell in a hazy pillar through the well above.

'What *is* this place?' Robin whispered, awed by how it so resembled some grand cathedral – the dome of light, the central aisle, that hollow echo of one's own inadequacies – and yet there was nothing godly about it.

Beneath the weak light of the well, where a place of worship should have held an altar or some symbol of the Almighty, there was instead a mound of bone, strewn wide and scattered like the leftovers from some grisly feast – limbs and ribs and all those intricate parts that hold humankind together. Fleshless skulls stared skyward, like flowers drawn to the light, their hollow eyes pools of darkness. Skeletons of the old and the young – some decayed and discoloured, others looked freshly licked clean. Coins shimmered like cats' eyes in their darkest recesses. And knotted between them were clothes, the most incongruent element amidst the whole ghastly spectacle. No flesh. No blood. Just bones and garments. Robin was surprised to see that their fabrics still held some colour. They must have been decades, not centuries old. These weren't the vestiges of some ancient ritual. The bones of those who'd built this place would have long crumbled to powder by now. Robin's weary eyes picked out a leather jacket, faded and pockmarked and yet unmistakably modern. And then he noticed a woman's shoe with a low heel. Amidst the ghastly pile there was some muddied denim and the torn sleeve of a yellow rain jacket. These people had died in Robin's lifetime.

All those deaths whispered about on the mainland like a dark conspiracy, could Robin's own parishioners have been the ones responsible? With their wealth lost and faith abandoned, had they turned on each other to pay the Bodach, offering up the weakest amongst them as sacrifices? What if the many sins of Croaghnakeela were more heinous than he could have possibly imagined?

'We have to get you out of here, Grace,' Robin said, so weakened by his own suspicions that he almost tripped blundering back to the door.

All those quiet pleas and prayers that had carried him to that moment, they'd all been for nothing. He was the sole reason why Grace had returned to the island. Her death was his doing and nobody else's. But he could still save her soul... even though his own may have been beyond redemption.

Robin expected the iron door to be ajar, as he'd left it, and yet it was locked. He fumbled around it in a panic, feeling around its every inch, searching for some handle or mechanism – any means to draw it open. But there was nothing. Not even a keyhole to suggest that it'd ever been a door at all.

'I don't understand,' he called back, kicking it in frustration. 'I didn't fucking close it.'

'You need to keep your voice down,' Grace whispered to him across the silence.

Robin turned, slowly, quietly, and crept up the aisle towards her.

'*Listen*,' Grace said to him. 'You can only hear them if you *listen*.'

Robin didn't understand what the woman meant until she tapped her ear.

For a moment, with his breath held, the dead air around him remained constant as the man's own confusion. But in each second that followed, Robin was sure he'd heard *something*. Weak and remote at first – wordless murmurs, the shyest insinuations of a sound – but it was getting louder, as if the very act of listening was amplifying their voices, and they were multiplying. Sharp little whispers now repeated over and over, fizzling in the air, coarse sand to the ears. There was weeping, too, amidst the chatter, like drawn-out strings – the most pitiable, dissonant cries to ever touch a human soul. It was impossible to fathom how many there were from their collective symphony. Robin knew only that each voice was that of a child.

'I can hear them,' he whispered, turning to take in the cavern around him. 'But... where are they?'

Only its uppermost heights by the open well were visible. All else was half-light and shadow – an elusive in-between that sired more questions than it did answers.

'The walls,' Grace replied. 'If you look closely, you can see them.'

Robin stepped towards the walkway's edge and faced the dark beyond. He'd prevailed against the dead before – souls so sinister, so septic, so mentally shattered that they'd taught him the true meaning of terror as a child – but this was different. The priest's trepidation wasn't born from those tried and tested fears of old. These were children. His fears weren't for himself. They were for them.

'My God,' he whispered as the horror harvested long trails of gooseflesh across his body.

Everywhere he looked, pits had been cut into the wall – hollowed-out little circles where the shadows pooled darkest – like a massive beehive, and each cavity in its honeycomb held at its centre a child. Those faces that Robin could make out amidst the gloom were pale and frozen in time, so long separated from love and happiness and the joys of youth that they knew only loneliness, caring for nothing, and hoping for less.

If Croaghnakeela's stony surface were a scab, then the priest now stood in the bloody wound of it – the source of all that pain, all that suffering. It'd been beneath him the entire time. The children, Wilberforce had told him, they're all Lavelle ever wanted. The Bodach was like a spider, cocooning their souls in the lining of its nest, feeding on their misery... and it could return at any moment.

'Grace, we need to get out of here,' Robin said, the words skipping off his tongue too quickly. 'What's the last thing you remember?'

Robin looked to the skylight above him, wishing only for some means to reach it. But there had to be another way out. The absence of any blood in the firelit corridor meant that Grace must have been delivered to the cavern through a different entrance. And only she and the Bodach knew where that was.

'Please, Grace,' he pressed, 'I need you to think back to how you got here.'

The woman pinched the bridge of her nose as she rifled through those empty spaces in her mind. But the fog of her own passing had yet to clear. In light of what he'd discovered outside her home – and the carnage of her abduction – Robin knew it was another of God's cruel attempts at kindness; another soul unable to move on.

'I don't know,' she replied, holding her head. 'I remember leaving Harriet's. Someone was watching me from her window. I got scared, and so I ran home to my mum's. There was a bottle of… whiskey, I think. But I can't… it's too mixed up.'

The priest needed a different approach if she were to remember.

'How long do you think you've been here?' he asked.

Rallying her thoughts to the present might force her mind to put it into some sort of context. Robin didn't need to know *why* she was brought to that accursed place, he just needed to know *how*.

Grace looked to him, brimming with despair. 'I've no idea. What even is *here*?' she asked him. 'Richard, what's going on? Why can't I remember anything?'

Robin had failed the woman in life, but if he could just guide her back to the coast – to the salty air and open skies – the truth of her passing might set her soul free.

'Don't worry, Grace, it'll all make sense soon,' he said as he approached the edge of the aisle, searching for some elusive passageway concealed amidst the mist. 'Just stay strong and stay with me. I'll get you out of here, I promise.'

The drop down from the bridge must have measured fifteen feet or more. It wasn't meant to be climbed. Robin guessed it was designed to keep it safe from whatever the hell was happening around it. A low flood of water had seeped into the cavern, a restless white on black, disturbed by the tides that'd found their way through. Shadows weaved through the mist like spools of wool unwinding in the air, but there were shapes below too – stone tables perhaps, or tombs. Fat chains and shackles snaked over every block. The light from the well above illumed only the flimsiest part of them, but that was enough to hint at the despair that'd once rung around those walls. But Robin couldn't trust his eyes. Was any of this real?

Or was this his gift revealing to him some different – some darker – plane of existence.

'What's down there?' Grace asked, standing in closer to him.

'I don't know,' he replied, lowering onto his knees for a better look. 'But I don't think this was a place of worship. Can you see the chains?' he said, pointing towards the iron links. 'Whoever built it, they were trying to contain something terrible, Grace, but...'

Brendan wasn't mad. And neither was his father.

'But what?' she said impatiently, stepping back as he rose to his feet.

'I think they failed,' Robin replied, sadly accepting his own thoughts as the truth. 'One of them must have gotten out.'

He strode up to where those skeletal remains lay strewn beneath the well, seeking out some passageway or recess that might lead them back to the light. The tides had found their way in, why shouldn't they find a way out? He had to step around the bones to gain a better look at the back wall behind them, and though the daylight there settled faintly as silver dust, he saw that which confirmed all Brendan had told him. Long recesses had been hewn into the stone, along the length of the wall and reaching as high as Robin could see.

'Stay back, Grace,' he whispered. 'Whatever you do, don't touch anything.'

Laid across the shelves were the relics that'd slipped through the eternal fog, the source of all those fairy tales and superstitions that the Irish people had carried like a taint in their blood for centuries.

'What are they?' Grace asked warily, keeping her distance.

'I don't know for sure,' he replied, guiding his feet around the bones, 'but an old friend once told me that they're something very, *very* old.'

Only when he rejoined her on the aisle did Robin notice how it still sparkled dimly with rock salt, as if it'd been worked into the very stone itself. The pagans – if that's even what they were – knew what they were dealing with. The flood was no accident. They'd used the salt water to keep them safe, for a time at least.

'I think I'm starting to understand why my mum sent me off this fucking island,' Grace said, pinning back her curls with both hands, looking distraught as the priest felt. 'How long did you say you've lived here for?'

'Six years,' was Robin's rueful reply.

'And you didn't know about any of this?'

The priest shook his head ashamedly. 'The… *thing* that did all this, Grace, was dead and buried before I ever came here. And the islanders made a pact amongst themselves to bury the past along with it. If I'd known, I would never have let you come here.'

'But this *thing* of yours,' she said, raising her voice, 'is the reason why my mum gave me away, isn't it? She wanted to keep me safe. She didn't want me to come back.'

And yet Robin had gone against the dying woman's wish regardless.

'I'm sorry, Grace,' he said, 'I just thought that—'

Something shifted in the corner of the priest's eye, and before he'd chance to turn his head an inch, a block of stone crashed down onto the altar and ricocheted into the wash. The echo of its impact rang in the air long after it'd come to rest. It'd fallen from the well above them.

Together they stared up towards that circle of sky, brighter than the priest ever remembered seeing it, and higher than he could ever hope to climb.

Grace spoke the priest's thoughts aloud as the silence steadied around them.

'There's someone up there.'

28

Sarah

Panic overruled all thought as she tore through the fog. There was only the desperate, breathless desire to find her father and save him from the death they'd each been sentenced to. Running blind, Sarah clipped her ankle on a rocky nub that sent her crashing to the dirt. Dazed, still moving, never stopping, she staggered back onto her feet, battling through the pain as it burned across the bone, cursing herself for wasting that single second with so much at stake. But hindering as the ancient debris was to her struggle, its many shards told Sarah that she was close, and that she hadn't lost her way in the maddening mists of Croaghnakeela's hilltop.

The well had been housed within a building once: a church, possibly, or a temple. Only the barest rubble of its four walls remained, but it'd left enough of a shape for Sarah's imagination to rebuild the basics. Its original purpose never troubled her like it did some of the others, rather it was the mystery of how so many stony fragments came to be scattered around its perimeter. It was as if they'd been blasted out from the inside – a theory that Sarah kept to herself having heard how they'd all turned on old Colman for speaking his thoughts aloud. Something came up that well – God knows when, but it did – and it'd risen with such force that it left the building above it in bits. Whatever horrors once stalked the shores of Croaghnakeela, Sarah had long suspected that the Bodach wasn't even the worst of them.

'We're over here!' she heard Wilberforce call out, bellowing loud as a sea captain.

But who could she trust anymore after they'd each fallen in line with Finnerty's attack on her? If just one of them had spoken out, all of this could have been prevented and the powers of judge, jury, and executioner wouldn't have fallen to the likes of Eoin Murray – the blackest seed to ever grow from the island's dead earth. And yet Sarah had lived amongst these people her whole life. She knew there was still some good in them despite the Bodach's best efforts to make them forget it.

When she reached the eastern side of the fallen wall, lungs billowing, it was as if a white film were being peeled from her eyes. The fog never crossed within that square of rubble – another phenomenon that defied explanation, making it seem terrifyingly sentient in its movements – and for the first time since scaling to the hilltop, Sarah could see beyond her outstretched arms. Now, as always, a dome of empty air rose around the well. There she saw her father, pinned to his knees, surrounded by the others, none of whom had come to the man's aid – too weak to rise against those chains shackling them to the past, even now, with so little left to lose.

There was a world out there beyond the shores of Croaghnakeela, but Sarah had visited the mainland only once, with her mother, when she was just a child. Theirs was the shortest day trip imaginable, and yet she'd memorised its hours like a collection of postcards, leafing through them in her thoughts for years after, doting over the same details, reliving those same moments. The land had stretched on for miles with no ocean on the horizon. Trees grew in shady woodlands, taller than any on the island. Shops sold wares and wonders that she never knew existed, and every road branched off into more just like it, hinting at a never-ending maze that she'd pined to someday explore. Colours there were different too, more vibrant, with flowering petals uncommon to the island – those she'd drawn and pinned around her bedroom wall like cuttings taken from some exotic land. The cars, the faces, the unfamiliarity, all of it was like some dream that she'd tried so hard not to forget.

And yet, after a lifetime of lonely reflection, all she had now were reprints of those same memories, dulled with each reiteration, becoming something less when all she'd ever wanted was more. It didn't seem fair that Grace had gotten away; younger than Sarah by a few years, she'd escaped the island when no one else could – the impossible dream made possible.

'Eoin!' Donal roared when he saw Sarah approaching him. 'Where the fuck are you, lad?'

The fiddler looked none too pleased that she'd arrived *sans chaperon*. He stood over her father, with Ray to his side, like two obedient dogs waiting by their dinner; neither had the mind to act without their master's order. She cast a cautious eye around their company, identifying who she could trust to keep her father safe. The Cunnanes had distanced themselves from the others, sheltered neath the tallest scrap of wall still standing, neither aligned with nor against Sarah's efforts. The widow Malley, Maggie, and Wilberforce were grouped together, seemingly united despite past animosities. Each looked relieved to see her safe, but Eoin could return at any second, and that bastard had enough rage in him to burn the whole island into the ocean.

She crept closer to her father, trembling on his knees, muddied from head to toe, squinting at her with a bizarre blend of joy and dread. His darkened nose had swollen to twice its size and split on the bridge, breaking the skin just enough for a line of red to seep out. He was quietly weeping at the sight of his *little girl*, still alive despite the odds set against her. She wanted nothing more than to run to him and dab the dirt from his cheeks. He was alive. That's all Sarah cared about. *He* was all she cared about.

'Best you let Connor go now,' Fergal said gruffly to the musicians, treating them like a single entity as he heaved himself towards them. 'There's no use in you keeping this madness up any longer. No one's going down that fucking well today.'

Donal glanced flightily around him. 'We were just doing what Eoin told us to—'

Finnerty collapsed into the open, chest heaving like a busted engine, more distraught and blundering than Sarah had ever seen him. And she knew that even the likes of Eoin Murray couldn't terrorise a man like that.

'What's happened?' Ray asked him, fastening his hand back around Connor's shoulder, brandishing his loyalty to the man who poured the pints. 'Where's Eoin at?'

'The Bodach,' Finnerty replied between breaths, hands held to his knees, scanning the low walls surrounding them. 'The Bodach got him. It's out there,' he gasped, waving towards the fog. 'We can't stay here. We need to get off this hill.'

Seething, Sarah squeezed her cold fists so hard they hurt. Did the bastard expect them to follow his lead after what he'd done to her? In taking his stand against Murray, John may have tried to make amends. But it all seemed too little too late by now. Executioner one moment. Her saviour the next. The coward wore so many fucking hats, she didn't know what to make of him anymore.

'And go where, John?' Fergal barked at him. 'Back to the fucking pub, is it? Wasn't it you who brought us up here?'

'Anywhere,' the publican shrieked, pacing on the spot, his brow glistening. 'I don't care where we go. Are you not listening to me? It's in the fucking fog, Fergal. I saw it take Eoin. We can't—'

'We're not running anymore,' Mary Malley flared as she rested her old bones on the stony lip of the well, stubborn as ever. 'The sooner you realise, John, that we're all going to die on this island, the sooner you might calm down.'

Was this really the end? It was fair to assume that whatever Brendan and Father Richard set out to accomplish that morning had come to nothing. Knowledge never was much use on Croaghnakeela. The same could be said for prayers. Sarah knelt beside her father and held him in her arms – the man who'd cared for her like a caged bird, keeping her safe the only way he could, out of love and out of fear.

She had never forgotten the day her mum brought her to the orphanage, and their shared excitement at welcoming all those new children to the island. They'd joked about who she was looking forward to meeting the most, the boys or the girls. Of course, it was the girls, though the boys were already becoming a curiosity to her. It was such a tall, funereal building, and Sarah remembered counting the many windows spread across its three storeys as they'd approached it. Given the hour of the day, the whole western side of the hill was still loured in shadow, and the air was bitingly cold. This was where the homeless children were to live for a time, but it was sad how little it resembled a home at all. In the room directly above its front door, watching her from behind a long pane of glass, stood Valentine Lavelle. Sarah had never seen the man before, but she'd heard the adults talking about him, and when they did, more often than not their words were spoken through smiles. There was no reason in the world, not then, to fear him. And yet she did the very moment their eyes met. For it was the eyes that froze her feet to the earth.

'What's wrong?' her mum asked, looking to her daughter before following her gaze to the upstairs window, where the man had since disappeared into the darkness of the room. 'Who did you see?'

Only a child could ask such a question so innocently.

'Why are Valentine Lavelle's eyes red, Mum?'

Sarah was one of the lucky few, having survived when so many children were lost. And yet, despite her father's many heartfelt assurances since that time, she'd always known that the Bodach would return, that those same eyes would someday look upon her again.

Donal was the first to run. And Ray soon followed him, keeping a slower tempo as usual, forever failing to play in sync with the fiddler's movements.

'Lads,' Finnerty called out, 'where are you going? We should stick together!'

But the publican was ignored. Life was more precious to those men than pints, apparently, though Sarah would never have guessed it. They'd done as they were told their whole lives – filling the silence with the same songs read off the same dog-eared music sheets – and it was rare to see them acting on their own impulses. They rushed off in the opposite direction that'd brought them there. If the fiddler's plan was to descend the hill's western side, then he was more fool than the eejit following him. Too sharp were its cliffs. Too loose its rocks. It'd demand a steady and near-perfect journey downward, and neither man was capable of that, especially not with the fear driving them on.

Sarah looped her father's arm over her shoulder and, still kneeling by his side, looked back to the others. Only then did she mark the absence of Gerard and Laoise. She couldn't tell which was sadder – the fact that they hadn't cared enough to even say goodbye or that no one had noticed they were gone.

'Everyone, closer together now,' Wilberforce ordered as he stood above Sarah, 'and keep your backs to the well so the bastard Bodach can't sneak up behind you.'

'And what if he comes up the fucking well, Fergal?' John asked him, jittery as a wasp trapped in a jar. 'What if he drags us all into it?'

'Didn't you say you'd seen it out there in the fog?'

The publican nodded, as close to tears as a man could come without breaking down.

'And where exactly was that, John?'

'How am I supposed to know, Fergal?' he replied. 'I couldn't see a thing out there.'

'Well, if he's in the fog, then he can't be in the well too now can he? Think before you speak, you fucking clown.'

A far-off scream – agonised and afeared – suddenly sounded from where the musicians had run off to. All heads turned like flags whipping in a storm. More cries. More unintelligible words torn from a dying man's throat. And yet their message was received loud and clear. Sarah felt her father grip her closer. As horrifying as it was to listen to, the men's cries gave them an understanding of the Bodach's whereabouts. The musicians were distinguishable only by their instruments. There were definitely two voices out there, but Sarah couldn't tell them apart at that distance. Never had a swan song comprised so many harrowing encores, and they'd all nestled together in quiet solidarity, waiting for the silence to pronounce both men dead.

'Gerard and Laoise are gone,' Maggie whispered, the first of them to notice.

Whereas Mary and John scanned the fog for the absentees, Sarah noticed how Wilberforce never took his eyes off Tadgh Scuffel's widow.

'With any luck they took off back to the path, Maggie,' he said to her. 'It's not so far that they'd wouldn't have made it by now. And sure the bastard Bodach is a way off west.'

It wasn't like the mean old brute to wish well on another. But maybe there was still a grain of goodness left in Fergal Wilberforce after all. With their deaths looming so close at hand, where was the harm in capping a life with a little kindness.

Sarah wished she'd had the chance to speak to Grace, just once, if only to imagine how her own life might have played out had she enjoyed the same opportunities. Had the woman fallen in love? Did she have a job... and friends... and holidays abroad? Of course she did. She would've had it all. Sarah was given one day and she cherished its every hour. Chrissy's daughter had thirty years.

'We should make a run for it,' Finnerty said, talking only

to Fergal, ignoring the fact that Sarah's father, the widow, and even Wilberforce himself were in no fit state for running any great distance.

'Do whatever you want, John,' Fergal replied after a long sigh of disappointment. 'But don't think I'll be coming to your rescue when you start screaming.'

'If we can just make it as far as the hillside,' the publican said, 'we'll be able to see where we're—'

'Listen,' Maggie snapped.

Something stirred amidst the silent mists surrounding them, by the ruined perimeter of the eastern wall. Without sight, no sound could be trusted. There'd been a step and a cry, like the crestfallen whine of some wounded creature lost to the fog. A whisper then crept on the breeze – the softest susurration, as words spoken in privacy, intended for no ears but their own. They carried no sense, only sorrow. There were two people it could have been, inseparable since the day they'd met.

Laoise Cunnane staggered into the open, weak-kneed and dazzled by the sudden clarity of sight. She was cradling her husband's severed hand against her chest, fiddling with its fingers. It'd been ripped off at the wrist, where streams of blood and sinew dangled from it like loose wires. The woman was muttering under her breath, studying Gerard's hand like a clue to some cryptic question that her broken heart now held in the centre of her world. She frowned at all those standing in front of her, taking in each of them individually, wondering perhaps why her husband wasn't present amongst them and why his hand now felt so stiff, so cold, so unlike the one she'd held for so many years.

'Come here,' Maggie whispered, reaching out. 'Laoise, get away from the wall!'

But the woman didn't understand what was being asked of her. And just as her lips parted ever so slightly – to speak, to cry, to scream – the Bodach's long fingers snapped around her ankle. With her eyes still staring at them, she was wrenched back into the fog. Gerard's hand skittered across the earth towards them, its fingers splayed open, searching in death for the familiar warmth of his wife's palm. She hadn't screamed like the others. The woman went without a sound, leaving a silence that lingered in the cold air long after she was dead.

For a while, nobody knew what to say and so nobody made any attempt to speak. Laoise's state of mind made a sort of sense to Sarah now. With any luck she'd have a similar self-destruct button in her brain to get through her own final moments when the time came.

'I'm sorry, Sarah,' John said, limp as a man who'd already given up. 'And you too, Connor. It's because of me that we're all here. I just wanted it to end. But it's true what the Bodach says, isn't it? He owns us. He's never going to—'

'Will you ever pull yourself together,' the widow snapped at him. 'For the love of God, if this day is the death of us, then I don't want to spend it listening to your moaning.'

Maggie's eyes were lured back to the fog, and that was enough to elicit a silence from the others. The woman's hearing was sharp as an owl's. And then Sarah heard it too – the faint crack of bone echoing through the fallen stone, like the hard legs of a hundred cockroaches scuttling around them.

'The bastard Bodach,' Fergal muttered angrily. 'Stay as you are. There's no use in running.'

Where the air was opaque as grimy glass, it was stalking around them.

'We're trapped,' Finnerty cried, wedging himself in between Sarah and the low wall of the well. 'What do we do?'

'Don't talk to it, John,' Maggie replied, looking back at him. 'It'll only tear your heart out.'

Sarah heard footsteps approaching. Slow and steady they came, like the toll of two iron bells ringing in the Bodach's arrival. It could move as silently as a snake if it so pleased, but where was the fear in that?

'Don't worry, Dad,' she whispered, refusing to loosen her hold on him. 'I'm here.'

The earth at her knees shuddered – one step, and then another, over and over, rattling through her bones, each one more thunderous than the last until the Bodach's red eyes glowed where the veil of fog hung thinnest. Maggie tripped back as its long silhouette emerged into the open, this revilement of the husband she'd lost, resembling more insect than man, so abhorrent as to decimate even her most cherished memories of him.

'My God,' Wilberforce whispered, his brave front faltering at the sheer size of it. 'What's he done to you, Scuffel?'

The dead man's skin had been stretched so finely across the bone, ripping apart at its limbs and hanging in sickly folds that'd hardened in the salty air, making every inch of its naked body a terror to behold. It'd torn open most noticeably in the hollow neath his ribcage, where its festering organs were on full show like an abandoned post-mortem. Sarah couldn't fathom how the foul parasite was still standing – still mimicking life when everything about it screamed only death.

Her father buried his head into her shoulder, but she couldn't look away. These were the same devilish eyes that'd watched her from the orphanage's window, before anyone knew what Lavelle really was: their corrupter, their destroyer, standing in the very trap they'd built for him, waiting for all that supple flesh to be delivered to his doorstep by her own mother's innocence. But the Bodach no longer cared to keep its presence hidden amongst them. Its days of deception were over. Having been denied the feel of a human body for so long, it was exercising its full nightmarish freedom over Tadgh Scuffel's remains. This was what Colman McMorrow had warned them about – the portal, and the monstrosities that clawed at its threshold, forever vying to break through, like a weakness between two dimensions. Maybe they would have tried harder to believe the man had they not been so terrified at the thought of it.

Aside from the few shrivelled threads of a moustache, there was nothing of Tadgh Scuffel left. The very bones of his face had been deformed, leaving no part of it unchanged. His chin had grown long and crooked, and the jaw hung gaping wide from the weight of it, clicking at the hinge, and drooling blood and bile in sickly strands. It was as if another nose had forced its way through the old, rupturing the cartilage and breaking the skin in knobbly ridges. And yet it was the eyes that terrorised Sarah most of all, reawakening those old fears that'd hounded her into adulthood. They burned just as she remembered, only now their sockets had been hollowed out, leaving a sickening emptiness around them, as if their eyeballs hung on by the barest vein.

'Whatever happens, Dad,' Sarah spoke into his ear, 'don't look at it.'

The most repulsive cackling gargled around the Bodach's black gums as it staggered towards them, legs crunching with every twitching movement, its handless arm dangling by its side. Everyone but Fergal retreated further back to the well. Finnerty looked as though he were about to throw himself into it as he'd clambered atop its stone, distancing himself as far as possible from the Bodach's reach. In his panic, one of its stones shifted out of place and fell plummeting into the darkness, startling the publican into putting his two feet back on the dirt. If it'd made a sound upon its impact, Sarah hadn't heard it.

'Look at you,' Wilberforce shouted, spitting his disgust at the Bodach, 'you ruined yourself. You can't even talk, can you? You've brutalised poor old Tadgh's body so that all you can do now is hiss and fucking snarl at us like a dog.'

Its red glowing eyes pulsated as they zoned in on the man.

'And you left your hand behind you in the pub too, didn't you?' Wilberforce continued his upbraiding, still standing in front of it. 'What use are you to anyone with one hand, eh? You're only good for rowing a boat around in a fucking circle now, aren't you?'

'Fergal,' Maggie whispered to him, tugging on his sleeve.

'It's okay,' he replied, guiding her back with a gentle touch of his hand as he held the Bodach's gaze. 'If you're ever to fool the likes of us again,' he said to it, 'then you'll have a hard time doing it looking like that, won't you, you ugly bastard. You're not much of a fucking trickster if everyone can spot you coming a mile off.'

Wilberforce broke from their group and took a step closer to the Bodach. By some miracle it hadn't killed the man already. But from what Sarah could tell, it actually seemed to be listening to him.

'You're a clever old bastard,' Fergal said, chin held high to meet it face to face, 'I'll give you that. You did a fine job of ruining all our lives, just when we thought our luck was changing for the better. But you got a little carried away with yourself this time, didn't you?'

Maybe Sarah imagined it, but the Bodach's cheeks cracked into the most devious smile as it drew itself nearer to the man. She'd expected it to slash out at Wilberforce at any second, splashing his blood across all those pressed against the well. But whatever Fergal was planning, he now held its full attention. And few men ever survived that.

'You need a new body and you know it,' he said, making a point of studying the Bodach's naked flesh, shaking his head in disgust, 'an old one at that. I might not be the prettiest man on the island but I won't put up a fight against you, and that's the truth of it. Take my body and do with it whatever the fuck you please. Just let these ones go.'

The Bodach stared Wilberforce down, motionless, its bones suspended in silence, as if it were considering the offer. It cocked its head to the side, eyeballing him, calculating the man's conviction. In response, Fergal hocked up something from the back of his throat and spat it down by the Bodach's gnarled toes.

'Do you fucking want it or not?' he said impatiently. 'My life for theirs; that's the deal. Take it or leave it.'

The Bodach's smile grew and grew, splintering fresh cracks through its skull before the coarsest laughter was scratched out from its throat. Fergal must have known better. No matter the covenant – nor how airtight the promise – it always came out on top. The man looked back again, seeking out only Maggie, as if she stood alone on the hilltop that day.

'There's no other way,' he said to her sadly. 'You're not

dying on this fucking island. You're better than all this, Maggie, and you deserve to be happy. I'm just sorry I didn't get to know you better. Who knows, things might have been different.'

The woman looked as stunned as the rest of them.

'Fergal,' she said, reaching out a hand towards him, 'but… why?'

'I suppose I love you,' he replied, squeezing her fingers as he considered his own words with a frown and a nod. 'Always have, always will, and there's not much that can be done about that now. But then, I wouldn't have it any other way.'

'Why didn't you ever tell me?' Maggie asked him.

'I was going to once,' Fergal replied ruefully. 'I guess we all got a little carried away with keeping secrets now, didn't we?'

A sharp crack of bone drew Wilberforce back to the Bodach, and he let Maggie's hand slip from his own. It was growing impatient, ogling the man like a hot meal going cold.

'Take care of yourself, Maggie.' He winked back before turning to face what remained of her husband – the monstrosity now salivating in anticipation of what was to come.

'Right, you bastard,' Fergal said, sounding more like his old cantankerous self, 'let's get this over with.'

Sarah felt her father's head turn by her shoulder as she held him. Even he couldn't look away from Croaghnakeela's most unlikely martyr. Together they watched as the Bodach's tapering fingers elongated around Fergal's head like the legs of a spider, trapping its prey. Sarah noticed how he held his clenched fists by his sides, forcing himself to follow through on his promise. Apparently, though it may have been the island's best kept secret, he wasn't the loveless bully that everyone thought him to be. The Bodach's eyes flared as its hand tightened around his skull, and its whole hideous body shivered in ecstasy. It was no different from a hermit crab crawling into a new shell. Fergal's limbs stiffened. His fingers splayed open. And after a parched gasp for air, the Bodach's bones crumbled into a pile by his feet – another living vessel, stolen, abused, and abandoned, draped now in the near-transparent folds of Tadgh Scuffel's skin.

Fergal lurched back towards the well, off balance and blind to those around him, gurgling as if he were choking on his own tongue. The Bodach was burrowing through him, eating the man alive from the inside, leaving only itself. He groped at the air, fending off whatever foul figments had infested his mind. Sarah hoisted her father up and hauled him away as Fergal dragged himself over to the well and fell upon its stone. She noticed how his fingers had already lengthened – how the bones shifted under his skin – but there was still some stubborn element of Wilberforce in there somewhere.

'South of the pier… in the cove… my boat,' he growled, his eyes aglow with the faintest tincture of red. 'Run, all of you, get off this island while you can. Go, now, and don't you ever look back!'

With that said, Fergal Wilberforce rolled himself into the well, taking the Bodach's foul spirit with him into its darkness. His last act in life was to deceive the very trickster who'd taken from them everything and left nothing but death and heartache in return.

Cautiously, Sarah inched over to the low wall and peered down into the pit. It was too dark to see its end, but no man could have survived such a fall. Death was a certainty given the unfathomable distance. And yet the Bodach was no man. All they'd gained from Fergal's sacrifice was time.

'Come on,' Sarah groaned as she held her father steady.

The widow was hugging Maggie close, consoling her, reconsidering their low opinions of the man who'd given his life so that they might keep theirs.

'Come on *where*?' Finnerty asked, agitated as ever, backing away from the well as if the Bodach were already climbing its way back up.

'We do exactly what Fergal told us to do,' she replied, cooly as she could. 'We leave this island and we never look back. I think we owe the man that much, don't we?'

Sarah had waited thirty years for this – to start the life she'd always dreamt of.

And she wasn't going to wait another moment.

29

ROBIN

From that circle of smoky sky, a body broke the air. Time and thought were doctored as it descended perfectly within the column of light, sinking like a stone in still water, darkening as it drew ever closer to oblivion, and there was nothing Robin could do to stop it. The bone-crushing impact came before he'd chance to accept what was happening. Coins tinkled off the surrounding stone like wind chimes flurried in a storm, and a landslide of dead parts and forgotten trinkets scattered across the altar and splashed into the shadowy depths below. And only then, when all that'd been disturbed had resettled, did the silence return. More bones for the pile, hollowed out with a dead man in its centre. There were so few left on the island, and – sure as the human body was as fragile as its soul – there was now one less.

'Wilberforce,' Robin said, blurting out the man's name.

'Who?' Grace asked, unacquainted, slipping in beside him. 'Is he...?'

'He's one of mine,' he replied, which was the strange truth of it. 'Not a bad old sod once you got to know him. But not many did.'

The man's head had borne the brunt of the fall. It'd come dissevered at the neck and clung to his body by the flesh alone, resting cheek to stone, facing them, exposing the worst of his wounds. Fergal's forehead had cracked open. A creamy white layer of bone was visible neath the skin, thin as a smashed work of pottery with a bloody lump of brain leaking out from its centre. Of identifiable features, there was little left. His nose had been pulverised out of existence, leaving only a cavity above his blood-soaked beard. And the man's teeth lay like maggots around him, where his lower jaw had detached from the skull, joining the mismatched bones strewn across the floor.

'What was he doing up there?' Grace asked, shivering as she tightened the folds of her arms. 'Did he jump down himself or...'

'No,' Robin replied, cutting across her, confident of the fact. 'Not Fergal. Not so long as there was a pint in his future.'

But could he be so sure of anything anymore?

His gaze returned to the well above – to that pale moon of light suspended in the black – as a garden of grim scenarios weeded their way around his thoughts. Had Fergal been thrown against his will or was this an act of self-sacrifice? It wasn't in the man's nature to put another's well-being before his own. Unless it were Maggie Scuffel, of course. Robin had seen how he'd watched her, gleaning some secret joy from her society whenever they shared the same room. Whoever was up there, the distance between them was too great to be heard from where he and Grace now stood, and the wind would always scream louder than their voices ever could. All the islanders had to do was wait in Finnerty's pub. They were safe there. Brendan had told them as much. The Bodach couldn't cross the salt that they'd—

Wilberforce suddenly sucked in a sharp lungful of air, jolting Robin back.

'He's still alive?' he said, disbelieving that anyone could have survived such a fall.

The man's injuries were too severe, surely. He'd landed face first, for Christ's sake. Even his spine must have split given how he lay, a twisted wreckage of humankind, too bent to ever breath again, and yet… Fergal's legs began to spasm violently in his last torturous throes of life. Robin prayed for it to cease, though the man couldn't possibly have been cognisant given the damage to his skull. Fergal was dead the second his body met the floor. But what terrors had chased his soul into the afterlife? What happened up there amidst the ruins that'd sent the poor man falling to his death?

Wilberforce's eyelids suddenly snapped open, and Robin beheld those blood-red irises glowing in the half-light.

'Get away from him, Grace,' he shouted, tripping back, sending more bones skittering into the flood.

The Bodach writhed amidst the pile, contorting its mangled limbs, struggling to crawl its way out. Robin backed further down the aisle, watching on in horror as it went about rearranging the dead man's bones, gathering their shattered pieces together into something resembling a working skeleton. The unnerving chatter of every split and fracture echoed around the darkness, circling them like a cloud of bats. It was only a matter of time before it would stand again. And with the iron door still sealed behind them, they were trapped in that pit with it.

'What the fuck is happening?' Grace shrieked, mimicking his retreat.

Robin had neither the time nor the mind to explain what

was now hauling itself towards them, and he still didn't know how to kill it.

'Stay back, Grace,' he said, forgetting in that moment that the woman had already lost her life to the damned thing. 'Don't let it get close to you.'

Its body was broken beyond repair. Whatever circumstances had led it to possess Fergal Wilberforce, the Bodach was trapped inside the dead man's skin like a genie in a fucking lamp until it found another host. In his desperation, Robin dashed back to the door. He clawed his fingers around its frame and again he failed to find some way to release it. The firelit corridor that'd once held him as its slave was now all he yearned to travel through. He may have lacked the strength to see the journey to its end, but he'd collapse in death a happy man knowing that Grace would be free of that place.

Wilberforce's fingers sprouted like skinny branches from his hands, and with these the Bodach was heaving the dead man's weight across the stone. So distracted was Robin that he'd lost track of Grace's movements in that moment. She had strayed to the edge of the aisle and was staring off into the darkness, as if she were preparing to jump.

'What are you doing?' he shouted, wondering now if she had the right idea; with the door sealed shut, there was nowhere else to go.

'*There hasn't been a child on Croaghnakeela for decades now*,' Grace said as though she were quoting another. 'I'm alive because my mum sent me away.' She glanced tearfully back at Robin. 'If she didn't put me up for adoption, then I'd be here too, wouldn't I? I'd be just like all these kids trapped in the walls.'

More bones cracked throughout the cavern as the Bodach

battled onto its knees. With its neck crumbled to powdered pieces, its head hung at a ghastly angle. And yet its unblinking eyes retained their terrifying fixation on them, as only a devil could lock on to a soul it so sorely coveted. It was working Wilberforce's body like a malfunctioning machine, jerking at its limbs, trying futilely to regain some control, its frustration growing with every failed exertion.

'You don't have to stay in this place,' Grace called out to the children. 'You don't have to let this fucking thing hold you here any longer.'

'Grace,' Robin said, pacing towards the side of the walkway where she stood, 'they can't help us. We need to find a...'

He stopped, awestricken, when his eyes met the darkness below.

All those innocents who'd inhabited the walls had crawled out from their cavities. They gathered now in the shallow water, their silver reflections intermingling with the mist, ever-changing, making it impossible to gauge their number. But there must have been hundreds of them, if not more. And in those fleeting moments when their bodies wholly manifested, each one was dressed as they were when their last breath passed their lips. Some of the girls wore dresses. A few of the boys wore shorts. And yet it was the children clad in their best pyjamas that affected Robin most of all. So many had come to Croaghnakeela for the false promise of a fresh start in life. And more had been snatched from their homes, leaving broken hearts and broken families mourning over empty beds. And now their many deathly eyes were all turned on the Bodach.

'*Look* at it!' Grace shouted down to them. 'It can't even stand!'

She was right. Wilberforce's bullish character had the strength of twenty men but his body was well past its prime. Too many lost years sinking pints had left him weak and shapeless. And Brendan's arthritis wasn't an isolated case amongst the island community. Fergal's bones must have been just as delicate, and his rolls of fat carried enough weight to strain even the Bodach's unearthly strength.

'Now's your chance,' Grace said. 'You might never get another one like it.'

What happened next came so silently, so quickly…

The spirits of all those children rose up from the darkness. They didn't gently lap the shadowy shores of the aisle, they crashed it with breathtaking force, like a flash flood exploding from below. Robin caught only glimpses of them – faces seen and lost in the same second, shifting with every strand of mist that curled up towards the light. If the Bodach were aware of his many victims flanking him on all sides, then it was helpless to save itself. They smothered it like a low cloud of phantom locusts, and though the foul thing lashed out against them, they were too many in number and its body too maimed to retaliate. And yet still it refused to yield.

The Bodach's voice filled the cavern like a dying behemoth roaring into the abyss. But the children were winning. Their many arms were like filaments of translucent web, coiling and trapping and turning its body towards the flood. It was dizzying to watch, and all the while the monstrosity hissed and snarled and fought for every lost inch, but it hadn't the teeth to snap back at them.

Robin had dedicated so much of his life to prayer, like a gambler chained to the same losing slot machine. But this finally felt like the miracle he'd been waiting for. The most agonising shriek tore through the air when the Bodach crashed into the water. He rushed over to see it flailing, squealing like a rat, its skin somehow melting from the bone. The fog enclosed it in a perfect circle now, where those rows of pale eyes glinted like crystals in the darkness, watching on as the water fizzled through the Bodach's open throat, eviscerating it from the inside, eating through its dead organs like acid.

'What's happening?' Grace shouted over its bawling.

Robin couldn't keep from laughing. 'The salt,' he replied, giddy from exhaustion. 'The salt in the fucking water… it's killing it.'

He felt a fool for not thinking of it sooner.

The Bodach's cries had weakened to a pathetic, raspy little whisper, and it came as music to Robin's ears. In the dim light where it lay prone in the shallow water, he saw what remained of its corporeal host. The salt was chewing through its bones, dissolving them, leaving only a wiry, withered frame and no trace of Fergal nor the wicked thing that'd taken his body for its own. Whilst amidst the fog, those shadowy details of youth had faded – childish features appeared less defined, their shapes less individual – and they began to blend into one another, unravelling into restless wisps that spread out from where the Bodach lay dead in its centre.

The children were dispersing where the daylight gleamed brightest beneath the well. They were no longer the Bodach's prisoners. Its sway over them had been released. And the fog lifted through the light, rising higher and higher until all those souls trapped within it finally escaped into the open air.

Robin thought of Harriet and that list of names in the church register who'd once called Croaghnakeela their home. Adults and children. Friends and families. Had they too been liberated from its curse? Was he so optimistic at heart to hope for such an ending after all he'd been through? And yet, much to his heartache, Grace remained. The one who'd guided all those lost souls to the light had been denied the same blessing – the same peace. Robin was the one who'd brought her to the island. And he would be the one to set her free of it once and for all. But first...

He lowered himself down onto the stone floor, succumbing to those pains that'd racked his body since he'd tumbled down the stairwell. Robin lay on his back, utterly spent, staring up at the sky, imagining the cool rush of wind against his face. And eventually, for he couldn't hold their weight any longer, his eyes fell closed like two downy duvets. Peace at last. No more secrets. No more lies. No more Bodach. His chest rose high and long with every breath as he silently pieced together his memories of what he'd just experienced, trying to put them in order. But it'd seemed to pass so quickly. The moments and their corresponding images hadn't yet fully developed in his mind. He could sleep; that's all he knew for sure. Given the chance he'd lie there till the end of time.

'Hey,' Grace called over to him, 'are you still with me?'

Robin groaned as he lifted up onto his elbows. The lighting in the cavern seemed different, as if a dark blanket of cloud had fallen over the well. Grace was standing by the door, waiting. And though he couldn't quite believe it, after all his failed attempts, somehow it was now open.

'I don't know about you,' she said, smiling over at him, 'but I think it's time we got out of here.'

Epilogue

ROBIN

The twilit sky was neither light nor dark but a dusty in-between, with night a few short, tired breaths away. Along the island's sea-splashed shore, shadows were awakening in its many crags and cracks, spreading black as oil through its deepest recesses. Robin and Grace stood side by side, facing the bay – that roiling plateau of pewter waves and silver strands, restless as his soul to set the woman free. He stole a glance at her coppered curls gilded golden in the evening light – the brightest colour on that dismal ledge of stone. Thinking back to the day he'd landed, lumbering onto the pier with his worldly possessions crammed into a single suitcase, it felt like a much longer stint than the six years he'd already served. But then, the past, the present, and the future were words of convenience – like the primary points on a compass – guiding humanity in the right direction and counting their days along the way.

Robin couldn't recall when last he'd journeyed this far east. Small as the island was, he never had reason to visit this part of it. Long before he'd arrived in the guise of Father Richard O'Malley, Brendan had been the ferryman's sole link to

Croaghnakeela. Those two men were no better than grumpy old dogs fighting over a bone, brandishing their teeth and bickering for the sake of something to do upon a Saturday. Robin had only spoken to Maloney in person on a handful of occasions and each time the man had stayed stubbornly on his boat, as if he distrusted the land to keep him afloat. He'd obviously heard the many rumours circulating about the island, though it was unlikely he'd still be making that crossing if he knew the reality of it.

A faint breeze brushed Robin's cheeks, soft as cold silk. All was stone, and so nothing stirred. There was only the ocean's ceaseless lapping of the shore and the gulp of it plunging in and out of the island's rocky pits. A thin pall of fog brooded on the bay, making the mainland seem farther away than it really was. Robin rubbed around his tired eyelids, warm against his fingertips. He'd lost track of the hour and when last he'd slept. But the time had come to tell Grace the truth, though this was one responsibility he'd have happily traded with another: to convince a young woman that her life and all the hopes and dreams therein could go no further; that her stock of memories – cherished or otherwise – would be replenished no more. It was the cruellest act imaginable and yet it came from a place of kindness and necessity. Even if Grace's soul were trapped in a state bearing some semblance to peace, she may have been born on the Isle of Croaghnakeela, but this island wasn't her home.

Complete honesty, that's what he owed her.

'I never had chance to tell you, Grace,' he began, steeling himself, 'but my name isn't Richard. It's Robin.'

'I know,' she replied, smiling coyly over at him, cold hands stuffed into her coat pockets, 'you've told me.'

'Did I?' he whispered back, confused, as he couldn't recall speaking his true name to anyone since the Vatican sealed it in their archives.

How would he explain *this* to the bishop? The mere mention of a phantom island might be deemed an act of sacrilege. Gods and devils didn't travel through portals, and no proof on Robin's part would convince the Catholic Church otherwise. He'd probably have his rosary and white collar revoked, like a maverick cop handing over his gun and badge, though perhaps a little less dramatic. So uncertain was his future, there was no knowing what tomorrow might bring.

'Grace,' he said with all the warmth he could muster, 'there's something I need to tell you. It's not going to be easy but—'

'Look,' she said, pointing north of the pier, where the darkening sky was melding into the ocean, blearing the long line dividing them. 'There's something over there.'

Robin was grateful for any reason to postpone that particular conversation.

'What is it?' he asked, overplaying his interest.

'I think there's a boat washed up on the rocks.'

Her eyes were clearly sharper than Robin's. It took him a moment to isolate it from the surrounding stones, but there it was, beached like a whale on its side. The rocks had torn a gaping hollow through its hull, putting its seaworthiness into reasonable doubt. And from what Robin could see of the boat's cabin, its wood was tarred black with rot and had turned the colour of old seaweed. Much of it had collapsed in on itself. It'd obviously been a long time since it had crashed the shore – years, if not decades. Robin wondered if perhaps it once belonged to the Corcoran family he'd heard mention of. That might explain why no attempt had ever been made to clear away its wreckage.

'Do you recognise it?' Grace asked, guiding him to inspect it more closely, though the dim light and the distance weren't allied to his efforts.

There were far more pressing issues to discuss other than the identity of a washed-up boat. But in light of the woman's spiritual circumstances, a little confusion was to be expected, and so Robin accommodated her curiosity. So few vessels remained on the island, and none had touched the water since he'd arrived for reasons that he now understood. But *did* he recognise it? Some faded flakes of paint still clung to its hull. Their colours had been washed thin by the tide, but they looked similar enough to those he remembered seeing on the sides of Maloney's tour boat.

'Is that...?' Robin was about to ask before he cut himself short.

It couldn't have been. Their last delivery from the mainland had only come on Saturday. This vessel had been shipwrecked for much longer than that. And yet, even its shape and size correlated with the little ferryman's pride and joy.

'It's Maloney's,' Grace said, paying close attention to Robin's confusion.

The more he stared at it, the more it made a sort of sense. Within the breach of its hull, a plastic seat had fallen through the decay of the upper deck.

'But how's that possible?' he asked her.

The woman steadied herself before she spoke. 'Because you've been here for a *very* long time, Robin. The children have all moved on. So, too, has Harriet. Even those who survived the Bodach – Sarah and the others – they left this island years ago. They took Fergal's boat to the mainland on the same day you died. We're the last ones left. And I wasn't going to leave you here on your own.'

He didn't understand, not until he looked down and saw the blood, and the red handle of Finnerty's knife protruding from his chest.

About the Author

A. M. SHINE writes in the Gothic horror tradition. Born in Galway, Ireland, he received his Master's Degree in History there before sharpening his quill and pursuing all things literary and macabre. His debut novel, *The Watchers*, was made into a major motion picture produced by M. Night Shyamalan.

Follow him on
@AMShineWriter
and www.amshinewriter.com